THE WELL
Sinclair Ross

The Well

Sinclair Ross

THE UNIVERSITY OF ALBERTA PRESS

This edition published by
The University of Alberta Press
Ring House 2
Edmonton, Alberta T6G 2E1

This edition copyright © The University of Alberta Press 2001
Text copyright © Sinclair Ross 1958, 2001
Introduction copyright © Kristjana Gunnars 2001
A volume in (cuRRents), a Canadian literature series. Jonathan Hart, series editor.
Printed in Canada   5 4 3 2 1

NATIONAL LIBRARY OF CANADA
CATALOGUING IN PUBLICATION DATA

Ross, Sinclair, 1908–
   The well
   ISBN 0-88864-359-4

   I. Title.
PS8535.O79W44 2001   C813'.54   C2001-910884-2
PR9199.3.R599W44 2001

All rights reserved. No part of this publication may be produced, stored in a retrieval system, or transmitted in any form or by any means—electronic, photocopying, recording, or otherwise—without the prior permission of the copyright owner.

Printed and bound in Canada by Kromar Printing Ltd., Winnipeg, Manitoba.
∞ Printed on acid-free paper.
Proofreading by Kate Hole and Tara Taylor.

The University of Alberta Press acknowledges the financial support of the Government of Canada through the Book Publishing Industry Development Program for its publishing activities. The Press also gratefully acknowledges the support received for its program fro the Canada Council for the Arts.

INTRODUCTION
Kristjana Gunnars

SINCLAIR ROSS WAS BORN in Shellbrook, Saskatchewan on January 22, 1908. His parents separated when he was a young child, and he lived with his mother into adulthood. At sixteen he left school to make a living as a clerk at the Royal Bank of Canada in Abbey, Saskatchewan. Banking became his lifelong career, and he pursued his writing alongside his work. He lived in the small-town prairie settings he wrote about, as well as in Montreal, which is the setting for some of his fiction. Upon his retirement in 1968, he moved to Greece and then to Spain; he returned to Canada in 1980 for reasons of ill health. Even while in southern Europe, however, Ross continued to write about the prairies he knew so well and which had such deep roots in his imagination. He died in Vancouver on February 29, 1996.

In 1934, Ross's first short story, "No Other Way," was published in London, England. Thereafter, Ross published stories with Prairie settings in Canadian magazines. His best-known short stories include "The Painted Door," "The Lamp at Noon," and "A Field of Wheat." These are classics of Canadian literature and have been widely anthologized. His first novel, *As For Me and My House*, was published in New York in 1941 and also ranks as a classic. The narrative is presented as the diary of Mrs. Bentley, a preacher's wife in the small town of Horizon, Saskatchewan during the Depression, and shows the workings of Ross's most enduring themes, including a form of existential despair or loneliness, intellectual isolation, suppressed creativity, family tragedy, sexual tension, and a close tie between human beings and landscape. In 1958 *The Well*, his second novel, appeared but did not receive the critical acclaim his first work did. In 1970 a third novel, *Whir of Gold*, was published and also failed to gain favourable reviews.

Not until his 1974 novella *Sawbones Memorial* did Ross's fiction regain the attention it deserved.

In *The Well*, protagonist Chris Rowe, who calls himself Chris MacKenzie, is a young man on the run from the law. Originally from Montreal, Chris has made it as far as "a prairie village called Campkin," two days northwest of Winnipeg. He stops at a diner and is befriended by a local farmer named Larson. After giving him dinner, Larson takes Chris home to his farm and offers him work, which the young man sorely needs. Chris also needs a place to hide out for a while, and a remote prairie farm seems to him as good a place as any. What exactly he is running away from does not become clear until much later in the novel, but there are intimations along the way that Chris has been involved in something serious, possibly a murder. Chris soon discovers that Larson, a man in his sixties, has been married to a woman named Cora. Cora has died, their son has been killed by a horse, and Larson has married a much younger woman named Sylvia. Sylvia was a waitress in Regina when she met the older farmer and has been rescued from a cheap life—a condition she does not appreciate because she does not love her husband. It also dawns on the young drifter from the east that Larson is projecting his dead son, who would be roughly the same age had he lived, onto him.

So begins what becomes a psychological thriller, mixing genres like a prairie wind that blows in circles and picks up particles and dust and pollen, until we are unsure what we are seeing. Ross uses his knowledge of Montreal to describe Chris's background, as well as his intense rootedness in the prairie to expand on the philosophy of life that is so unmistakably regional to Manitoba and Saskatchewan. Some critics have said that Ross does not delineate Montreal as well as he does the prairie. But that may be answered with the reminder that there is a different literary tradition in Montreal, which can be much more romantic in nature than the stark realism of prairie literature. Urban romanticism, such as we find in Gabrielle Roy, is not far from the kind of film noir atmosphere Ross creates when depicting a life of crime and the goings-on of the Boyle Street gang, to which Chris belonged. It is impossible for Ross to narrativize rural prairie life without becoming ruthlessly psychological and naturalistic. The psychological emphasis is partly the result of isolation. When there are fewer people to delineate, each individual's inner life becomes larger, more dominant, and even more oppressive.

In some ways the format of the story Ross tells here is another clever way of talking about the prairie spirit. Chris does not know this landscape and its people at all. He comes to the prairie innocent of its ways, and thinks he can hide in an empty and benign element. He believes he has come from the centre of urban communities, where what people do really matters. Little does he know that the opposite turns out to be true: what happens in the urban centres is much less real, less significant, and less powerful than what happens in the isolated prairie. It is in the prairie that life is dynamic; in the prairie real love, real hate, and real crime take place. By comparison, the urban story he has left behind is cheap and insignificant, lacking all tragic dimension. Chris has, ironically, gone from a life of petty crime to a life of tragic dimensions, where real cruelty is inflicted for epic reasons. It is this relationship to classical tragedy that some critics have noted as a special feature of Ross's work, and *The Well* is no exception. The young Chris is a kind of Odysseus on his epic journey to personal redemption, and his search for a father is paralleled by the father's search for his son, in Homeric style. As the young man slowly discovers what land he has entered, the reader is shown what the prairie is about as well.

Some of the criticism levelled at this novel says it is not a satisfactory detective story or mystery or thriller. It has been suggested that some of the characters are one-dimensional, the plot is at times unconvincing, and the motivation for people's action in the story is not thoroughly delineated. But rather than reading *The Well* as an inadequate work of genre fiction, or as a partly unrealized work of prairie realism, it might be better to see this text as an exploration of the prairie spirit. To call this raising of the spirit of place a prairie "mystique" would be a misnomer. There is a real sense of hauntedness in the land and the weather, and in the people, depicted here. The haunting we notice makes times past, present, and future swirl together, and the human mind becomes possessed. This is Chris Rowe's actual journey. More than a psychological journey, or a moral and ethical journey, the young man is on an ancient errand where he is met by inexplicable forces that act on him. The whole emphasis of story, narrative, character, imagery, and motifs, such as the well itself, points to the encounter with the inexplicable.

The novel begins with an opening irony: namely, that as the young man heads out of the village into the open prairie, he begins to feel closed in instead of released or freed. As he and Larson ride on towards the farm, he realizes, "The prairie was closing behind him." Chris is afraid that "he would never find his way back." The fear of being lost while the journey proceeds is not uncommon in classical literature, and a guide is needed. Here the guide is Larson himself. The effect of the prairie on the traveller is immediate and clear:

> [he] felt oppressed, uneasy. It was his first contact with the open country; the bare expanse spread out before him now seemed gaping, mutilated, as if a giant shovel had sheared away something essential, like features from a face. He would never fit in, never survive. The feeling of exposure and inadequacy was so strong that it cost him an effort not to retreat to the truck and slam the door.

Chris loses his composure as soon as he comes in contact with this landscape in all its expansiveness. There is a sense of violence in the air which he does not understand and cannot explain. A tension hangs about him, which oppresses him until he wishes to be safe inside somewhere. Ross therefore turns the idea of inside and outside around, and the leitmotif at work—the well that surfaces later—is a perfect illustration of how a world that is too wide and large and open and bare can constrict a mind until it becomes like the shaft of a dry well. These feelings expressed at the beginning, of course, foreshadow actual events and set the tone for what is to follow.

Space itself, and how it expands and contracts inexplicably, becomes a force in the narrative that takes on a life of its own. Another force acting on the protagonist is sound. There is a stillness in the prairie which he is not used to, and he is in a way terrified by his encounter with it. Any sound imposed on that stillness becomes menacing and harsh. This is the case when a wind blows, or rain falls, or horses' hooves are heard, or footsteps or shouts ring in the distance. We get an early description of how the contrast between extreme stillness and harsh sounds affect Chris when a sudden whirlwind rushes past as he and Larson are talking. The whirlwind tugs at them, and Chris can feel the pull as if an actual being was pressing at his clothing: "When it was past the stillness tightened to a burning ache. Chris put his hand to his eyes and squinted at the sun. He felt the menace of the wilderness again." The blinding light, the unexpected interplay of sound and silence, the experience of exposure, all add up to a "menace" the city youth is unprepared for.

Chris's sense of self, his identity, begins to erode when he arrives on the prairie. The motif of the mirror therefore becomes a necessary and interesting device. In an unpopulated place, where only a few characters occupy the stage, his own image takes on the aspect of another character as well. He looks at himself as he would at a stranger. His idea of himself was shaped in an eastern city, with the help of half-realized peers and unsatisfactory responses from the environment. He has, in fact, no secure identity to bring with him and is at pains to discover who he actually is. As soon as he arrives at Larson's farm, the process of eroding and rebuilding the self begins. He meets the young wife Sylvia, who scoffs at him and makes him feel diminished. His first task is to wash up and shave, and to look at himself in the mirror to find out what he is really like. He finds his own image not so bad, after all. We are told that for Chris, "Restored good looks would mean restored self-respect. They would also be something to work with, a weapon." He wishes to return to Sylvia's presence looking good, the way he thought he did. In this attempt he is confusing outward appearance, which he can use as a "weapon," with real character. Much later in the novel, he is still unsure enough of himself to need to pay attention to how the townspeople see him. He goes to church with Larson and Sylvia, and is aware that people are looking at him. "He liked to be looked at," we read, "and remembering what the barber shop mirror had shown him a few minutes before, he felt at ease and confident."

What we will learn, of course, is that appearances are deceiving, and Chris' confidence is ill-founded. What the novel is about, at its essence, is how Chris "looks" on the inside: what his character is like as it is mirrored by the his landscape. The actual mirror that he shaves in front of at the outset offers him false hope, like a siren that leads him into wrong thinking. He spruces himself up and finds "the rediscovery of his good looks. After their brief eclipse they seemed even better than he remembered. For despite himself, he had half-believed the mirror, and now, as if wakening from a bad dream, he felt relief, a kind of gratitude." He uses his good looks as a tool to win over Sylvia and gain power where he had none. However, it will be, as he is to discover, a false triumph. The mirror lures, appearances lead astray, and the tools he brought with him from Montreal will not suffice in this new land.

The more philosophical conceptualization of appearance and reality, which underlines the whole novel, is literalized here in ways that may seem deceiving to the reader. Touches in the narrative that are so subtle they might be missed, but when considered are obviously important to the theme, simply reinforce the way in which the narrative problematizes itself. When Larson shows Chris the old house he built for his first wife, "he seemed trying helplessly to explain to Chris their [the wallpaper's] importance, the difference between appearance and reality." What Larson is unable to explain is what is in his head: his dreams, hopes, desires. Likewise, Chris is frequently unsure of how to take the others. He thinks he sees them, then he does not. He thinks he is secure, then they turn around and do something unpredictable. People are friendly, but then "suddenly he saw the friendliness itself as a trick to give him a false sense of safety." The land and its people exist before him in a kind of mirage, and we are not far from the possibility that here is where one may lose one's mind. It often happens in Ross's fiction, in fact, that a person literally loses her mind, such as in "The Lamp at Noon." That is part of the still inexplicable; part of the power of the prairie.

Chris arrives with his "tough hard strength in which he took such pride," only to find his self-reliance threatened repeatedly. His times with Larson can be happy because Larson seems to trust him. But he also feels threatened and wonders about the older man's sanity. He discovers that the more he gives in to his trust and wishes to like Larson, the more he can get hurt. And he does. In the centre of the prairie reality he is experiencing is the cold, hard fact of betrayal. And betrayal, "when it came, made suspect even the memories of his happy times." He is unable to remember clearly, because betrayal itself acts like a broken mirror and does not reflect things accurately. When he goes over what he is living through, he finds himself easily hurt: "He looked back through the hurt as through a cracked lens, and saw everything askew and darkened." In this manner, human emotion colours reality itself, and memory, history, and experience are all suspect in the same way one's vision is blurred by a prairie blizzard or a dust storm.

Ross goes to some length to narrate identity and memory through the use of mirror imagery. Everything for Chris becomes a mirror of sorts, which reflects him back to himself. Even the Boyle Street gang in Montreal, before he left, operated like a mirror for him, because "he existed only in the reflections they gave back." Chris thinks that since those characters are not with him here, he is free to create his own identity. It is a discovery he makes a quarter of the way through the novel: that he can, in fact, start to think of himself on his own terms. He ruminates that "here he could relax, slip a little, and it concerned no one but himself. No mirrors, no reflections—it was almost freedom." But he is wrong. It is still too early for him to know that the landscape he is in, the reality of the prairie itself, will be a more relentless, threatening and powerful mirror than any he has so far encountered.

He is not "free to create his own identity," as he thinks. He is not free until he has looked directly into the glaring land and the people that crack and distort it, and seen what there really is to see. In a way, this is a re-enactment of Zoroaster meeting himself in the garden. Because Chris is literally running for his freedom, away from the near certainty of being apprehended by the law if he is found, and because he has not been free on any level before this, *The Well* becomes a novelized essay on the notion of freedom. When is a person really free? What does freedom mean? How is it achieved and at what cost? To produce the image of an old, unused well ("our honeymoon well") in this context is interesting. A well contains water, and water reflects. But at the bottom of such a dark, narrow shaft (mentioned by some critics as a phallic image as well), we end up becoming very interested in what exactly Chris can or will see.

As usual with Ross, the story focusses sharply on the landscape, the weather, the horses, creating a double of itself on a psychological realm. Ross's work often sets itself up as a duplication, as if there were real space and cyberspace, or reality and virtual reality, already in his time. The prairie mirrors the human interior, so stories that are grounded in very earthy ways, on farms where work in the fields and in barns and in kitchens needs to be done, end up becoming ethereal: everything that happens is mirrored in the flux of human emotion and psychology. *The Well* is a stark example of this narrative duplicity. Ross's fiction does not operate symbolically in the way D.H. Lawrence's work might be seen as doing. With Ross, a horse really is a horse and not necessarily a symbol of some force of eros or brute strength. What distinguishes Ross's images is that they are not necessary images. They are objects that the characters, and by extension the reader, are unsure they can apprehend accurately. They, and we, are lost in what we thought was reality. In this novel, Chris begins to understand the value of being lost, and finds that the lack of certainty may be a way to freedom for him. He recognizes that "he had to get lost again, trim himself down to anonymity," because as soon as he settles into a certitude of some kind, he will be trapped in it, discovered, and lose his freedom. This will happen psychologically and emotionally as well as literally.

We are used to reading the family drama, or the family romance, when we read Ross, and *The Well* is no exception. His best-known novel, *As For Me and My House*, deliberates extensively on the nature of isolation and loneliness in the face of family emotions. Mrs. Bentley narrates a journal to herself about her life and what is happening, and through this diary we understand the story. In that book, therefore, the text as a mirror of reality, duplicitously presenting itself as two identical texts, works on the reader the way the family landscape works on Chris Rowe in *The Well*. Chris becomes unsure of who belongs where. He begins to feel that he belongs with Larson, while Sylvia does not: "it struck him that she was the intruder, the one who spoiled things." At the same time, the plot proceeds on the assumption that Larson is the intruder and spoiler, and it is he who has to be eliminated so Sylvia and Chris can be free. But this uncertainty about the exact nature of the nuclear family—is it Sylvia and Chris? Larson and Sylvia? Chris and Larson?—is part of the problem of the mirage the novel sets up on so many levels. It appears they cannot all three inhabit the same house at once. One of them has to go, and go into the well, which is described at first sighting as "the grey cribbing of a well projected two or three feet above the ground, with uprights and a cross-piece like a make-shift gallows." Larson has built this well for his former wife, as if to remind us that someone has to die before the novel is over.

Inside the family drama are emotions that will, like the well and the police and the townspeople who gossip, either entrap the protagonist or set him free. Late in the novel, when Larson offers Chris a position in the household of three, "just like a family," Chris immediately wonders, "Was it a trap?" Chris does not know. On the one hand, love and gratitude are freeing emotions, but he recognizes that if he gives in to Larson's goodness and accepts what he is offering (life on the farm, a position in the family, a secure job, and possibly part of an inheritance in the end), the young man will be "living under a perpetual obligation, owing him perpetual gratitude." The family itself becomes yet another force of entrapment for Chris, and the location and meaning of freedom remain an open question. Even back in Montreal, with the gang he put so much faith in before he left, he realizes that he had a "dread of committing himself to an organization that would henceforth have power over him." He could lose his freedom there too, before the shoddy crime happened which made him run. Freedom can be lost anywhere.

Chris has a sexual relationship with Sylvia through most of the story. This relationship in itself turns upside down the security of family relations. In Oedipal style, with the nod towards classical drama that distinguishes so much of Ross's work, Chris is the son who kills his father and sleeps with his mother. Yet at the same time he is not. He is neither son nor murderer, but more like a young Hamlet haunted by his nightmares, which he cannot distinguish from reality. Like the tortured Hamlet who has to face both father and mother, "He was frightened—frightened of them both, as a child is frightened of a nightmare that may return." Chris is frightened and repulsed by Sylvia's cold-blooded, calculated plans for killing Larson, as Hamlet is frightened of his mother's cold-bloodedness. He does not wish to run away, and he does not wish to stay. He knows of a crime he needs to relate, but is unable to speak it. Like Hamlet, he is torn between his visions and his knowledge, and his growing sense of self which is beginning to override all other stories.

We learn what is happening in Chris, the maturing of his character, when he says to himself in self-examination, just as he and Sylvia are executing their own "crime," that "it was less his actual crime which haunted him, than the ignominy and misery of flight." He sees how cowardly it is to flee, and that is what he has been doing all along. The face he sees reflected in his attempt at a real crime, therefore—a crime which presents to him the real, terrifying mirror of who he is—is the face of a coward. He realizes he has always been a coward. His "crime" in Montreal was really something he had "magnified and distorted" and was "nothing but a piece of stupid bungling." Fleeing was itself cowardly. In the end, he realizes he has walked into yet another trap, and he has done so out of cowardice. But self-realization brings redemption, and finally *The Well* is the story of the redemption of Chris Rowe. The young Montrealer has to come to the prairie and face the isolation, the uncertainty, the perpetual mirage, the depths of human despair and greed and misery and ineptitude, to find his way to real freedom.

Fanny, the horse in Larson's barn, gives birth to a colt late in the novel, when Chris is present. He has never witnessed a birth before and is both terrified and worried. The colt is not coming out right, and he does not know how to help it be born. This episode can be read as another material manifestation of what Chris himself is going through. He is being born, in a metaphoric sense, and he has to help himself. There is no one else to assist, and he has to rely on his own courage and wits to make it all come out right. As with the colt, Chris does not know he is in the process of rebirth, yet he knows this incident matters to him a great deal. Critics have noted the importance of the figure of the horse in this work, and much can be made of the meaning of horses here; for example Old Ned, and the horse that caused the death of Larson's son, which the farmer had to shoot. The animals on the farm are part of the prairie landscape, and part of its haunting. Fanny's colt begins to walk soon after it is born, which surprises Chris. More importantly, Larson appears and is the one who provides the final assistance. Ironically, Ole's son Chris, the namesake of the protagonist, who is quite ill and frail, dies at the same time as the colt is being born. In a novel such as this one, these seeming coincidences are meaningful. They amplify the reality that something weak and frail in Chris Rowe has fallen away as a brute strength, along with real compassion, have emerged in its place.

Another noteworthy feature of this novel is the relationship between speech and violence. The characters here seldom communicate with each other. They seem unable to express their feelings, although they sometimes try. Sylvia's account to Chris of her background, her way of explaining what amounts to prostitution, and the fact that she has prostituted herself to Larson on a permanent basis, becoming his wife in exchange for regular installments of cash, is dry and hard. Larson's explanation of his plans for his first wife and the way his son died is ineffectual and fragmentary. Chris himself is not actually able to express what has happened to him in the past, and he is unable to tell anyone about it. There is something clumsy about the way people interact, and something wooden in the telling of it. The whole narrative has, as a result, a tinselly feel, as though it is still fragile and could collapse under too much pressure. This quality in the narration and the dialogue may account for the scant critical attention *The Well* has received. But again, rather than searching for well-rounded situations and fully realized characters, which we will not get here because the people in the story are all unevolved in some way, we may look at the placement of violence instead. Domestic violence happens when people are unable to express themselves in other, more effective ways. Incidents of violence in this novel are significant for what the characters express through it. Ross may be insinuating that in a non-verbalized, or unarticulated, civilization, violence becomes the mode of speech. We go from one violent episode to another, one form of cruelty to another. It is the absence of speech, therefore, that partly haunts us in the novel. The overwhelming silence that is experienced on the prairie, which Chris cannot get used to, is mirrored in the tense silence between its inhabitants. While in the landscape the great hush is broken by bursts of whirlwind or storm or blizzard, a force which is terrifying and unpredictable; among the inhabitants the great hush is broken by outbursts of uncontrolled anger, either verbal or physical. Here is the haunting that permeates *The Well*, an echo that is cast back and forth about the walls of a narrow shaft. It is partly the fact that so much of the land is actually uninhabited, unspoken, unarticulated, that haunts. When it is lived in, on farms and in villages, the prairie is further haunted by people's inability to express their thoughts and feelings, and consequently to understand one another. It will be noticeable to any reader that all the characters in this novel are inept communicators and are acting out instead of talking together. What makes Ross's earlier novel *As For Me and My House* seem like such a breakthrough by comparison is that the narrator is in fact articulating herself. She is writing down her thoughts and processing her feelings, which is more than can be said for characters in *The Well*. But this latter novel may, as a consequence, be more telling about the reality of prairie rural life in decades past. Significantly, Chris is only free in some sense at the end when he becomes prepared to face the consequences of his actions, look himself in the face, and tell all.

The characters in this novel are haunted by their dreams. Chris dreams of being a fugitive no longer. Sylvia dreams of owning her own life, and not being owned by another, an older man who calls himself her husband. Larson dreams of getting on a train and riding away, never to be seen in the area again. All of their dreams amount to the same thing: they dream of freedom. While freedom is a universal human desire, it is also, more particularly, a Depression-era motif. Much in this novel hearkens back to the Depression of the 1930s, and the memory of it. Riding the rails, looking for work, difficult farming, cheap labour, running from the law, poverty, family entrapment—all are played out in great detail in literature that deals with the Depression. Sinclair Ross's works have, in fact, often been likened to the works of John Steinbeck. Both authors show us people who are engulfed by the difficulties of their lives, both materially and emotionally. But with *The Well*, the theme of freedom is so pervasive that it takes over the whole work. It is paradoxical that people are not free in this landscape, which is open, bare, expansive, and invites forward movement. But what entraps is so overwhelming that it is the absence of freedom, however we define it, that becomes the major haunting in the book.

The Well

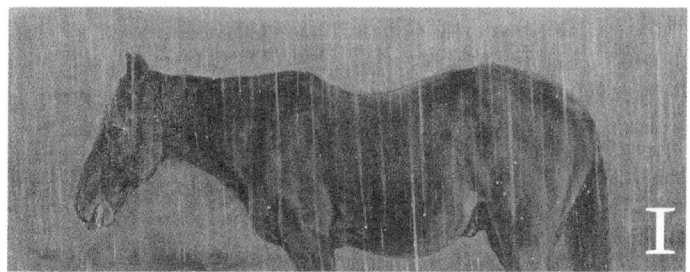

Two days north-west of Winnipeg, early in the afternoon, he left the freight at a prairie village called Campkin. It was wheat country and the beginning of the harvest season, but he was in search of food now, not work. The train would be probably two or three hours unloading freight and uncoupling empty grain cars, and he hoped in that time to beg a meal, perhaps a little bread to stay his stomach through the night.

The nights were the worst. Every creak and jolt was a footstep or whisper; nightmares dissolved into the reality of what he had done, where he was; and his fear, driven from his mind where it mocked the intrepid ruthlessness on which he had always prided himself, took refuge in his stomach as a gnawing hunger.

There was a town about every ten miles, but apart from the larger stations, where there was no help for it, he showed himself only once or twice a day. In case Baxter was dead—when he left, according to the radio, he had had a good night, was holding his own and a little better, but there was always the chance of relapse. In case the police knew he had left town, and had given his picture and description to the papers. The fewer who saw him the safer—even this far. The little towns, for that matter, were the worst. You stood out. Everybody looked at you.

Besides, begging a meal wasn't easy. Looking grateful went against the grain. It gave him a sense of furtiveness. It sapped his illusions of strength and importance. And somehow he couldn't shrug it off as a ruse, an exigency of the moment. It went deeper than that, involved his integrity. His way was to signal a waiter and bring him on the run, slap a bill down and say "Keep the change."

Yesterday—until then he had had enough for coffee and sandwiches—a woman had set him down on her back doorstep to stew and potatoes and half a prune pie. Farther along, on the same street, another had given him a stale loaf and a few slices of bologna. But today there were only sour faces and slammed doors. Perhaps because the appeal and boyishness of his smile were beginning to lose out to his filthy shirt and the stubble of his beard, because he was taking on a haunted look. Or because the crops had been a long time ripening, and the Campkin housewives were tired of hungry harvesters getting by on hand-outs while they waited for a job. He knocked at seven or eight doors without success. At the last one a shrill woman said, "There's a restaurant if you want to eat—that's what it's for."

He started back towards the train, a little sick with sun and hunger, then decided to take her at her word. There was time. If he offered to work for an hour in the kitchen they might give him at least some soup and bread.

It was a small, dingy restaurant, with cracked yellow blinds and a ceiling that a tall man could have touched. Flies swarmed through the hot gloom. There was a rancid, weeks-old smell of grease and cooking.

The proprietor, a fat, bland-faced Chinaman, lolled against the cigar and candy counter half asleep. There was only one customer, an old man with a white bald head who sat at a table near the door that led to the kitchen, eating soup and swearing at the flies.

The smell of food made him ravenous. Encouraged by the flabby look of the Chinaman, he decided to order a meal and offer to work in the kitchen afterwards. He had talked his way out of worse spots. Even if the Chinaman turned ugly and got help, there was nothing they could do. Broke and without a job—they weren't going to lock him up for the price of a meal. It would pay the town to let him catch the freight.

But when he approached one of the tables the Chinaman straightened. "Pay first," he said sharply, "then eat."

He hesitated, his hand on the back of the chair he was ready to pull out. The Chinaman continued, his voice singsong but threatening, "Good meal one dollar—soup, pork chops, pie. Too many like you. Pay first, then eat."

Remembering that he was hungry, he said quietly, "I can't—I'm looking for a job."

"No job here. Maybe you ask first I let you. Now go."

"I could help a while in the kitchen ..."

"Lots of help in the kitchen. Now go."

As he started out the old man who was eating called him. "Better have something to eat with me, son. Maybe I can fix you up afterwards with a job. Big crop coming in—always lots to do." Spoon in hand he motioned him to his table, then with the same gesture beckoned the Chinaman. "How'll pork chops suit you? They've got hamburgers too, but I wouldn't trust them—not with the flies. Double order for the boy."

He was a man well on in his sixties, stooped, broad-shouldered, bony. His hands were big and rough, his jaw stubborn; his eyes, in contrast, had a dreamy, clouded look, something about them lost and vacant. He gestured expansively, gave his order to the Chinaman in a clear, slightly strident voice, yet his smile when he looked up was timid and uncertain, almost as if he were afraid of being laughed at or rebuffed.

"Name's Larson. Swede—away back—don't speak a word." He held out his hand. "That's what everybody calls me, even the wife—just Larson."

"Chris MacKenzie."

The Chris was on his own. The MacKenzie he had decided on a week ago—the name of a teacher who once had tried to persuade him to quit his gang and spend more time studying. He had been repeating it to himself ever since, with a kind of

The Well / 5

wry humor, even laughing sometimes, because if you laughed things couldn't be so bad: "Me, will you, Chris Rowe, calling myself after that silly bastard!"—so that now he spoke it without hesitation.

"We've got a Chris in the family too. Only seven and his heart's no good. Born that way—doctor says he won't last another year. First wife had a sister—her grandson—but he calls me Uncle."

He looked at Chris searchingly a moment, as if seeking resemblances, then added, "Real name's Christian. His dad's a Swede, too. How about you? Christian or Christopher?"

"Christopher, Christopher MacKenzie."

"It's all right, doesn't matter." He shrugged concedingly. "Saw you get off the freight. Just like a kid for trains myself. Any time I'm in town I never miss one. You ought to hear Sylvia carry on about it."

He pushed away his soup bowl and wiped his mouth with the back of his hand. His pale blue eyes stared past Chris absently. "Always thought I'd like to do it too. Like you, riding the rods. No bags or parcels—no slicking up first."

His eyes brightened, came back and rested on Chris, soft and envious. "At night, riding along in the dark with the whistle blowing. Just going anywhere, not giving a good goddam."

Another Chinaman, old and withered, with a palsy-like shuffle, brought Larson a plate of pork chops and potatoes. "All fat and bone," Larson said critically, tapping on one of the chops with his knife, "but it'll keep us going in the meantime. You're getting double. Can't stand anybody hungry."

He held up his knife, squinting along the blade to see if it were clean. "Tonight, now, you'll get a real meal. Better than in one of those fancy hotels. Lots of it and clean. A couple of weeks and Sylvia's going to have you up ten pounds."

The old Chinaman returned with Chris's soup. "Swede, too," Larson continued: "Can't speak a word either, but she looks it—all this yellow hair. I've had her now round five years."

His eyes had gone vacant and soft again. "Five years just about now. I took a few days off before harvest that year and went to Regina for the fair. She was waitressing in a little place near the station—had her home inside a week. Big crop ready, couldn't wait for a honeymoon. Got her a fur coat for Christmas instead."

It was sinking in. Even as he gulped the greasy soup, Chris was looking for an angle, wondering if it was a set-up where he might fit in. Play along with the old fellow till he'd had his meal, then catch the freight again; that had been his intention when he sat down, but now it struck him that the job might be worth his while.

The police were probably still watching Boyle Street, all his old hangouts, trying to work something out of his mother and the boys; but even if they'd moved out of town, even if they'd put the screws on Helen, the last place they'd look for him was a farm. Not Chris Rowe. Handling a hayfork or whatever it was you did—that wasn't his speed.

Try glasses and a moustache, Helen had said. Try a crewcut; change all the little things they maybe know about you, like the kind of cigarettes. If you ever play pool don't show off how good you are. But this would be better still. For a few weeks, a couple of months even. Till he got steadied up again, had a chance to think things out sensible and straight.

Above all, till he had a little cash. He had always leaned on money. It had bought him approval, given him a kind of license for contempt and insolence. Without it he felt helpless, disintegrating, like an alcoholic locked in a dry room.

It was a craving as indiscriminate as an alcoholic's—a quart, a mouthful, rye or raw alcohol—whose imagination, paralyzed by need, can project itself no farther than the moment of relief, the glow and tingle of the first swallow. So with Chris it was money itself that was important: the idea of it, its feel, color, rustle, smell—and for the moment, without so much as a coin to finger, it seemed that even what he earned as a farmhand would remove the feeling of disadvantage that had seized him, would restore his self-esteem.

And on another level, nearer the surface, he needed cash for clothes, perhaps a gun. And he had to move on and make contacts, get in on other jobs; perhaps find Rickie, who was somewhere on the west coast; eventually make his way to Mexico or the Argentine. It wasn't clear. His mind wasn't working well enough to attempt a program. He only felt the need of getting started, trusting vaguely, with a reflex-like vestige of his old conviction of luck and uniqueness, that once under way he would be able to handle himself and hit his stride.

Besides, on still another level, he rather liked the old man, somehow felt safe with him. For the last ten days he had been alone, unnerved, all the familiar haunts and faces that might have reassured him lost somewhere on the far side of a wilderness of shunting cars and darkness; and his response now, unknown to himself, had in it something of gratitude. The inherent softness of his nature, everything immature that had been held in place by nerve and vanity as a rupture is held in place by a truss, was swollen out painfully in need of protection and security.

His meal came. He ate for a minute or two in gulps, then leaned forward and looked hard at Larson. "This job you've got for me," he said, "how much does it pay?"

"Depends on what you can do, son. I pay fair."

"That makes it pretty one-sided." Although he had never had a job—it was an especial pride—he was instantly alert to his rights as a worker. "After I've been with you a while you maybe say I'm no good. I've got to take it—just what you feel like giving me."

"Nobody's trying to make you come. I pay fair."

His jaw came out. His eyes were hurt, unyielding. Chris met them a moment, then said submissively, "Sure, we can talk pay afterwards."

"You've got nothing to worry about. You won't be sorry."

But it was a new experience: to trust someone and to be trusted, to show his hand and show that it was empty. He felt exposed, uneasy. "I'll try it for a week anyway," he said, skeptical, aloof, trying to regain a little of the ground he had lost; and then, yielding again, "If you'll keep me that long. At first I won't be much use to you."

"You've got soft hands. You've never worked much—on a farm or anywhere."

They were good hands, slender and shapely, but not effeminate, and it piqued him that Larson should describe them as soft. They were one of his vanities. They even served as a justification for what he was, the kind of life he lived. The things he would have been good at, that he was meant to do, that would have earned him a place in the world—he'd never had a chance to do them. The wrong street, the wrong home—what could you expect? "Look at the hands on him, will you! He's not cut out for a pick and shovel, that one," his Aunt Rosemary used to say when he was small. "One of these days you'll have to be getting him a piano."

Sometimes when alone, in a restaurant or bar—never among his crowd, to whom hands were strictly utilitarian, for slugging or cards—he would pose a little, holding his glass or cigarette to show them to advantage; and sometimes, losing himself in a fantasy or day-dream, he did play the piano, not so much now to display his hands as to win the approval and acclaim of a world which in these moments he forgave and—the envied now, not the envying—forgot to despise.

"They're not soft. And this isn't either."

As he spoke he pushed his sleeve back and brought up his forearm. His muscles were good; he worked at them. Only in spurts, but hard and intelligently enough to keep them where they were worth showing off. A stretch and a yawn, then his fingertips to the back of his neck, elbows out like wings; in summer, when he was wearing a sport shirt or short-sleeved sweater, it was an almost unconscious routine.

Larson nodded respectfully. "But what I mean, your hands look soft like somebody living in town. See mine now..." He held them up to show the cuts and bruises. "That one's barbed wire, and there's the nail coming off where I jammed it fixing the windmill."

Chris scarcely raised his eyes. Sensing that he had offended him, Larson went on, "But you've got real nice muscles there— nice a set as I've ever seen. Been training?"

"Off and on." Chris kept his eyes down, and spoke with his mouth full. "Not so much lately."

"You mean the gloves? A real fighter?"

Chris cleaned a bone, then puckered his mouth in qualified assent. "Kid stuff—they used to say I wasn't bad. Some of them talk like I've still got chances."

There was a little truth in it. Six or seven years ago he had been a promising youngster, with the beginnings of style and a fearless will to win. But before long, realizing that the ring offered no future, only sport, he decided that the occasional small-time thrill of victory in a police-sponsored boy's club was hardly worth the risk of cauliflower ears or a smashed nose. His nose was a particularly good one, and his profile, like his hands, was already important to him. The moments of conquest and admiration in which he sometimes indulged would not have survived disfigurement.

"Sure, you've still got chances. All you need right now is some sleep and a few of Sylvia's meals inside you. Come far, son?"

"Montreal."

It was a slip—Montreal was where Chris Rowe came from— and he added quickly, "But the last couple of years I've been pretty well on the move. Right now Montreal's where I'm heading for."

"But you're going the other way. Going west?"

"No, just doubling back. They said there were better chances of a job. I want to see my old lady—she sort of worries. I left Vancouver a couple of weeks ago."

"Right across." Larson's face lit. "That's a lot of travelling round for just a young fellow. You must have seen a lot of places."

"A few—right across the States too. A couple of times— and a while in Mexico."

It was the sudden scent of prey. He lied now less to make an impression than because he realized Larson was eager.

His eyes had taken on a rapt, childlike look, and Chris sensed that he was in the presence of something abnormal, perhaps exploitable. Keep on talking, feed out his line gradually; his reward might be special consideration, a few privileges. Better pay, time off—for the moment his mind went no farther. For his response to the scent was instinctive. He had not yet identified it.

"It sort of grows on you. I got as far as Cuba once. Just a kid, seventeen. One of these days I'm going back."

The name came readily. It was as far as a friend of Rickie's had got before they caught up with him. "Maybe after Christmas I'll be heading south again ... this time maybe South America. Can't stay in one place—seems I'm just made that way."

"Me, too, if I had the chance. And you're right to do it now when you're young. Before you get rheumatism and stiff joints. Later on there's always something to hold you anyway."

"The palm trees and the blue sky—that's for me." It was travel posters and technicolor movies now. He was doing it for Larson's benefit, guilefully, not quite knowing why, but as his words conjured up the scene a kind of wistfulness made them ring sincere. "The beaches and the boats coming in ... everybody taking life easy ..."

"I know exactly. And if I could I'd do it too."

The approval in Larson's voice was emphatic, as if he were trying to establish, despite superficial differences, a kinship with Chris. "The track runs just about a mile from my place. Sometimes when I can't sleep I lie and listen to the whistle. Always a lot of freights in the fall; nights it's so still you can even hear the engine. I keep on listening after it's gone—sort of riding along, leaving everything behind. Wheat and fences and no-good hired men and goddam things always breaking. Sure—even Sylvia."

He blurted out her name angrily, then went on with a slight touch of grievance in his voice. "I thought once I had her I wouldn't do it any more, but it's just as bad." His eyes had settled on Chris again, defiant, defenceless. "It's crazy, a man my age, and I figured she'd fix it for me. I mean so I'd be satisfied, never hear the trains. Nice young wife ... you'd think so."

The shuffling old Chinaman returned with their coffee and two pieces of raisin pie. Chris took a small bite and swallowed slowly. He broke off another piece, worried it a moment, then pushed back his plate and took a sip of coffee. He wanted the pie, but his hunger, now that it had eased a little, seemed a humiliation. It was as if he had yielded to Larson, grovelled before him. His impulse was to straighten, give the lie to his need and helplessness.

"There's pudding too, but it's worse." Larson watched him solicitously, apologetic for the fare he was offering. "If you're still hungry you'd better eat a couple of candy bars."

"I'd rather have a pack of cigarettes—if you'll stand me."

"Sure, son, but why not get makings, like I do? Just as good, comes a lot cheaper."

"If it's all right with you I'll get a pack too. I've never rolled and I don't feel like taking time right now to learn."

Larson brought out his wallet and gave him a dollar. "That'll do you for now. Somebody always comes to town Saturday night, so anything else you want you can send in for."

"Could you make it two?" He ran his hand over his cheek and chin. "Feels like I'd better get some shaving cream and a razor."

"I've got a spare razor. Just get yourself some shaving cream. But there's another dollar anyway."

Chris ran the bills through his fingers slowly, as if testing them. "Two dollars—you'll keep it out of my first pay."

"Cash two dollars, meal one—that's three." Wetting his lips, as if working with a pencil, Larson tilted his head slightly and frowned. "No, just the two dollars cash. We won't count the meal."

Something in his voice, the set of his mouth, made it plain that the decision had been reached over the protests of an ingrained parsimony. "It'll be more than a dollar for the meal—you had double pork chops—but we won't count it anyway."

Chris drew down the corners of his mouth, nodded without looking at him. Crossing the street to the drug store he muttered, "Tight old bastard—Jesus!"

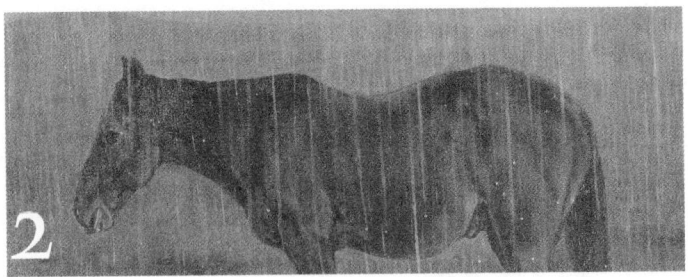

2

"Mine starts here. Soon as we're over the ridge you'll see the buildings." About four miles out of town Larson slowed a little and motioned towards the land on his right. "Three sections: two here that I farm myself, and another piece over that I've got rented out. Young Chris that I was telling you about—his father."

The fields were brassy with wheat and sun; a scattering of high, small cumulus clouds, white-tipped, grey-bottomed, sprawled loose blue shadows over the slow dip and heave of prairie. Even in the truck Chris could feel the sultry hush. They seemed cleaving a passage through it, just as the last few nights the train had seemed to cleave a passage through the darkness. And the light was no help—it only added hostile, eye-like glare.

The austere serenity of the landscape was lost on him. Roads, telephone poles, fields with men and horses working—the foreground at least was to human scale, but his imagination, fixed in its alley-doorway patterns, shrank from the stark, sky-and-earth immensity. It seemed desert-like and sinister.

And again, as on the train, he felt lost, cut off. The prairie was closing behind him. He would never find his way back. Grasshoppers flew up and dashed themselves against the windshield with crunching little plops. A black whirlwind twisted viciously across the road in front of them, and then, like a crazed reptile, sped teetering into the adjoining field.

They changed direction, south to east. On the crest of a slight rise in the land Larson pulled to the side of the road and stopped. "There, you can see them now," he said, nodding towards a clump of buildings. "If you like we'll take a minute and get out."

A big white house, a big red barn, a gleaming, silvery silo; but Chris's eyes slipped past them, unarrested. From where they stood the prairie fell in easy, wrinkled undulations halfway to the horizon, spread out a few miles, flat as the surface of a lake, and then, gathering the last faint momentum of its descent, slid smoothly to a standstill like a spent toboggan against a range of stubby sand-hills. He still felt oppressed, uneasy. It was his first contact with the open country; the bare expanse spread out before him now seemed gaping, mutilated, as if a giant shovel had sheared away something essential, like features from a face. He would never fit in, never survive. The feeling of exposure and inadequacy was so strong that it cost him an effort not to retreat to the truck and slam the door. He wanted to shout to Larson to take him back to town.

"I always like it the way you come up the hill and there they are."

Larson's voice was shy and mumbling. He glanced at Chris as if for encouragement, to satisfy himself that it was safe to continue. "Sometimes I stop by myself the way we're doing now. Just a few days ago old man Martin came along and caught me—one of my neighbors, a couple of farms over. Told him I heard a knock in the engine. We both listened and sure enough he heard it too."

"How much is a section?"

Larson stared at him a moment, then laughed. "You sure haven't spent much time around a farm, now have you? Like a new fellow once I told to harness a team and he got the collars on upside down. Only he let on he was an old hand, and you told me first."

Set back a little, Chris reached for his cigarettes. Larson went on, the faint tone of contempt and incredulity—countryman to city dweller—giving away to complacency again. "A section, son, is six hundred and forty acres. But you don't know how much an acre is either, so let's say a square mile. And like I said already, I've got three of them."

"You mean you actually own them?" Chris spoke with half-closed eyes, trying to convert three square miles into city blocks. "That's a lot for one man, isn't it?"

"Clear title to every acre." Larson took a step into the field and shelled a head of wheat into his hand. "My old man started with a quarter—what you call a homestead. You used to get it free from the government. When he died and I took over forty-one years ago there was a half."

"You're doing all right then." Chris threw away his cigarette and began shelling a head too.

"Sixty-five." Larson blew off the husks and began giving the kernels a rough count. "I've been checking every day for the last week and it's always sixty-five. Forty bushels to the acre easy."

"And that's good?"

"People round here think it's good when they get twenty. Land's been worked so long it's starting to play out. But I do it scientific." He leaned a little on the word, pleased with it. "I rotate. I grow alfalfa and raise cattle. And I make money every year."

"Then you've got the right idea. What's alfalfa?"

"It's good feed, and it puts something back into the land that wheat takes out. That's what I mean, doing it scientific. I had a boy once. I got it from him."

He stood for a moment looking past Chris, trickling the kernels from palm to palm. "Cora—that was his mother—I lost her when he was eleven. She made me promise I'd keep him at school, scared I guess he'd turn out like me. He was smart at school, too. Maybe just a little too smart. Not much fun in him, always a book. But you could trust him. And willing. All kinds of little things I didn't know about till afterwards and I had to do them myself.

"Only he got so goddam critical." He tossed the kernels away, then spat. "Twelve or so, and starting to tell me I didn't know how to farm. He got it at school. Mostly it's women teachers, but a couple of years there was a young fellow called Norris. Quiet, something like a preacher, but all right what little I saw. The boy, though, took a real shine to him. Every time we sat down to a meal it was some smart new idea he'd got from Mr. Norris. I was growing too much wheat and wasn't doing my summer fallow right and I didn't know how to feed hens. Same with the women. After Cora died I had to keep one for running the house and looking after him, and he was always telling them they had germs in the milk and everything ought to be boiled."

He returned to the truck and stood bunting his toe against the front tire. "Then I lost him. The school's three miles, so he had to ride. A fast little sorrel called Minnie. Smart and mean and pretty. People were always telling me she was no horse for a boy. She'd get the bit in her teeth and go anywhere she wanted. Sometimes she threw him—more times I figure than I ever heard about. But I was sort of proud. Skinny little fellow you could have picked up with one hand, and all that nerve."

Chris held out his cigarettes, but as if they were a suggestion rather than an offer, Larson began to roll his own. "It was the saddle; she had a trick of taking a deep breath so you couldn't get the girths tight, and this morning, just as they were going through the gate, it turned. Soon as she felt him round her feet she went crazy—it didn't take her long. And right at the last, like it was an old joke between us, he said 'Grow alfalfa.' Same as his mother, digging her nails in and saying 'Keep him at school.'"

There was a sentimental streak in Chris that a tough street had taught him to control. It threatened now, and he said defensively, "So it was a good tip—the kid knew his stuff. You've been growing alfalfa and making money ever since."

"Something like that. Not quite so fast or easy. If you're going to grow alfalfa you've got to have cattle to feed it to, and building up a herd takes time. Right now I've got around sixty, after shipping a carload in June."

He, too, was throwing up his defences. His voice was self-consciously dry and business-like. "There was a section for sale right across the road that was still three-quarters pasture: a ravine cutting through it and some scrub poplar and a creek in the spring. So I took that and left the pasture. Good grass—they do pretty well for themselves till snow. A dry spell and I've always got plenty of feed to help out. You can't always depend on wheat, but a few steers to sell and you've got your groceries."

He smoked in quick, nervous puffs. "It's work. Most farmers lay off a little in winter—up some of them as late as eight. Me, it's the same as summer, half-past four or five."

"Jesus—half-past four! You mean you still do?"

"Sundays just the same. Couldn't stop now if I wanted to."

"But what's the good of making money, then? Why don't you hire yourself a couple of men?"

"Just never satisfied unless I'm doing things myself." Larson spoke patiently, as if not expecting to be understood. "I don't like too many around—spoils it for me. It's not my farm any more. Six or seven months a year I need help—like now, getting the crop off—but when I can manage alone I do."

He looked at Chris and smiled. "Getting old—full of old ideas. I've got my truck and car—new Cadillac, just this spring—but for the land and hauling I still like horses. Twice as many as I need, just eating their heads off. Right now we're combining with the tractor. Ole's running it, I'm keeping out of the way. Young Chris with the bad heart—Ole's his father. Rents from me, and I can always get him to help out. Better than strangers; keeps it in the family."

Another whirlwind sprang up behind them over the rise in the land, spun so close they felt its tug at their trouser legs, then reeled down the long incline of prairie. When it was past the stillness tightened to a burning ache. Chris put his hand to his eyes and squinted at the sun. He felt the menace of the wilderness again.

"The same day I shot her. She'd gone back to her stall and I did it right there. She put her nose out, thinking I was going to take off her bridle, and I climbed into the manger and let her have it right between the eyes."

His face looked pinched and fallen-in. He began nervously rolling another cigarette. "Didn't think—just let her have it. In a way, though, it helped—took my mind off him. I'll show you their picture sometime, the two of them."

He finished rolling the cigarette, hesitated a moment, not wanting it, then thriftily put it in the breast pocket of his shirt. "The alfalfa helped too. Started paying off my debts, buying more land."

Chris gave a short laugh, still on the defensive. "Up at half-past four—Jesus, you ought to be able to buy land!"

"But it was the alfalfa that made the difference—his idea. Spring and fall all farmers get up at half-past four. You don't find many, though, that own three sections."

He gave a quick glance up the road, then turned to Chris confidingly. "Here's something else. All along it's him I've been doing it for. Sure, he's dead—sort of a game I keep playing—thinking things up for him, supposing to myself he's going to drop in on a visit and look the place over."

He glanced up the road again, leaned towards Chris and touched his elbow. "Then he comes and I start showing him around. Asking him how he likes it, talking away. Sometimes they catch me at it, and say I'm crazy. But I'm not talking to myself like they think. I'm talking to him."

Chris watched him uneasily, wondering if he might be getting in for more than he had bargained.

"It's not right carrying on like that, and all along it kept worrying me. I'd think sometimes maybe I'd got queer, living too long alone. So I figured what I needed was a wife again, like a lot of people kept telling me."

He shook his head and began stubbing his toe against the front tire again. "But Sylvia's been no help at all. Four years ago I put in electric light—that was for him. Last summer I painted the house over—that was for him too. No difference. And I keep on thinking about the trains, listening and taking off on a trip. Her lying right there beside me. Just turned thirty—nice a shape as you'll see anywhere, and all that hair.

"I don't mean she's no use to me." His voice rose, boastfully. He turned to Chris and winked. "But afterwards I lie going places again, or playing the game with the boy. Actually, he'd be a big fellow like you now, supposing he did show up. Sometimes that's the way I play it: I get him a wife and a new house of his own. He's been away, seeing places, just like you. Then he comes home and I've got everything ready waiting."

He turned and looked at Chris thoughtfully. "He had black hair too; that was Cora. And if he took after me he'd be about your build. It's hard to see him grown up, after thinking about him small so long—but allowing a little, you'd just about do."

Then abruptly he motioned Chris back into the truck, and the rest of the way they drove in silence.

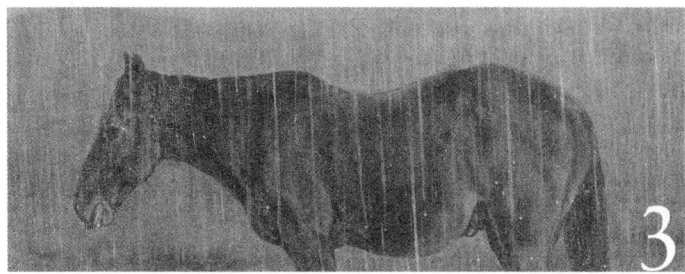

3

"There's a bunkhouse—that's what it's for. You're not bringing him in here."

"It's full, Sylvia; we've been out looking it over. I thought he'd be all right for a night or two in the little south room—just till I can fix up something else."

"There's enough cleaning up to do already. This is no flophouse."

"There'll be nothing extra. He'll make his own bed, won't you, Chris? Just like the boys in the bunkhouse."

"You heard me—get him out."

She was a handsome, big-breasted blonde. Even in disarray, caught up carelessly behind the ears, darkened along the forehead with perspiration, her hair had spark and lustre. The nose was strong and straight, with flared nostrils that gave her a look of suppressed, hard-breathing energy. The mouth had a sinewy twitch when she spoke, as if it were an exposed muscle. As she advanced towards him across the kitchen her deep-set eyes had a look of contempt that she made no effort to conceal. Meeting it, he drew his lips in thin and retorted silently, "Bitch—before you're finished you'll be begging for it. Crawling!"

"You've got to be reasonable, Sylvia. I'm telling you the bunkhouse is full."

Her nostrils quivered. "Couldn't you find a clean one?"

"He's got shaving cream in his pocket—let her see it, Chris. Asked for a dollar as soon as I hired him. Shows he *wants* to be clean."

A second woman, thin and grey-haired, was sitting by the window with a pan of vegetables in her lap. "Back where you come from, Sylvia," she asked drily, "was everybody always slicked up and clean? Never see your old man with a three days' whisker?"

"Mrs. Paynter, my first wife's sister. This is Chris, too, but Christopher. Her daughter's married to Ole, the one that's renting my other place. Mrs. Paynter lives with them, but sometimes she comes over and helps out when we've got extra men."

"You look beat, Chris." She gave a friendly nod and went on scraping carrots. "Want something to eat, or can you wait?"

"I can wait all right. Mr. Larson got me a meal in town."

"Get him out of here." Sylvia's voice shot up dangerously. "Him or me—I'm not arguing."

"It's harvest, Sylvia ..."

"You're telling me it's harvest! Who do you think's dishing up the meals around here?"

"I'll set him helping you too—digging potatoes and a lot of things. Good steady boy—we've been talking. He's got to sleep somewhere."

"What's wrong with hay? Give him a blanket and put him in the loft."

"I treat my men fair. Nobody's sleeping in the loft unless I say so." His voice went hard. A rush of blood washed out the dividing line between his sunburned face and white bald skull. "Come on, Chris, don't mind her. I own the beds around here."

Limping slightly, but his step firm and angry, he led the way through the kitchen into the hall and upstairs. "Not very big, but the bed's all right. A real good mattress." He held the door open for Chris, then sat down on the bed and bounced a time or two to demonstrate the springs. "Sleep here myself sometimes when Sylvia's having one of her spells."

He looked up and winked again. "Not such a bad idea giving it to you. There's a big spare room next to ours, but it's all fixed up fancy. She'd never stand for me messing round in the frills. So if you're here, spell or no spell, she's got to let me stay where I am."

It was a small, clean, hot room, furnished with a white iron bed, a golden oak dresser and a kitchen chair. Chris stood still a moment, trying to breathe out the smell of varnish and linoleum, then began tugging at his unbuttoned shirt collar. In its effect on him the close, cupboard-like room was an inversion of the open prairie. Driving along in the truck he had felt exposed, conspicuous. Here he was trapped, a prisoner.

He was vaguely ill-at-ease, too, at being shown into a room empty-handed—nothing to set down, suitcase or parcel, with which to make a gesture of acceptance and possession. Involuntarily he brought the tube of shaving cream from his pocket, and with a shrug on nonchalance turned and tossed it on the dresser.

In the same instant he saw himself in the dresser mirror. It was the first time in several days, and at the sight of the haggard cheeks and the stubble of beard he stared incredulous a moment, then wheeled on Larson. "Is there some place I can shave?" His voice shook, urgent. "If it's not too much trouble—I mean right now."

"Sure, son, but what's the hurry? The farm's not like town. You shave when you feel like it—nobody cares. Sometimes when we're busy I go a week. Happened I did this morning, just because I was going to town."

"No, I'd like to, now. If you don't mind, right now." He couldn't help it. What others saw—that was what he was.

"No girls here to give you the eye." Larson stood up and slapped him on the back. "Just take it easy. After supper we'll get you fixed up so you won't know yourself. My shirts ought to just about fit you, and I'll look you up some overalls."

Chris turned back to the mirror furtively, as if hoping to find that the reflection he had just seen was a false one, that the red-rimmed, derelict eyes had been a trick of mind and nerves.

"But it won't take long—and I just don't want to wait."

This time his own ear caught the entreaty in his voice. He went on, trying to give his insistence a more rational turn, "What I want even more than a shave is a good wash. It's nearly a week—more than that. And the freights were hot ..."

"Sure, son, when I've been out in the dust I like a good splash too. It makes Sylvia sore, so a lot of times I do it in the bunkhouse."

"Couldn't I go there now? Start paying me tomorrow, and dock me for my meals today."

"Just cold water—no use asking Sylvia."

"I need hot all right—the shape I'm in." He looked in the mirror again and stroked his cheek dubiously. "But maybe with a new blade ..."

"Sure, Chris, one that's still got the paper on. How'll that suit you?"

The way the words came out, hesitant, then emphatic, as if there had been a momentary blockage, another gritty calculus of thrift in the duct of good will, suggested that he made his own blades last.

"It's just the way Sylvia's acting up. When she gets that look I don't like crossing her. Harvest's on. Any other time there's all the hot water you want."

"I can't say I blame her at that." Turning back to the mirror, touching his cheek again, Chris understood her contempt. He shrank himself from what she saw; no wonder she shrank from it too. Yet at the same time he remembered vindictively the way she had looked at him. The cut still smarted. His resentment, underground but undiminished, still called for a settling of the score.

It made the need of a wash and shave more urgent than ever. Restored good looks would mean restored self-respect. They would also be something to work with, a weapon.

He turned and went out, but Larson called after him. "In here—the bathroom—your razor and new blade."

It was the largest bathroom he had ever seen or imagined. Besides the fittings, basin, toilet and bath, there were two chairs, one a wicker armchair, one an old-fashioned rocker, a gramophone, a chest of drawers and a table on which were carefully arranged brushes, trinkets and perfume bottles. The curtains on the windows—two windows, one on each side of the bath—were stiffly frilled. Red carpet was laid right to the walls, even under the bath and fitted around the toilet. Larson gave a hitch to his overalls and said, "Quite a place, eh? Ever see anything like it?"

"Can't say that I have. Only, what's wrong with using it?"

"Oh no—Sylvia'd never stand for it. Not when you're just new. Besides, there's no hot water. Only in winter—we connect it with the furnace." He turned the hot-water tap to let Chris see. "We've got to bring it up from the kitchen."

"But Jesus! what's the good of it then?" For a moment Chris had thought he might be able to have a bath as well as a shave. Now, hotter and sweatier than ever, he could not control his anger. "A bathroom to look at—it's so goddam phony!"

The events of the last ten days had shaken him. He had done jobs before—tough, safe, little jobs—but this was the first time he had been in real trouble. Baxter might be dead for all he knew, and when it was murder there were no angles. Flight, somehow, confirmed his fears, even magnified them. He could not think through his situation rationally. He could not even believe what he remembered—that when he left, Baxter had been practically out of danger.

"What's the good of it?" he repeated, seizing a towel off the rack and slashing it across the bath like a whip. "You've got electricity, why can't you have hot water the year round too?"

"Sure, I've got electricity. And it works." Larson met his rage evenly, unimpressed. Naïve as a child he put his hand to the switch, on-off, on-off, looking up at the pale glimmer of light with a smile of triumphant satisfaction, as if the bulb's confirmation settled everything. "There you are—it works."

"Then why don't you put in a heater? Scared it'll break you?"

"Heater? What's that got to do with electricity?"

"A hot-water heater, so you'll have hot water *all* the time."

"I don't know anything about that. The electricity I got's just for light. And freezing, so we can keep meat. I make it myself. I've got an engine."

He switched on the light again, then looked at Chris and shrugged. "Sure, I know what you mean all right—Sylvia keeps talking about a heater too—and something rigged up so it'll run the washer. But you can't have everything at once; it's got to be gradual. There's not another farm round here that's got *any* kind of electricity. Instead of picking on me and wanting more you ought to be thankful."

"Why can't you have it all at once? You say you're making money. What are you holding out for?"

"Because it's no fun that way—it's all over." He swallowed, switched off the light. "I've got nearly everything now. The farm's just about where I want it. So if I don't go slow I'll run out of things to show the boy. New things ... surprises."

Chris hesitated. "You still mean the dead one?"

"Sure I mean the dead one. He's the only one I've got."

His voice quavered. His flat eyes blazed up a moment with indignation that seemed directed not so much against Chris as against a heartlessness and incomprehension that was all around him. Then, picking up the towel that Chris had flung into the bath, he said, "You oughtn't to have done that. It'll only start her off again. For your own good you ought to try and get round her. Meals and washing—things like that—she can make it a lot easier for you."

He smoothed the rumpled towel across his knee, then put it back carefully on the rack. "I know—you think I'm crazy talking like I do about the boy. But Sylvia's been no help at all. That's what I got her for, and I'm as bad as I ever was. Show her something new and it doesn't mean a thing. Nothing's a surprise—just looks for more."

Chris turned to the door again, but still Larson detained him. "You ought to hear the boy, the way he carries on. Like the new barn; he remembers what the old one was like. And the electric light; he remembers the lanterns and the coal-oil lamps. Don't suppose he's *ever* going to get over it. But Sylvia, she's just like you. Always wanting something more." There was no resentment; it was just an aside, an illustration. "Everything at once, nothing to look ahead to."

Again his hand went to the switch, on-off, on-off, the clicks quick and angry. "Besides, why should she? Cora had to wait. Sometime I'll show you the well we dug. Just the two of us, the first year we were married."

He straightened one of the brushes on the table. "It was on her account I put in the bathroom. Takes a lot of money in the country; no pipes or sewers to connect up with. But in her time we were living in the old place—everything she'd been looking forward to came after, and I figured it was as good a way as any to show her. Take a stone—you don't work up much feeling. The cemetery's too far away anyway. Here I can look in as often as I want to."

Chris wondered if it would be all right to sit down. "That was hers," Larson said, following his glance to the rocker. "Same as everything in here. It's her room."

He set the rocker gently in motion. "I got it for her when the boy came. We had another but she couldn't nurse him comfortable in it because it had arms."

He halted the rocker, gently still, as if it were a live thing that might tire itself, then turned to the wicker chair. "Never made a fuss about things we couldn't afford, but she did get it into her head she wanted this one. Had to be wicker—just a notion. You see all this stuff the way it twists ..." He squatted, and with his fingertip followed the pattern of whorls and curlicues. "She used to dust it with a brush. Every little corner, every day, she was that proud and careful. Sylvia just gives it a flip now and then, so I go over it regular myself."

He straightened stiffly and turned to the gramophone. "Something else she had to wait for. Supposed to be a wedding present, but it took a few years. Never got round to many records—always something we needed more."

He lifted the cover, peered inside a moment, and then, as if afraid Chris might intrude, closed it again quickly. "Never play it now—hardly ever. Lots of music downstairs anyway: a victrola and a player piano and a radio. Don't play them much either. Sylvia can't carry a tune."

His voice faded, came back crisp with malice. "Used to play it at night sometimes when she first came. Nights she wouldn't ... to make her sore. 'All right, *don't* then,' I'd say, and I'd get up and come in here and start putting on tunes. Till one night she came in and said turn it off or she'd get a hammer; so just in case, I didn't any more. I had to think of Cora. When Sylvia gets that look in her eyes I don't like crossing her."

Chris looked curiously at the table. "And all these things you've got spread out—they belonged to your first wife too?"

"Everything. This is her room."

"And Sylvia—Mrs. Larson—she doesn't mind?" He spoke slowly, his mouth drawn sidewise in a faint smile. Perhaps it was for the satisfaction of seeing her knuckle under to a worn-out old man that he asked the question, to have the picture elaborated, confirmed.

"Sure, she minds. When she first came you should have heard her. But we've got nine rooms and a basement, so I figure Cora's got a right to one. Sylvia can use it, but she's got no say. That's what I told her: 'If you don't like it, stay out. I'll just lock the door and keep the key.'"

"Anyway, there's no hot water." Chris suddenly felt his weariness again. He stood swaying slightly a moment, rubbing his knuckles into his eyes. "Maybe I can have that blade and razor."

"Sure, Chris. A brand new blade like this one, you don't really need hot water."

They went downstairs and through the kitchen quickly. Mrs. Paynter nodded. Sylvia, busy at the stove, kept her back turned.

"Just the same, I give in on a lot of things. Take pigs—smell didn't suit her. Keep them clean and they don't smell so bad anyway, and I had their pen on the far side of the barn. But she'd come out on the back step and stand sniffing, just working it up. So I said all right—for the sake of peace. But the men I feed you can figure what it costs me buying pork."

He cuffed down a young collie that came bounding at him. "And cows—ever hear of a farm where the woman won't milk? Makes me do it. Comes from a farm herself at that. Sure, she does. I got her in Regina, but that wasn't where she belonged. Won't lift a hand outside; says it's not a woman's work. Good cook, everything clean, but she'd be a poor one for a bad year if you were just getting started."

Chris snapped his fingers at the collie, and Larson said sharply, "None of that. Every time he comes at you slap him down. He's nearly a year old and he still just wants to fool."

There was a hint of rebuke in Larson's voice. Chris answered touchily. "I like dogs. I had a pup myself once, the same color." He hadn't intended to lie, and he hesitated a moment, surprised. "Friendly, just like this one. He got run over."

"Sometimes I wish *he'd* get run over." Larson stopped and looked after the pup that was loping off crazily in pursuit of a hen. "Supposed to be a cattle dog, but he just wants you to throw sticks for him."

His eyes had their lost, vacant look again. It seemed to Chris that they followed the pup, overtook it and then kept on into the distance. "Looks the same—sometimes I could swear it was. The white ear, and the way the tail goes."

"Maybe if you give him time—he's friendly."

"Not Norris. Better if I took him out some day with the shotgun."

"Norris? For a dog?"

"Didn't suit me either. It was the boy's idea."

"But it's just a pup—you mean ...?"

"I was telling you about the teacher he liked, the one that was always talking alfalfa. Felt bad when he left, so he called his dog after him. There's been one ever since."

Norris had forgotten the hen, and was sniffing the front wheel of the truck preliminary to cocking his leg. "From here even *he'd* be fooled. Must have looked over a dozen litters easy, trying to find the right one. Sometimes there's no way you can tell."

He paused a moment, his face brooding, then glanced at the sun and led the way to the bunkhouse. Inside, pointing to a tin basin, he said curtly, "Don't take all afternoon, and soon as you're finished, yell. This time of year there's lots to do—you've got to learn to make yourself useful."

4

AS SOON AS LARSON WAS GONE the pup came in. It stood quiet a moment, ears cocked, tail wagging, and then, taking Chris's silence for invitation, let out a yelp and leaped at him again.

He staggered back a few steps. He had never had a dog, and at the scrape of the big-nailed forepaws on his chest he thrust out his elbow defensively. But the next instant, realizing that this was still only play, he began to laugh and hugged the pup to him in sudden affection.

For a minute or two they rocked and stumbled around the narrow space between the beds in a kind of bear dance, Chris's face thrust into the shaggy coat, the pup frightened now, whimpering, but still trying to twist its head and lick his neck. Then Chris tripped and toppled backwards across one of the beds, and the pup, freed by their fall, stood over him, growling and tugging at his shirt in mock attack. Chris seized it again, and they struggled and rolled like wrestlers. At the wet swift dab of the tongue he kept bursting into laughter. It was a kind of hysteria, a release of shored-back terror and exhaustion. Then simultaneously they quietened and lay still. Chris felt drowsy and relaxed. His blood still seemed to throb with the rhythm of the train. The pup snuggled close, its muzzle on his shoulder watchfully.

The sound of voices roused them. Apparently Sylvia, at the kitchen door, was quarreling again with Larson. Tumbling the pup off the bed Chris bounded to his feet and began straightening the blankets. He had barely finished when Larson returned. "Brought you overalls and a shirt, and socks. Left more in your room. You're going to need a shaving brush too."

He frowned as he turned to go, apparently wondering why Chris had not even put water in the basin or taken off his shirt. But with a glance at the pup he only said, "Looks like he's taken to you. Just see to it when he tries to play you slap him down. Six months slow—it's getting so I'm ashamed of him."

When he was gone, Chris filled the basin with water from a pail beside the washstand. His spirits were high now. As he looked into the mirror and fitted the new blade into the razor he began to whistle. This time he didn't flinch even at the sight of his beard. The pup, crouched near the door, subdued but watchful, thumped its tail hopefully. He ignored it as he began to shave, but his confidence somehow was restored.

In such a mood cold water was an affront. After a dab or two at his face he threw the brush into the basin, then stood motionless a moment and smiled. The irritation, mingling with his high spirits, had served as a precipitant: now his old cocksure insolence was beginning to crystallize. He splashed the cold water on his face to remove the sweat and dust, ripped off the shirt he was wearing and put on the clean one. It was khaki, a fair fit, and almost new. He left two or three buttons open and creased the front back to show his chest. Then, after running his comb through his hair, he smiled experimentally. An appealing smile, boyish, a little forlorn. Mouth pulled sidewise, knowing, disillusioned, and at the same time wistful. Not a bad fellow—just up against it, misunderstood. Nobody's fool, though, either. He'd been around. He knew the score.

"Now what?" Sylvia greeted him harshly as he appeared at the screen door with the basin. "Supper's not till half-past six. I don't stand for anybody hanging around between meals."

"I know. Mr. Larson told me." He gave his smile exactly as he had practised it. "It's this beard of mine—I wondered if you could spare me a little hot water."

Her nostrils quivered. "One thing for sure, a little hot water won't do you any harm. Stay there and I'll see what's in the kettle."

When she returned he knew by the way she was carrying the kettle that it was full. If she would let him take it to the bunkhouse he would have enough hot water for an all-over wash as well as a shave, and he would also have an excuse for a second visit. "I'd like to take the kettle if you could spare it." There was no smile at all now, just the appeal. "Like you say, I can stand it, and I won't be long."

"It's heavy—don't stand there looking at it." Kicking open the door, she thrust the kettle towards him. "Are you supposed to be working round here, or taking a rest cure? There's plenty of time for shaving after supper."

She snapped the door shut and turned. He smiled as he went down the steps, then began to whistle again.

When he finished shaving his spirits were still high. It was the transformation, the re-discovery of his good looks. After their brief eclipse they seemed even better than he remembered. For despite himself, he had half-believed the mirror, and now, as if wakening from a bad dream, he felt relief, a kind of gratitude.

There was still more than half a kettleful of water. He washed his face and hands, then stripped and sponged off his body. He took a pride, almost excessive, in personal cleanliness. His fastidiousness, somehow, set him apart from the Boyle Street gang, even from Rickie, to whom he had once submitted, whom he still acknowledged—gave him the right to despise them. It was a qualification, like his hands and profile—a proof that the larger life he dreamed of was in reality his due.

"Your kettle, Mrs. Larson."

This time his smile had nothing practised or deliberate. Now that he was rid of his beard and dirty shirt, appeal was no longer necessary. "It's made me feel a lot better, " he said politely. "Sometime maybe I'll be able to make it up to you."

She took the kettle impassively. "Aunt Bessie's just made coffee. Do you want a cup?"

He hesitated. "I'm afraid Mr. Larson's waiting."

"Another five minutes isn't going to hurt—now that you've been this long."

"I wouldn't mind. I'm supposed to learn chores."

"*Learn* chores?" Her voice climbed as she held the door open. Her deep-set eyes dilated. "You mean a farm's new to you?"

"First time—I'm just about as surprised as you are."

She carried the kettle to the stove and then stood motionless as Mrs. Paynter poured his coffee. "Tell me, Chris," she said after a short silence, asking the question slowly, with apparent reluctance, "are you sure Larson met you in the restaurant?"

He watched her curiously as he sat down, wondering at the change. "That's right. He heard me trying to talk my way into a meal."

"Where did you come from?" She released the words carefully, her arms rigid at her sides. "How long had you been in town?"

"Half an hour—I'd tried a few houses before the restaurant."

"There was a freight about one o'clock. I heard the whistle." She turned to the table now and stood over him. "You came in on it and he saw you get off. That's right, isn't it? He just told you to let on to me he met you in the restaurant?"

"No, he'd been down watching the freight—he told me afterwards. But it was the restaurant where I first saw him. They were just ready to throw me out."

She gripped the edge of the table as if for support, her knuckles bone-white. "It's nothing to do with you," she said quietly. "Pay no attention and drink your coffee."

"Don't take on so about it. Here, you have some coffee too." Mrs. Paynter came towards the table with the coffee pot, but Sylvia wheeled, biting her lip, and half-stumbled out of the kitchen.

"What did I say?" Chris looked after her in bewilderment. "That's exactly how it happened."

"It's not so bad as she tries to make out. Anyway, she's no right to be talking about it in front of strangers."

She poured herself a cup of coffee and sat down facing Chris. "Larson's all right, but he's had a lot of trouble—lived too long alone. He keeps talking about trains, and she's afraid some day he's going to catch one."

"And the way you've got it figured out she wouldn't mind too much if he did?"

"You're just starting here, Chris—you don't want to get mixed up in things." She stirred her coffee severely a moment, then looked up with a conspiratorial nod. "Just the same, take my advice and keep clear of her. He's the one you're working for, and he's not such a fool as she'd like to have you think."

"Thanks, Mrs. Paynter. I'll remember."

He rose and went out slowly, rubbing his knuckles into his eyes again. For a few minutes after his wash and shave he had felt revived; now, as if in reaction, his weariness was settling on him like a drug. He stood in the doorway blinded by the sun a minute, trying to force himself into it; then from the bottom of the steps Larson said, "I was coming to get you. We've got a lot to do, and I want to show you the watermelons."

"Sorry. Mrs. Larson gave me a cup of coffee."

He staggered on the last step, and Larson gripped his arm. "Never mind—talking away so much I just didn't realize. Plenty of time tomorrow. You'd better get up to bed right now."

"It's just the sun. I'll be all right as soon as I get started."

"Your eyes are sticking." Larson started up the steps, taking him with him. "If Sylvia says anything I'll handle her. I'll call you for supper, and then you can go back again."

But when Larson woke him it was morning. "Shook you a couple of times last night," he said, "and you just turned over. Grinding your teeth and muttering away—thought I'd better leave you. No time to lose now, though, or you'll miss breakfast too."

5

"THIS IS THE TEAM I ALWAYS DRIVE MYSELF. They think they're going to get more oats—that's what all the fuss is about."

He slipped between two big greys with dappled rumps that had begun to stamp and whinny at the sound of his voice. "Walk right up. Put your hand on them good and firm so they know what it is. Makes them scared if they think you're scared."

Chris hesitated, then slipped in quickly past the threatening hooves and pressed close to Larson. "They're just sniffing you because you're new. Go on, do like I tell you. You've got to let them know you're boss."

Chris gave them a few light strokes on their shoulders, then slipped out again. "I told you in town—I've never handled horses." Larson had followed him, and he retreated a few steps. "You'll have to give me time, I've got to get used to them."

"Nobody's asking you to handle them. Your job's going to be cleaning out."

Contempt of country for city flashed again. "I'll show you. You load up a stoneboat and take it down the pasture a piece to the manure pile. It takes a horse at that, but you'll be all right with old Ned. His stall's further along. He's up close to thirty, and blind."

His face softened. "You've got to lead him. That's all I ever let him do, just so he won't feel out of things. Starting to get old myself—I know what it's like. I ought to shoot him too, but he's helped bring in a lot of crops."

The contempt was gone without a trace. Expansive and guidelike he continued, "First you'd better come up and look the loft over. You've got to feed, so you might as well start where it comes from."

At this time of the year, before the new crop was in, the loft was less than a quarter filled. It soared up, vast and arklike, seeming to sway a little, as if afloat. "Big, eh?" Larson's face had a wondering look, as if he himself were still impressed. "Best time now, when it's empty. You can see it. Right from here to the end—that'll be oat sheaves solid. And hay at this end—I'm bringing in a couple of carloads."

"I didn't know what she meant when she said the loft. It wouldn't be a bad place to sleep at that."

Larson watched him and smiled. "Sure, Chris, you're just a no-good tramp like me. I get the idea sometimes I'd like to sleep out here too. When it's raining—you can lie and think. But for nights I've got a bed. I'm crazy enough already as it is."

He stood for a moment looking up towards the roof again, then turned on Chris sharply. "You're not sleeping out here either. Like you heard me stand up to Sylvia and tell her—I treat my men right. There's a bed for you too."

"It's so still—makes you feel sort of safe and shut away."

"Come up for a while this afternoon. Nobody'll know. I'll chase you out in time for supper."

"Maybe I will. You don't get much sleep in a box-car, and it was about ten days."

"But you wouldn't change with me. You'll get up some morning and pull your pants on and say to hell with him and his chores. Just like that—and it'll be the last I'll see of you."

He put up his hand to ward off an interruption. "And you'll be right. Never let anybody talk you out of it. Me, there's always been something. Crop ready to cut, a mare going to foal—you can't just walk out and leave them. Now I've got rheumatism, and I guess for freights you've got to be quick on your feet."

"I don't get it. Why freights? If you want to go somewhere take a plane. Enjoy yourself—have fun."

"There's more than one kind of fun. What are *you* riding round in freights for?"

"That's different. I'd fly if I had the price."

"You could get a job and settle down if you wanted to. You don't need to beat your way around the country any more than I do. No, son—it's the way we are. Born right in us. Except that you do it, and I lie listening to the whistle."

Then, apparently forgetting that he had brought Chris to the loft to show him how to put the feed down the chutes, he turned to the stairway. "Wasting too much time—you've still got a lot of things to learn. First, there's Ned. You'd better come along and meet him."

Ned was a gaunt, rangy bay. His ribs showed; his hide was rubbed and worn in places like the elbows of an old fur coat. "Can't fatten him up—poor teeth. Lately he's been doing better on mash, but I don't think he'll last till spring."

Ned gave a wheezy sigh, swung his head till it met Larson's shoulder, then let it rest there. "Had him from a colt—back to Cora's time and the sod stable. Deaf and blind both, but like I say I can't shoot him. It would be murder again."

He ran his hand lightly along Ned's neck. "Whatever you do, never lose your temper. Never get sore. If he's slow starting, just coax him. And afterwards always give him a little slap like this on the belly, so he'll think he's done a good job."

Some of it reached Chris. He said earnestly, "I'll treat him all right. I'll be careful."

"Now we'll go and see Minnie, the little mare I was telling you about. See if *she* suits you."

Chris took her in in silence for a moment. Then, without turning, he said, "I'll trade you a box-car for her any day."

"Better see what she thinks of you. Go on—talk to her."

Chris glanced at him. "By the way, is she what you call a sorrel?"

"That's right. You mean you've never seen one before?"

"The boy's horse—didn't you say she was a sorrel too?"

"Spit of the first Minnie, except she's bigger. But that's going to be all right for you."

"You think I could?" Chris's face lit. He met the fine, curious nose turned towards him with his fingertips, and then, to redeem the timidity of his approach to the greys, stood motionless while she rubbed her head against his sleeve.

"Sure, son. She needs exercise anyway. Take her out every day if you like. Nothing to be scared of. No tricks except sometimes she shies."

He stepped back to the corner of the stall and eyed Chris up and down. "You'll look fine. She's bigger and *you're* bigger—like you've both been growing."

Now Chris saw himself astride her. And though it was a strange, unexpected picture, it pleased him. Somehow it fitted in. But as he looked round at Larson his eye caught a saddle set on a peg behind the stall, and thinking about the boy he said dubiously, "I don't even know how to put on one of those things. There's a lot you'll have to show me."

"Nothing to it; maybe we'll see, this afternoon." Larson stepped out of the stall, and reaching up gave the saddle a little shake by the pommel. "There wasn't much left, but I mended it so you'd hardly know. You see, it didn't come off—it just turned. After she got rid of him she could still feel it dangling between her legs." He hesitated, then began tracing with his nail the design stamped on the leather skirt. "You can still see the marks, but you've got to look close. Good as new. It's been hanging right here behind her ever since."

He looked at Chris with a faint, wavering expression in his eyes. Then, as if identification were not quite complete, he swung round abruptly. "Over here on this side," he said. "This is the saddle we always use."

A shrill neigh rang out, followed by a thud of hooves. "North's heard us talking—always wants to know what's going on. But first we'll look in and see old Fanny."

Fanny was a few stalls farther along, an old, rusty-black mare, dejected-looking, rheumy-eyed, her belly distended so enormously that to Chris it seemed ready to burst. "Good colts," Larson said, "but she's getting too old—nearly up to Ned. This one'll be sixteen—I figure it's her last." He scratched her affectionately between the ears, then looked in her manger to see whether she had been eating. "No sense to it—eight or nine horses just loafing round the pasture already. But that's what I built the barn for. I like seeing them around, and I like coming out to talk to them."

"She looks bloated," Chris said, putting his hand on her big, drum-tight belly. "Like she'd been eating something."

Larson laughed and scratched himself. "Come on, then. We'd better go and see who's been feeding her."

He led the way to a box-stall at the end of the barn, its door divided at breast-level and the sections opening in. "He's quieter when it's closed. When he can see out he's always kicking and neighing. Gets the others worked up. Keep back a bit. Somebody he doesn't know, he's likely to turn ugly."

There was another neigh, so shrill this time it was almost a squeal, and as Larson pushed open the upper section of the door a black stallion thrust its head out. Chris jumped and retreated a few steps; then, ashamed in front of Larson, he edged forward warily.

"Careful, son—one snap and he'll have half your face."

But unheeding, Chris drew closer, slowly raising and extending his hand till only a few inches separated his fingers from the outthrust nose. His face was white and tense, fear mingled with wonder. It was as if he were compelled, as if here were something—an imperiousness, a brute beauty—to which he could respond, yield unstinted admiration.

"Careful," Larson warned again, seizing the stallion's halter with both hands. "You're asking for trouble. He's no time for strangers."

But Chris's hand came closer, trembling with the strain like a compass needle, till at last it reached the stallion's nose. There was a little snort of consternation—feigned, exaggerated—and then indulgently the thick black lips began nuzzling Chris's fingers.

Chris shivered, flushed. Recklessly he stepped forward and drew North's muzzle against his cheek, while with the other hand he reached up and stroked his neck.

"You're the first one he's ever let do that." There was excitement in Larson's voice, something like respect. "He's taken to you. He knows you're not scared of him."

Chris caught the respect and laughed. "Let me inside, I want to get a good look at him." He shook the door impatiently, as if he had subdued the stallion by force of will, as if its docility were a conquest.

"Easy, son—it doesn't take much to make him turn." As he spoke, though, he was opening the door. "He's used to me, so I'll go first and hold him off. In case he starts playing rough."

But today, as if to reward Chris's admiration, North was a model of good behavior. The snorting and stamping were pure showmanship. He champed, pawed, nosed them as they entered; then, suddenly aloof, flung up his head and neighed again. Chris quailed a moment—the neigh was like a trumpet, the walls reeled before it—but his vanity, the need to live up to Larson's praise, regained control swiftly. The sleek magnificence of the brute, the dramatic listening pose he had struck, head high, ears pricked forward, straining for an answer to the challenge of his neigh—Chris rose to it, awed, and yet fearless, with a conviction that he had imposed himself.

He circled North a time or two, then laid a hand on his shoulder, confident and familiar. Too familiar: ignoring him a moment, North pealed out another neigh, establishing the proper distance between them; then, swift and accurate as a beak pecking a bug from a leaf, he caught Chris's sleeve with his teeth and ripped it from shoulder to elbow.

"Don't be scared, son—that's only play." Larson sounded as if it were important to him that he should not have to think Chris scared. "He'd have taken a piece out of you if he'd had a mind to."

Chris laughed shakily. In the same instant North began scratching his head against him, gentle as a pony. "I'm sorry about the shirt," Chris said. He suppressed a desire to laugh, afraid he might not be able to control his voice. "Did a neat job, didn't he?"

"Doesn't matter. We'll get Aunt Bessie to mend it. Look at him, rubbing right up against you. And I'm the only one he's ever let lay a hand on him."

"How did you get round him?" There was a shade of resentment, of rivalry, in the question. It would have been even better if Larson were afraid too.

"I've had him a few years. He knows me. Besides, I guess he knows what side his bread's buttered on."

"You mean it's just because you feed him." Somehow Chris was relieved as he turned back to North and ran his fingers through his forelock.

"Not so much because I feed him. I'm the one that leads him out when there's a mare. He wouldn't want me to get sore and cut that out."

He looked into Chris's face and laughed again. "You've sure got a lot to learn about a farm all right. He's a stallion. We can't let him go chasing round on his own. Anybody brings a mare it's a business deal. There's a charge."

"You mean he doesn't work? You keep him just for that?"

"Just for that." Larson gave North a little slap under the belly. "Kind of job I wouldn't mind myself."

"And the others—like old Ned?"

"You fix a colt when he's about a year. He never knows what he's missing."

"Who does it? You?" His curiosity was off-hand, yet at the same time he shrank a little.

"Here you are. It's got a special blade." Larson went into his pocket and brought out a jackknife. "Good steel; I keep it honed up just like a razor. Go on, feel it—nothing to be scared of."

It was the wrong word. Involuntarily Chris had taken a step back, and now the look on Larson's face was the same as when he told him his job was to be cleaning out after the horses, not handling them. "Sure, I'll feel it for you." A sudden hot rage filled him and he had to bite his lip a moment to control himself. Chris Rowe scared! If the old bastard knew some of the jobs he'd done with a switch knife! Real jobs, that took real guts! If he let him feel *that* kind of steel ...

"You've got to do it," Larson was explaining. "If your horses were all stallions you'd never get your work done. There'd be a fight and a runaway every time they smelled a mare, to say nothing of the scrub colts they'd throw. For breeding, you see, you've got to have a purebred."

"He's purebred?" His hands were still clenched, but his voice kept its tone of off-hand curiosity.

"Belgian—paid twenty-five hundred cash. And now, counting his keep, I don't clear a hundred a year. Just a notion I took; something for the boy."

"What's wrong? Didn't you say you make a charge?"

"Sure, fifty dollars. But I never get it. Neighbors mostly. They let it slide. Ten or fifteen down; promise the rest after harvest. He throws good colts too—hardly ever misses."

"Then you're crazy." Now it was his turn to show contempt; at the same time his voice took on a ring of authority. Maybe he didn't know how to handle horses, but nobody could tell him anything about double-crossers. "Let them see you're soft and they just take you—every time. You'd clear a lot more than a hundred a year if you had me looking after him."

"But there are other stallions. I get tough and they just take their mare somewhere else. I lose what they do pay, and turn them against me besides. They say I'm mean and crazy as it is. They're sore because I've done better, got more land."

"So what have you got to lose? Put the screws on—they'll be eating out of your hand." The scorn in Chris's voice now had a faintly protective edge, as if he despised Larson for being so soft and easy, and at the same time felt it his duty to wise him up to what the world was really like.

"Maybe that's how I'd feel if I had the boy behind me. But when you're alone and starting to get on you need your neighbors. It gives you a feeling, just knowing they're there.

Sylvia hasn't worked out. Thinking about the boy the way I do—that doesn't always work out either."

He shrugged disconsolately. "Got to think about North, too. How'd he like it if they started taking their mares somewhere else? Never near enough for him anyway."

He stood still a moment, moistening his lips and admiring North, then reached for a bridle that hung outside the door. "Want to take him? I haven't had him out to water yet."

As if he understood, North gave a whinny and crowded against Larson. Instead of resisting the bridle, he thrust his head into it. "That's one thing he learned the first week I had him," Larson said, buckling the throat latch. "No bit, no water; no bit, no mares. You won't have any trouble."

Chris watched and listened respectfully. It was acceptance again. Like a boy, he wanted to please Larson now, prove himself worthy.

"This is a special bit," Larson went on, handing him the reins. "A snaffle—see? Pull on it and it cuts into his mouth and tongue. Pull hard, or jerk, and you can bring him to his knees. So take it easy—unless he starts something first. But don't get any smart ideas you can handle him without it. If he wanted to cut loose he'd swing you like a cat. Me, I give him a little play so he can throw up his head and show off. But keep a good grip, and remember he's always figuring out how much he can get away with."

Chris put out his hand for the reins, a little impatient now. As they started along the cement-floored aisle between the rows of stalls, North clopping meekly majestic, he felt like a small boy unexpectedly in charge of an elephant. If only there was someone to see him! As they stepped outside into the light he slackened his grip of the reins in obedience to a sign from Larson, and North flung up his head and neighed again. And at that moment Larson was not enough. Indiscriminate in his need for someone to see him and be amazed, he glanced towards the house, hoping that Sylvia or Mrs. Paynter might be on the back steps. Then his mind leapt to Boyle Street—if only the boys were here! Or Rickie—or Helen! But with the wish came the realization of what happened, where he was, and his elation collapsed as quickly as it had soared. Even the farm, the big house and Cadillac—his mind made another leap, this time to the futility of possession. (There was no surprise at the leap, as if already, secretly, the idea of possession had taken hold.) What use would it be without someone to know and be envious?

"Not too much play," Larson warned. "Slip your hand up close to the bit again. Never let him get a start on you."

"Supposing he did get away?" Chris's voice was suddenly scornful. All his pride in North had vanished. "Would it be so serious if he did find a mare and tried having a time with her?"

"Could be serious. If there was a fence he might cut himself. Or if she was hitched up with other horses he might start a runaway."

Now they were at the tank, and North began to drink greedily. The bit was in his way; he sucked in the water with a squeaky, slobbery sound. "You've got to let him take his time," Larson said. "There he goes, trying to scratch off the bridle. Knows you're new—thinks if he works on you you'll maybe do it for him."

Chris's lip curled. The bit was cruel, unnecessary. For a moment he hated Larson.

But Larson, missing his glance, pointed to some clots of green scum floating on the water, and told him the tank was to be cleaned. "Stuff grows fast in the hot weather and the horses don't like it. Drain it and then get right in and swish around with a broom. First day there's a good wind, so it'll fill up again."

He looked up thoughtfully at the windmill. "And there's something else. I want you to get in the way of keeping an eye on it and as soon as the tank's full shut it off. Makes mud when it runs over. Little things like that—it won't take long till you're seeing them for yourself. My idea's to train you. If you turn out all right you can stay on."

Again the implication was acceptance, and Chris, forgetful that a moment before he had been hostile and withdrawn, swung back impulsively. "If you'll just give me a day or two, till I get on to things." He wanted to please again. The old man's opinion was important to him.

But Larson wasn't listening. He stared up absently again at the windmill fan, then leaned over the little stream of water running into the tank and cupped his hands and drank. "Good water," he said, wiping the wet from his chin. "Had to drill through the rock for it—three hundred feet. Found out too late I'd picked the wrong place to build. The drilling machine was here nearly all one summer."

He leaned forward and cupped his hands again, then let the water trickle back into the tank. "Drilling machine and an engine and a crew. They got the water all right, but some day we'll go over to the old place and I'll show you a real well. Sixty-five feet—by hand. Did it with Cora, the first year we were married. Never filled it in. Haven't used it for fifteen years now, but all that digging it wouldn't be right."

North had finished drinking, and like an amiable old plow horse was rubbing his mouth on Chris's shoulder. "Better take him in," Larson said, suddenly brightening. "Morning's nearly gone already, and I've still got to show you the watermelons."

He caught Chris's glance and gave a hitch to his overalls. "Everybody says it's too short a season, but wait till you see them. Last year was the first time I tried—big as apples and they froze. This time it looks like I've done it. There's one anyway, if the frost holds off a couple of weeks."

Chris nodded, trying to show interest. "I've only seen them in stores. Once when we were kids a couple of us snitched one."

"*He* always wanted them. I'd tell him this far north we were lucky to get cauliflower and peas, but now I keep trying new things—surprises."

They reached the stall, unbridled North and started out again. "This big one that's coming along, it's going to be for us, just you and me. Not a sniff for Sylvia—she's been working it too hard for laughs. *Buy* a watermelon, for Christ's sake, she says. That's all she thinks about, buying things, but it wouldn't be the same. I couldn't keep coming out to watch it. It wouldn't be for him."

Chris softened again. To be preferred, singled out for a favor—a preference that Larson's simplicity guaranteed, that even he could not adulterate with a motive or a low-down—it gave him a feeling of place and acceptance. It was a kind of fulfilment, a license to relax and trust. But it was also a threat to his self-reliance, to the tough hard strength in which he took such pride. He half yielded a moment, then thrust it away scornfully. "Crazy old bastard!" There was no time to be inventive. "His goddam kid and his goddam watermelons."

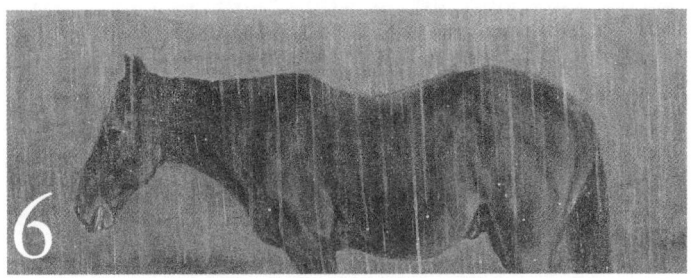

6

"WHAT ARE YOU DOING HERE, CHRIS? On the run?"

They were alone having coffee in the kitchen. Larson had gone to town for the afternoon and taken Mrs. Paynter with him. Sufficiently alert to realize that the abruptness of the question was deliberate, an attempt to throw him off his guard, Chris gave an easy laugh and tapped the ash off his cigarette. "Anyway," he said, "I'm not running very hard."

"Running or keeping out of sight—it's the same thing."

He laughed again and met her eyes. "Why? Do I look the type?"

"Not the farm type, that's for sure."

"I'm on my way home. I don't want to walk in looking like the day I landed here." He sobered, inhaling slowly. "I want clothes and cab fare. I've got friends—and my old lady. They'd be disappointed."

He spoke plausibly, with ease. For the last few days, in anticipation of such questions, he had been drilling himself. "I got cleaned out in a crap game in Calgary on the way back from Vancouver. Two crap games, as a matter of fact—sort of took my nerve. I wasn't planning to work on a farm, but a job's a job. Larson said he could use me. I figured it would do."

"A couple of crap games and your old lady—so that's your story." She waved the smoke from her face, smiling, then drank her coffee.

"That's my story." He looked surprised, a little hurt—a practised, finely shaded look that often in the past he had used to advantage. His words as he repeated her had the finality of innocence. At the same time the little shrug accompanying them made it clear that her opinion, whatever it might be, was of no particular interest to him. The shrug, too, was practised. All his life there had been people to defeat and wither.

"If that's your story, Chris, then you keep right on sticking to it." She smiled again and leaned slightly forward. He wasn't fooling her, but he had nothing to fear. "If we didn't stick to our stories we'd get nowhere. That goes for all of us."

"You make good coffee." In his smile now there was a kind of greeting. "When I met Larson he promised me good meals."

"Swedes like their coffee. Drop in for a cup any time."

"Thanks, but I'd better watch it. The men look at me already like they're wondering where I get the drag. With him, I mean. Ole especially."

"Ole's got his own troubles. It's that boy of his, young Chris. They've been taking him to specialists ever since he was born, and now there's another on the way. Naturally he's anxious."

"When we're talking I catch him trying to listen—like he thought Larson was getting too interested."

"I wouldn't let it worry you." She rose abruptly, dismissing him, and carried their cups to the sink. "I wouldn't let it chase you away too soon either. You never know. Play along with Larson and he may make it worth your while to stay right through the winter. It's not such a bad life, once you're used to it."

She was right. Things were working out better than he had expected. He had come hoping to lie low a while, save a few dollars, get back his nerve—nothing more than that. And already, in a little over a week, he was settling in, finding himself involved.

Sylvia was only part of it. He was attracted, increasingly aware. Watching her and making comparisons he even admitted, sometimes grudgingly, that he had encountered few her equal. But at the same time he was sure of her. And after the high-handed way she had begun, he owed it to himself to let her wait. It would be in his own time, on his own terms. There was no reason to deny himself, but there was no reason to hurry either.

More absorbing, more to his taste right now, was the game of property. (Strictly a game; he hadn't got round to thinking even remotely of the details of transfer, how farm and Cadillac and horses were to be acquired.) In part it was simply a device to save face. He have never worked, had always prided himself on being sharp and resourceful enough not to have to; so now, to avoid the humiliation of chores and early hours, he kept busy preparing himself for his new responsibilities, acquiring first-hand knowledge as a preliminary to taking over. But it also gave him scope. He rode and supervised and made improvements. There were endless things to do. Rickie and the Boyle Street boys were still necessary; to keep them impressed he brought about changes swiftly, with style. The farm became a ranch, pulled up its fences and rolled back to the horizon. The fleet, graceful Minnie multiplied into a stableful of saddle horses, a herd of broncos. The farmhands with their baggy overalls gave way to cowboys with chaps and sombreros—a touch of malice here, for the men in the bunkhouse maintained a careful, disapproving distance. And the land itself, with its roads and telephone poles and cultivated fields, grew stark and wild again.

For himself, he chose silver-studded chaps, dark blue shirt and scarlet bandanna. Minnie served him briefly; then he rode a hot-eyed, jet black stallion that no one else had ever dared to ride. Fierce, untamed—to mount him was to provide a spectacle of outlaw fury and consummate horsemanship. Watching him, even Rickie sometimes blanched.

Meanwhile, he was riding Minnie. Actually riding her. She was swift, but courteous; high-strung, but tolerant. The first day, the first mile, she restrained herself to a walk. The second mile, taking the bit in her teeth, she cantered gently, giving him time to adjust himself to the rhythm of her lope. Even on the way home, running hell-bent for her stall as if it were a winning-post, she was careful of him, and at the finish, instead of bringing up with a jolt or flourish, shaded off her speed so finely that he sat dazed and quiet a moment, scarcely able to believe that it was over.

Larson had been watching. "You're just the right build, both of you," he said. "Loosen up a little—a couple of weeks you'll be looking for a job roping steers."

From then on he rode her every day. He lost his awkwardness and fear. The rush of wind exhilarated him. The first few days the prairie had seemed aloof and desert-like; now he felt himself part of it, at home. Each time he turned reluctantly, wishing he could ride all day.

And frequently, when Larson wasn't around, he found time for North too. In his stall, or leading him out to water or his corral, he was still the small boy, impressed and wanting to impress. Secretly he was a little afraid, and to give the lie to his fear he took foolhardy liberties. When North nipped at his shirt, he would come back with a light cuff, or tweak his forelock, or smack him on the belly with the flat of his hand, and then leap out of the way across the stall; and North in turn, ears flat, teeth bared, feinting an attack, would rear up or lunge after him with a squeal of rage. There were moments when Chris sickened as the hooves hung over him, then slashed past his face with a little swish of wind, but he always stood his ground. And North, for his part, enjoyed the fun too much to spoil it. For he was a young, high-spirited horse, and there was not a mare for him every day. He was restless and bored. Chris was just what he needed, just the right age.

For Chris, it was sometimes a dubious kind of play. He kept his gang around him, even in the stall. Not only to impress them with his nerve and recklessness, but also to settle old scores. For there were humiliations behind him that still rankled, even fifteen hundred miles away. The ones that had talked tough and tried to throw their weight around—up against North they showed themselves for what they really were. One snap of his teeth and away they went, fighting and falling over one another to get out of the door.

But still it was play. The showmanship was intermittent. The old humiliations weren't always there. Sometimes, excited and released, he would forget the spectators, and when it was over go back to his work with feelings of regret and satisfaction and eagerness for the next time all mingled, like a boy called home to his supper from a game.

His own boyhood had been different. From a small, troubled child he had graduated straight to a precocious, wizened maturity. There had been excitement sometimes, gratifications. He had boxed, played baseball and hockey, all well, but none of it had been play. To outwit, score, defeat, survive—Boyle Street had permitted nothing else, had never let him relax or drop his guard. A game for its own sake would have been a lapse, would have left him disqualified or exposed.

So the job was proving better than he expected—better than he knew. It was a kind of therapy: sometimes, now, he did drop his guard. The edges of the old patterns were blurring. He was beginning to work, not even minding, forgetting himself sufficiently at times to play. Belatedly, growth was setting in.

The horses were part of it. They were responsive and affectionate. They looked to and sometimes needed him, imposed a sense of responsibility. In return he was safe with them, could trust them.

Not to trust—that was part of the old pattern. The boys who acknowledged and deferred to him, the girls he made love to, even Helen—the thought of trusting them, that they might be trusted, never occurred to him. In his distrust there was not even bitterness or hurt. That was the way things were. It was one of the lessons you learned early.

The little decencies and illusions he had taken to the street had given way quickly before what he found there. He had learned to accept others as they came, and they came tough and hard and crafty. Some of them he liked, even admired, but there was none who mightn't turn, who couldn't be bought, whose instincts were not as sharp and predatory as his own.

There had been trust, of course, in the beginning. Just the two of them: a room with a cretonne curtain up a splintery stair, canned soup heated on a gas ring in the hall, stale cakes sometimes that she smuggled home to him from the bakery. But the betrayal, when it came, made suspect even the memories of his happy times. He looked back through the hurt as through a cracked lens, and saw everything askew and darkened.

"Why, Chris, you're home early. Come in and shake hands. This is the gentleman who owns the new flat we're moving into. You're going to have a nice little room all of your own." Then a bright false laugh that he had never heard from her before. "Run along and play again—we've got some business to talk."

The hurt itself had been brief. The next day he had pocket money and new shoes. The meals improved. They moved to the new flat and he had his room.

For a while, as a result of the change, his difficulties increased. He hated the room, and sat in it estranged and unrelenting, making it an excuse to keep to himself; and at school and in the street he was a newcomer, conspicuous and vulnerable. But one morning—excluded—as he watched a boy break and share a few cigarettes, it occurred to him that he too had spending money now. He experimented, in a single recess period discovered that it took as little as a quarter to win allies and make bullies knuckle under.

He rose to it. He was neither ashamed for having bought, nor disappointed in the others for having sold so cheaply. So that was the way it was! A few quarters in reserve, then, and he could hold his own with the best of them. The street would be his.

It wasn't quite his, but from then on he did a little better than hold his own. To take, never to be taken—he worked on it. He too became tough and crafty. He trusted no one, and from not trusting derived a sense of self-sufficiency and initiation.

At home, he came to terms with the new situation quickly. (An instinct of survival, perhaps; like a live wire, the hurt of the first few days required insulation.) There was no for or against. He simply sized things up for what they were, and cocked an eye to his own advantage. Embarrassment became his standby. He learned that with a certain expression he could extort hush or conscience money; then, with the same money, he could extort approval and obedience in the street. It was a good system. It got him what he wanted.

As he grew older he laughed at and rather liked her. She was his Old Lady, his Old Doll. He moved away and back again as it suited him, according to his luck and finances. When things were good he bought her flowers and perfume—partly because he liked to think of himself as tough and big-hearted, partly because her doting gratitude somehow relieved him, as if there were still guilt fragments imbedded in their relationship. Such little burst of generosity, moreover, gave him sponging rights when times were lean.

But all along his self-sufficiency had been a goal beyond himself. Could he have stood back, detached, impartial, his verdict would have been "small time." Behind the façade he was dissatisfied and uneasy. There was a soft streak, even a gentleness. He wanted some of the things that he despised.

And now, with doddering old Ned, it was beginning to come out. He would stand minutes at a time, stroking and talking to him, pretending not to notice that he had stopped again. It was a kind of respect. Bad years and debts, survival, the struggle with the earth and seasons—all that was part of him—and the farm itself began to take shape in his mind as something more than a long-drawn money-making deal.

The same with the old mare Fanny, so repellently bloated with foal, so prompt with her sociable little whinny when he came to feed or curry her. There was respect here too—it slipped up on him imperceptibly—respect such as he had never felt for a woman. Sixteen colts, twenty-five years on the wagon and the plow; now, at the end of it, grateful for her oats and a friendly word. There was a serenity and fulfilment that disturbed him. At times it was almost as if he were missing something, had all along been wrong.

To respect a man who had worn himself out on a job—fool, sucker, stooge—would be to lose respect for himself. It would be a kind of treason, a sign of weakness. But with Minnie or Ned he could feel whatever at the moment it was in him to feel. There were no required attitudes.

Most important of all, he was alone. As it suited him he could gather his old crowd round him, or leave them half a continent away where they belonged. For on Boyle Street even his thoughts had never been quite his own. There was always the need to think and do according to the expectations of the gang. Because he existed only in the reflections they gave back, he was at their mercy, even while he went among them, assured and slickly superior. But here he could relax, slip a little, and it concerned no one but himself. No mirrors, no reflections—it was almost freedom.

That too was what made the work tolerable. When reality pressed too hard, when imagination and the game of property were powerless to transform it—cleaning out the barn, or staggering bleary-eyed into his clothes in the morning—then again he left Boyle Street where it belonged and availed himself of his isolation. Work in itself wasn't humiliating, but only in the eyes of Boyle Street.

And as the reality of his work forced itself upon him, so at times did the reality of his situation. There were bad moments when Baxter died, when the world refused to accept what he had done as an accident or himself as a wayward boy who needed only help and sympathy. Moments when he was simply frightened, when he broke and buried his face in Minnie's shoulder. But each time, when the crisis was past, he felt relieved, a little steadier. It was the beginning of a new kind of self-sufficiency. Each time Boyle Street dimmed a little, seemed farther off.

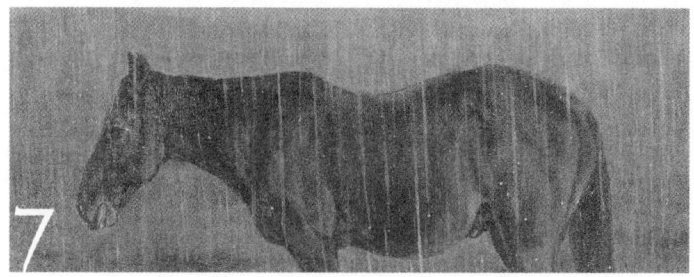

7

THE MAN IN CHARGE OF THE GASOLINE DEPOT put out his hand formally. "Name's Potter. Larson phoned you'd be picking up a couple of drums. Can't say as I've seen you round before."

"Chris MacKenzie. This is the first time I've been to town. I just started working for Larson two weeks ago."

"That so." He was a lean, stooped man with a large Adam's apple and intent, confiding eyes. "No smoking here—have a stick of gum. Can't trust myself, so I never carry cigarettes. You related to Larson?"

"Just happened to be looking for a job."

"That so." There was something constrictor-like the way his Adam's apple worked while his soft eyes clung. "Don't know his wife then either?"

Chris stripped the paper from his gum without answering.

"Never knew old Larson to let anybody drive his truck except himself. Car the same—just like a kid. You're doing all right."

"Everybody's busy and they're getting low in gas."

"Even so—new Cadillac last spring, and they say he won't even let *her* drive it. You've got round him pretty fast."

"I've got no complaints." Chris was at once curious and aloof. He half-turned, as if to jump down from the platform and return to the cab of the truck, but let Potter intercept him.

"You hear a lot of stories. All that money, and in winter he's too mean to keep a man—up feeding cattle in the middle of the night."

"Like I say, I'm just new. Maybe he hasn't got as much money as people think."

"That's right—sometimes you're fooled. Far too much talk in this town anyway." In response to the curtness in Chris's voice he retreated slightly, then edged forward again. "His case, though, you can see a lot of funny things for yourself. Now take trains ..."

For a second or two his Adam's apple was motionless. Then, sensing Chris's interest, he thrust his head out and drew a step nearer. "Hangs around town sometimes a couple of hours waiting for a freight. Just to watch. A man his age, you can't tell me it's normal."

Chris stood half-smiling, distantly receptive.

"What I mean, you can't help wondering. You must see a lot of things yourself, living right there." He hesitated, hurried on. "Even his wife—she tells round town herself she doesn't know what's wrong with him—scared he's going to clear out some day and leave her a grass widow. Making a joke, but sort of upset just the same."

Chris leaned over the platform and spat out his gum. "The set-up he's got out there, I can't see him leaving it."

"Can't see him leaving her either." Potter thrust out his long neck and winked. "A shape like she's got."

Again Chris made ready to jump off the platform; again he let Potter intercept him. "More likely she'll be walking out on him one of these days. Bleeding him fast. She's got a fur coat that the wife says must have cost a thousand, easy. See her sailing round town like nobody here's good enough to talk to. Used to be a waitress in Regina at a little place near the station. Sure, all kinds remember seeing her. Somebody's always going in to get new teeth or see a doctor. A couple of fellows say they even got to *know* her—if you know what I mean."

"She's a good cook. I'm starting to put on weight."

"Good worker, too, they say. Keen after the dollar, just like him. Making her hay while the making's good. The way I hear it she pretty well runs things—the old man can't call his life his own."

This time he did jump. "The way you tell it, though, he calls the Cadillac his own."

Everywhere he went it was the same. More discreet, more circumspect, as if they were taking into account the value of Larson's good will and the possibility of Chris's loyalty, but the same surprise that Larson should let a new man drive his truck, the same inclination to gossip about the trains and Mrs. Larson.

There was also an interest in Chris himself to which, despite his caution, he responded. It was a friendly, neighborly interest. The surprise at his driving the truck was accompanied by a faint deference. Even as Larson's man, it seemed, he had a certain standing. As someone privileged to watch and listen to the domestic scene, his confidence was worth winning.

He sensed approval, too, and here, as in Boyle Street, it was spark and sustenance, what he lived by. The needle under the skin of his vanity, the shot of euphoria, the little glow of poise and confidence—it was a familiar sensation, and yet he had never experienced it quite as he was doing now. Word seemed to run ahead of him. People shook hands and asked how he liked being a farmer and how he was getting along with Mrs. Larson. It was a welcome, rather than acceptance, as if they had been waiting for him.

In Nesbitt's General Store, when he went to buy socks for one of Larson's men, three or four women were shopping. There was an abrupt silence as he entered; then Nesbitt, a smiling, paunchy man, introduced himself and said, "Saw you drive in a while ago. Somebody tells me your name's MacKenzie. Larson's new man?"

Chris nodded and the women smiled. Like all the others, Nesbitt said it was the first time he'd known Larson to send somebody else to town and miss a chance to watch a train come in. But his laughter was without malice, and somehow he made it stand out that the real point of his remark was Chris's dependability.

Chris selected and paid for the socks and conversation resumed self-consciously among the women. Then, as he was about to leave, one of them cleared her throat and took a step towards him. "I don't suppose you remember me," she said apologetically. "You called a while ago. I'm afraid I was terribly rude to you."

She was middle-aged and stout, with a flat round face and touched-up hair. Her expression was conscience-stricken and childish. She wore a pink sleeveless dress from which her arms protruded like thighs. "You see, we'd been having so many that week, and my jam had just boiled over."

His throat went tight; his eyes filled with heat. With an effort he smiled and said, "It's not the sort of thing I like to do, but I was hungry."

"We'd had the most horrible man the day before. I let him wash and he took the soap." She wiped her chin with her handkerchief and patted the front of her dress daintily. "I'm ashamed because I take church and things like that seriously. I don't like to be a whited sepulchre. Ask anybody—I do try. So sometime I wish you'd come and have a meal with us. Just phone, any time you're free. I'm Mrs. Tillie."

He thanked her and went out. His step was firm, his shoulders relaxed; outside he lit a cigarette and flicked the match away; but there was a sense of exposure again, an inner furtiveness.

Mrs. Tillie had recognized him after a shave and a change. She would recognize his picture just as easily if she came across it in a paper. They all would. The eyes around him were friendly, but they missed nothing. Already they were wondering where he came from, what had gone wrong. And suddenly he saw the friendliness itself as a trick to give him a false sense of safety. They were just encouraging him to talk, hoping he would give himself away.

He had been a fool. He had forgotten he was on the run, and it was what he must never forget. First thing in the morning, last at night. They had his fingerprints and picture. It would be five to ten years even if Baxter had recovered, the rope if he had died.

Panic seized him. He looked at Larson's truck across the street, and for a moment his impulse was to take it and escape. Someone was coming; he steeled himself, brought his comb from his pocket and ran it through his hair. In the same instant he realized there could be no escape. Taking the truck, even if he left it and jumped a train, would only put the hunt on him. Lie low for a while, trust that no one chanced on an eastern paper with his picture; for the time being he had no alternative. Lie low, keep up a front, save what he could and disappear again.

Disappear, catch another freight, thumb a few more rides, move on. Suddenly he wondered where. The west coast, a chance to meet up with Rickie—that, all along, had been his intention. But now the prospect blurred, was no longer to be believed in. Trains, buses, cars—town after town after town. He saw them as clearly as he saw this one. All denied him, all enemies. The panic ebbed, leaving him tired, self-pitying. As he crossed the street to the truck his impulse was no longer to escape in it, but to go home. Back to Larson's place. Somehow, it seemed he would be safe there.

But besides the socks he had promised the bunkhouse magazines and hair tonic. He remembered as he reached the truck, and re-crossed the street to the drug store.

When he entered no one was in sight. Presently, in response to his cough and tread, a girl appeared in a doorway at the rear and asked him curtly what he wanted.

She was about eighteen, with short black curls and a freckled, turned-up nose. The mouth was large, soft-lipped, the eyes clear and frank and grey. She was wearing slacks and sandals and a blue cotton blouse, unbuttoned and turned back like a man's shirt.

He kept his eyes fixed on her as she served him. A few minutes before, outside Nesbitt's Store, his anxiety had flared. Now, as if there was a connection, as if vanity or self-respect had resented the humiliation of fear and were trying to redress it with the excitement of possession, he was suddenly attracted, roused. Her breasts showed small and firm through her blouse. Her hands had a lingering, soft way of touching things which made him imagine them on his flanks and shoulders. And there was an almost childlike self-possession that challenged him, a provocative innocence, something untouched and untempted.

She looked up and caught his glance, but there was no embarrassment, no snatch at her open blouse. "Razor blades and hair tonic—I know there's something else." Her smile made his pretense of forgetfulness young and clumsy. He went on self-consciously, "You're to blame—when I'm watching you I can't concentrate."

"Then I'll leave you a few minutes so you can pull yourself together. I was just starting to shell peas for supper—when you're ready, kick the counter."

"I remember now—magazines."

"Right behind you." She came round the counter quickly and pointed to a rack near the window. "We got some new ones in just yesterday."

She ran her hand from magazine to magazine with the same slow touch that he had noticed when she was wrapping his purchases. "Here's the one I was reading last night. I see I've got a smear on it."

She stood close beside him, absorbed in the array of bright, shiny covers. Pressing towards her till their arms touched, he said, "I'll take a detective and a couple of westerns. And the one with the smear."

"Oh no—it's a movie magazine. You don't want that."

"I go to movies sometimes. And I can look at the blondes."

"You don't need to. We'll sell it all right." Her voice went abruptly hard and independent. "Just pick your westerns."

"I mean the smear will be just like an autograph. Every time I look at it I'll think of you."

She gave a bright, easy laugh. "Sure enough it's my thumb. That's caramels in bed for you."

He moved forward and pressed against her arm again. "Speaking of movies, I hear there's one every Saturday night."

She nodded and touched another magazine. "Mostly they're pretty old though. And the film's always breaking, and the boys throw peanuts."

"Sounds like it might be fun. And there's a dance afterwards?"

"It's fun sometimes except there's such a crowd. You get fixed up for it, and then you feel stepped on."

"What about this Saturday?"

"If you're there I'll maybe see you."

"We couldn't go together?"

Their eyes met for a moment. She buttoned her blouse. "I go with my girl friend. That way we can dance with anybody we want to."

"You might like me for a change. There'd be no harm finding out."

She began self-consciously leafing through a magazine. After a few pages, without looking at him, she said, "You're Larson's man, aren't you? The new one?"

"Word gets around—who told you?"

"I remember you from the first time. There's been a big improvement."

"I was in here once before, but it was a man." His voice rose edgily. He was uneasy again.

"That was Dad. You didn't see me because I was at the back, peeking round the door."

"Why? Did I look so bad I scared you?" His lips felt stiff, as if he had had too much to drink. He had to force his smile.

"You didn't scare me. I just thought you wouldn't want people looking at you. I mean not a girl."

She put back the magazine and went to the window. "I was standing here when you were coming across the street, sort of sideways, as if you were trying to keep out of sight. So I went behind and called Dad. He thought I was scared too."

"Sort of sideways is about the way I felt. I don't as a rule go round needing a clean shirt and a shave."

She gave an approving nod. "Like I say, it's made a big difference. And I'm glad you're holding your job and getting along with Larson."

He was at ease again. His desire returned. But now, as if for the first time aware of the pressure of his arm, she glanced up and saw the way he was watching her. For a moment her eyes took on a frightened look. Then she reddened, backed away. Her mouth set scathingly. "These are all we've got. I don't think you'll find what you're looking for, so there's no use hanging round."

He reddened too. Small-town all over her—not even looks—the type that ordinarily he wouldn't even see. Yet somehow he couldn't cut her down to size and just walk out. There was something that controlled even his slapped-down vanity. "These two look all right, and maybe a detective." His anxiety was on him again, as if with her rejection his defenses had crumbled. "Just a minute—don't forget the one with your autograph."

She had recognized him just as easily as Mrs. Tillie had. All it needed was someone to come across his picture. He gave her a bill, and as she rang it up said offhandedly, "I don't suppose you ever get New York or Montreal papers?"

She stared. "Who'd ever want New York or Montreal papers away out here? They'd be so old."

"I just thought I'd ask. It's a long time since I've seen one."

"You mean that's where you come from? New York?"

"I've been there."

She came round the counter slowly, her expression almost respectful, and as he met her eyes he was in control again. She was right—who'd want to read eastern papers out here? It wasn't likely that they had sent out "Wanted" notices either. Not this far. The kind of job he'd done didn't rate them. He was just imagining things, working up a scare.

"Right now I'm heading back to Montreal. That's where I come from, but the last two years I've been out west—Vancouver. I just get the feeling sometimes I'd like to know what's going on."

"New York's where I'd like to go." Bypassing Montreal, she made a little gesture of small-town discontent. "You're lucky! Out here we're so far away from everything."

"Just overnight—makes a good week-end. But right now I'm more interested in getting home. I'd have been there a couple of weeks ago—not riding the rods, either—if I hadn't let them take me in a crap game."

"I hear they're bad sometimes." Her expression made it clear that she had been wondering. "Clean you right out, I guess, if you're not careful."

"Two crap games, as a matter of fact." People talked in Campkin—better tell his story exactly as he had told it to the Larsons. "I got as far as Calgary, stopped off to see somebody I used to go to school with." He shrugged, spreading his hands to reveal the extent of his stupidity. "So when I made it this far and Larson offered me a job I decided I'd better take it—earn enough for some clothes and a ticket anyway."

"You lost even your *clothes* in a crap game?"

"Not exactly." He hesitated, feeling caught out, and then, to account for his embarrassment, said with deliberate shamefacedness, "I'd been on a bit of a tear, that's the real story. Even my watch disappeared. I couldn't pay for my room, so they locked me out. Me out and my clothes in."

"They have crap games here too, and poker. Saturday night, back of the poolroom. If you're that way you'd better watch yourself."

"I'm that way all right. Seeing you Saturday night would be a lot safer."

"Now you're making fun of me. I suppose it does sound crazy, handing out advice to somebody that's been around like you."

"I'm the crazy one—advice is what I need. Maybe you can give me some more on Saturday."

"You wouldn't listen anyway. I'd rather just let you talk."

"It's a date, then?"

"If you're there I'll see you." With a quick shy smile she retreated behind the counter. "I'll be with the girls. Dad thinks it's safer that way—till there's somebody serious. There's just the two of us and he worries."

"You never know. My name's Chris MacKenzie."

"Mine's Elsie Grover."

She flushed, gave her curls a shake as if in defiance of the part of her that had yielded, then slipped out quickly to the back. And climbing into the truck he felt adequate again, restored. Their little game was over—he had won. It wouldn't be worth the trouble anyway—the love-me-forever type, all guilt and tears. Ten to one he'd be feeling guilty too before he got away. And somehow he shrank from the thought of handing out a line she might believe.

8

AT THE SUPPER TABLE he made no mention of his purchases in town. He felt the men watching him, expectant first, then sullen, but when the meal was finished he let them go, hanging back a minute to talk to Larson, so that he would have an excuse to visit the bunkhouse later on.

They had never asked him. Their manner made him afraid their welcome might be cool. But bringing what they had asked him to bring—bringing a little more—he would not be intruding. Whatever their welcome, he would at least save face.

For despite his need to save, he had spent a little on them. He had bought favor and approval so long that it had become a way of life. It carried no shame. The men were strangers, their lives and problems were of no real interest to him, yet it was important that he win them over. To sustain him he needed at least the trappings of good fellowship.

He entered casually, made no explanation of the delay, as if it hadn't occurred to him that they might be concerned about such trifles. They in turn were aloof and silent a minute, unable to relinquish the ill-will they had been working up since supper time.

And then, when they did begin to thaw, he spoiled it again. He had brought three magazines instead of one, cigars and candy bars all round, and at once they brought out their wallets or felt for change. He shrugged, said "Forget it," and they became insistent. He wasn't one of them. Sleeping in the house somehow put him on Larson's side. They sensed favoritism; sensed, too, perhaps, the city man's attitude of superiority. They didn't want to be under an obligation to him. The small favor he had done them today would be his license to ask a bigger one in return tomorrow.

"No, better keep it straight," a grizzled, broad-shouldered little man called Charlie said. "So there'll be no hard feelings."

"But it's just a few cents—Jesus ..."

"Charlie's right. It'll spoil it for the next time." Now it was Steve, a big, lanky boy with a loose mouth and a lick of sandy hair across his forehead. "You'll be going in again and we'll want something and we won't feel free to ask."

He felt a sudden hardening towards him, a tension. Steve found a pencil and began a painstaking calculation on the back of an envelope. Charlie said stiffly, "We're trying to get ahead a little, that's why we asked you to bring this stuff instead of going in Saturday night ourselves. Never fails—we get a few drinks and start throwing our money away."

He paused a moment, glancing at the others as if afraid they might not approve of such confidences. "All of us staying home it's easier. I want to see about renting a place for myself next year. Steve here's planning to get married. We've all got something. It's been nice of you to go to so much trouble."

He spoke hesitantly, but with precision. It was a setting down and ruling off of what had passed between them as emphatic and final as Steve's big grubby figures. Everybody knew now exactly where he stood. Steve had spoken about feeling free to ask him to do things for him the next time, but Chris knew there would be no next time. They had a little world of their own; they didn't want to be patronized by a chore boy from the city. He pocketed the money they paid him and it was time to go.

But still he delayed a little. As he turned to the door his eyes lit on a guitar that Steve had been strumming when he came in, and he said, "You do all right—sometimes I stand outside and listen."

Steve grinned shyly, eager to accept the praise and be happy with it, afraid it might be Chris's way of laughing at him. But Chris, shy and uncertain himself, continued, "I've always wanted one myself, ever since I was a kid. Just never got around to it."

It was the moment between his rejection by the men and the setting in of scorn and derision by means of which he would conceal it from himself, a moment of acknowledged loneliness, and the humility in his voice was genuine. Steve sensed it, and said quickly, "Come over sometime and try this one. I'm just catching on myself, but if there's anything I can show you ..."

Only for the others watching and listening he might have suggested that they begin right then and there. But there was a silence, an awkwardness, and Chris, resorting to a shrug as an expression both of leave-taking and indifference, thrust his hands into his pockets and went out.

He had taken only a few steps when the pup bounded up at him out of the darkness. Startled, he cursed and kicked it. There was a yelp, then, a few feet off in the darkness, the thump of its tail on the ground and a reproachful whine. He whistled softly, called it by name, and presently, with a little whimper of appeal, it crept back and lay at his feet.

As he squatted to stroke it, it licked his hand. Suddenly it struck him that he was the only one to whom it could come for a clap or greeting, that Larson and Sylvia and the men all treated it with contempt, a fool that wouldn't grow up. The value of its affection dropped sharply—it was almost as if he had been cheated, as if it had made friends with him on false pretenses. But the next moment, his own affection stiffening to loyalty, he felt drawn to it in a kind of fellowship. When he rose and started towards the house it followed close at his heels, without resentment but subdued now, as if matured by the hazards of devotion.

There was a quarrel going on between Sylvia and Mrs. Paynter. He listened at the steps a moment, then turned and walked back across the yard as far as the gate. The thought of his room with its persisting smell of varnish repelled him. The night was warm and still, and he felt relaxed in the darkness.

At that, he wasn't quite used to it yet. Darkness in the city was a back alley where the light came feebly. At its darkest it was a diluted grey. But prairie darkness on a night when there was no moon seemed less absence of light than a substance, as if a smooth black smoke had drifted in. Sometimes when he stepped into it out of the light he had a vague feeling of surprise at being able to breathe so easily. Even here in the yard, where he was at home now, he still lifted his feet and brought them down with exploratory care.

There were a few notes on the guitar, like an introduction, then silence. As he waited he imagined Steve plucking at the strings, setting himself for another song, and then deciding it was too late. On the highway a wagon clattered past, a brisk, disconsolate sound, as if it felt its rashness in venturing so noisily into the night and was pretending to be unafraid. The pup whined and flattened itself on Chris's feet, and he bent and clapped it again.

"That you, Chris? I didn't know you listened too."

It was Larson, hurrying and out of breath. "I've been out seeing to Fanny again. Another couple of minutes I'd have been late."

"Late for what?" Tired and depressed now, Chris would have preferred to be alone.

"There's a freight coming. I thought that was what you were out here for too."

It was still three or four miles away. The whistle blew, frail and urgent through the darkness; then Chris could hear the faint, oncoming roar. "You've got good ears," he said. "I can hardly hear it now."

"Maybe I feel it first—been listening such a long time. It's a good night for it, nice and still."

The roar was crescendoing impressively. One whole side of the night shook and filled with it. The whistle blew again and Larson edged closer to Chris, so that as they leaned on the gate their elbows touched. "Sort of mournful, coming from away off and going on again. Watch now—there's about half a minute you can see the light."

Chris shifted. "Maybe I don't feel it quite the same."

"Gives you a sort of left behind feeling. Sets you thinking—wishing you were on it too."

"You ought to try riding a freight sometime. The bumps and the smoke—twenty miles and you'd be cured."

"What's wrong I should have done it long ago, when I was your age."

"There's nothing to stop you starting out now. After harvest, a trip south for the winter. But do it right. You've got your Cadillac—or fly."

"Maybe it's something to do with the farm. Coming from a big place you wouldn't know. I was a boy here. My old man took up land when I was four, over sixty years ago. If we've time Sunday we'll go and see it—the old sod stable's still standing. They were here ahead of the railroad—fifty miles overland by wagon. They'd go for supplies maybe once a month, two or three neighbors together. Once for a couple of weeks right before Christmas we were out of sugar. Another time it was coal oil—we could just burn one lamp. Nobody gave you credit in those days. Nobody was handing out relief."

There was a silence, then he said explosively, "Like slates—the boy used to get me so goddam mad about slates."

The gate shook in his grasp. "The scratching used to get on the teacher's nerves. In my time there wasn't even a school till I was eleven, after the railway came through. And then I've seen it when we didn't have enough coal, let alone fancy books to write in. We'd take turns sitting near the stove.

"When the railway came through it just missed us. Nothing worse for cutting up a farm, but at the time I felt sort of cheated. Take Lamb's place—it goes right past the house, you can wave—and they got twenty-five dollars an acre for about ten acres. I remember they had new suits and shoes all round and a new cream separator.

"It would have been better for me at that if it had been farther off. Hoeing potatoes or riding the plow, all by yourself five or six hours at a stretch—you've got to put the time in doing something. So I took trips. Only natural—had the trains right there. That's why trips like you talk about in a plane or the Cadillac wouldn't be any good. I'd have to hear the whistle.

"There was Fred Lamb—he went. Couldn't have been more than fifteen. Caught a freight one day, stayed a year. Came back and told me all about it. Stuck around home a couple of months or so, then did it again. Last anybody ever heard of him.

"Left me wondering how I'd do if I ever tried it—if I'd have the nerve. We'd always done things together, but now he had something on me. The way he talked when he came back made me feel sort of no-good and ignorant. Then he went again and it was worse. I was always thinking where he'd be now, how he was getting along.

"But there were a lot of the Lambs, and it was a help to be rid of him. And me, I was the only one. There's always something on a farm they need you for—you can't just pick up and leave. And then first thing I'd got round to seeing Cora Salter, a couple of farms over—one thing leading to another. And now I'm sixty-six."

"And you've never tried getting away, even for a while?"

"There was Cora, then the boy; then more land and paying off the mortgages. Sure, I've been to Regina and Saskatoon a few times, but never so it meant anything. Anybody can buy a ticket. It's too soft. Not like starting out and seeing where you can get and what you can do.

"I've told you already—Sylvia was supposed to help me get over wanting trips, but she's too young, she just puts up with me. When it's over it's over. Cora now—with her it lasted. All night, or all week, depending. But we were both young, and maybe it's not fair putting all the blame on Sylvia. I've no right to her; I'm only getting what I pay for."

In the darkness Chris could hear him rolling a cigarette. He waited without speaking, absorbed by the small busy sound of rustling paper, and then, just as he was blinking in readiness for the flare of the match, he felt Larson's hand rub against his arm. "Here, son—you take this one and I'll roll another. I'll have a light for you in a minute."

For a moment Chris softened. A glow spread through him, intimacy and warmth. To have something done especially for him—it was a good feeling, a feeling of being safe and cared for. But as Larson struck the match he seemed to see himself, to detect the weakness, and suddenly Rickie and Boyle Street seemed to be looking on as well.

They had trained him. He owed it to them to take hold and get results. He had something here; he ought to be working on it, giving it the right touch, bringing it off. All at once he felt at fault; Rickie was accusing him. As they walked back to the house he reminded himself that he hadn't even scored yet with Sylvia.

"So you've got Chris listening too. Planning a little trip together?" She was waiting for them on the back steps. Against the light, arms akimbo, she loomed up big and domineering.

Larson stopped short a minute, then hurried up the steps placatingly. "No sense carrying on about nothing, Sylvia. You know how much chance there is of me ever walking out on you."

"Keep on and I'm the one that'll be walking out." She turned and they both followed her into the kitchen. "There's your milk. I was just going to call you. I've still got some washing up to do, so drink it and get upstairs out of my way."

"Put the eggs in?" He had an eggnog and asked the same question every night. Now he took a long drink, smacked his lips and winked at Chris. "Makes them good. You ought to have one too. Go on, Sylvia—make him one."

"Everything's in the pantry—he can make it himself."

"I wouldn't mind a glass of milk—just milk."

She brought it for him herself, ill-temperedly, and set the glass down so that a little of the milk slopped over. "That's all you need, too." She wiped the table, then tossed the towel into the pantry. "Eggs and sugar and vanilla—like a baby. You'd think you'd be ashamed, instead of telling him."

With another wink, he sidled up to Sylvia and ran his hand possessively along her thigh. "No use talking like that—

you know what it takes to keep the old man in good running order."

She remained motionless, letting his hand continue, but Chris saw her lips twitch and thin. It was almost as if she were submitting to his touch the better to work up her hatred, to help fix and harden it. But Larson smiled at Chris, heedless and even a little boastful. "She knows what it takes," he repeated. "Never forgets, thinking about me all the time."

She wheeled suddenly. "Stop making such a fool of yourself in front of people. Get up to bed out of my way."

"I'll be waiting for you." He reached out and patted her again. "Coming, Chris?"

"I want to wait till Sylvia's finished so I can shave. I'm just going to sit on the back step and have another cigarette."

"You're the worst one for your wash and shave I ever ran into. Wait a few weeks—you'll get over some of your city ways."

"I wish you'd try catching on to some of them. Everywhere you go the stable goes."

She stood motionless at the sink, her face to the wall, while Larson's plodding step receded into the hall and up the stairs. Chris walked over and set his empty glass on the draining board. She turned her head towards him, her shoulders and body still square with the wall. For a moment or two they looked at each other in silence.

"I saw you watching me. I'm afraid I'll forget some day and look at him like that in front of Aunt Bessie."

"And you're that much concerned about what Aunt Bessie thinks?"

"Right now I am. There are some plans she could spoil. Like as not she's still awake, so keep your voice down."

"And all this talk about trains—are you really scared he's going to catch one? If that look you gave him means anything, I'd say a couple of thousand miles would still be on the close side."

She rinsed and dried his glass methodically. "You saw for yourself just now—he never asks. That's what he married me for. He expects his money's worth."

Stepping back a little, he looked her up and down appreciatively. "Well, I can't say I altogether blame him."

She turned on him, her eyes searching and slow. He hesitated a moment, wondering if he had gone too far, and then, her expression somehow forcing him, blustered it out with a laugh. "Sometimes at night when I can't sleep—I mean if you were my wife I'd have the same ideas ..."

"Well then?"

She spread the dishtowel to dry, then without another glance at him walked to the door. He followed, outside on the steps drew her into the shadow. For a moment his eagerness was just a little in excess of his desire, as if this time her appraisal had extended to his initiative. (He had delayed to show his indifference, but perhaps she had missed the point. To her, perhaps, it only meant that he was young and inexperienced.) But at her response he flared and lost himself. Tightening his embrace he pressed her backwards against the railing until with a little struggle she freed her lips and buried them out of reach against his shoulder.

"Where can we go?" He forced her head up and kissed her again. His hand moved slowly from her throat to her breasts.

"Not tonight—he's waiting."

"Call up you'll be a while yet. He'll maybe fall asleep."

"There's no place, anyway. Aunt Bessie might hear us ..."

"Round at the side of the house—it'll be all right. We can get a blanket."

"Not tonight." She yielded a moment, limp, almost passive, then twisted away. "He's no fool. If he gets ideas about us it'll spoil everything."

She tried to push past him towards the door, but he set himself. "Do like I say and call up. There's the loft. I can feel my way without turning on the lights."

"Let me in." She shook him off, angry and offended. "If you think you're taking me up in the hay with you you're crazy."

"But it's clean. So long as it's safe what difference does it make?"

She thrust him aside; he followed her back into the kitchen feeling slapped down and young. Even striding ahead of him she seemed to blaze. There was a clatter of pans when she reached the pantry, and his impulse for a moment was to plead with her, ask what he had done. But when she reappeared a slight movement of her head indicated that the noise had been for Mrs. Paynter's benefit, and reassured, feeling the need to make up for his failure to assert himself, he crossed quickly to where she stood and took her in his arms again. She swayed a little, only half-resisting, and as his desire began to mount again it struck him that even now Larson was upstairs waiting for her, that in a few minutes she would be going to him. "There's no reason why we can't—you're just scaring yourself for nothing." She drew back a little and his grip tightened. "Lying up there listening to you—I tell you I can't stand it any longer."

"Leave it to me. It's Saturday tomorrow so that's no good, but maybe Sunday." Ignoring the insistence in his voice, she broke away again. Her eyes looked past him, calculating and narrowed. "There's not much misses Aunt Bessie, so don't say anything or catch my eye. Soon as I can I'll let you know."

"What difference is Sunday going to make?" His attempt to take a strong tone only made his voice petulant. "Where are we going to go then? It'll be exactly the same."

"No. Sunday, maybe I'll be able to give him something."

"You mean put him out?"

"Don't look so scared—it's not poison." She smiled, gave a slow, catlike yawn, stretching back her head and throwing out her breasts. "At that, don't you think it would be worth it?"

"I've never had to go to that much trouble myself." He straightened and looked at her coldly. After all, he was Chris Rowe, one of the Boyle Street boys. He didn't chase; he let them chase him. "Maybe I've just been lucky."

"Or maybe just easy to please. Anyway, you don't need to worry. It's something for his rheumatism—the doctor gave it to him last winter when he couldn't sleep. But he's not taking it now, and I've got to have an excuse to give him a drink too, so in the morning when he feels heavy he'll think it's a hang-over. Mostly he's down on liquor—being true to Cora—but when you get round him he likes a drink as much as the next one. Bell and Ole are coming over Sunday—maybe I can work it then. And besides, Aunt Bessie will be going home."

He resented her brisk, managing competence, and at the same time he relaxed against it. He felt vaguely that he ought to be taking a stronger stand, having his way with her instead of submitting to her shrewd little plans, and yet within himself he didn't mind. All at once she seemed much older than he was, and he didn't mind that either.

"Keep the sink clean and put out the lights." She turned a moment as she left the kitchen, raising her voice in case Mrs. Paynter might be listening. "And don't make a noise when you come upstairs."

He stood still a while, listening to her step recede just as earlier they had listened to Larson's. Then, careful not to splash, with a compliance of which he was completely unaware, he dippered out a basinful of warm water from the reservoir at the back of the stove, stripped off his shirt and began to wash.

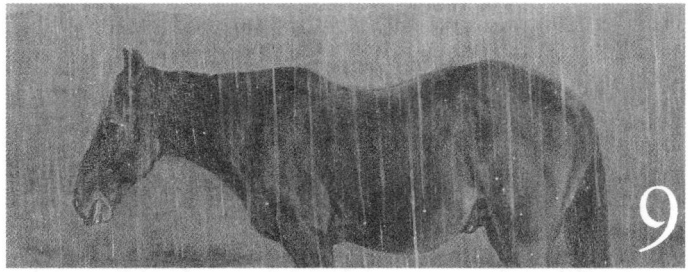

9

HE SLEPT BADLY. It was seldom he slept well, right through. There were nearly always dreams or nightmares, and often he woke with a feeling that he had just screamed or shouted—so convinced of it, sometimes, that he was surprised when Larson didn't call out or come in to see what was wrong. But tonight his dreams hung heavier upon him than usual, were harder to throw off, and the fear and anxiety they roused persisted even after he had struggled out of them, merging with actual fears and actual memories, so that the break between dream and waking was never quite distinct.

It was Baxter again. Usually, just as it had happened, he stood over him, watching helplessly while the blood trickled into the sawdust and the pale, staring eyes took on a look of recognition. Usually there was a numbness in his arm that made his efforts to raise the gun and fire a second time unavailing; and usually he was trying desperately to explain to someone (the numbness now in his throat and jaw) that he hadn't meant to do it, that he hadn't even intended to put the bullets in. (Actually, he had changed his mind at the last minute, afraid that if something went wrong, and it was in the papers that he had tried to do a job with an empty gun, the rest of the gang would think him yellow.)

But tonight Baxter was getting ready to do it to him. He had his apron on and was rolling back his sleeves. The apron,

Chris noticed, was smeared with blood—just like it used to be when he went to his store for meat—and he thought indignantly that for once he might have put on a clean one.

His nose itched and it was dark. There had been a shift; he was hiding from him now in the storeroom at the back of the shop—hiding, and at the same time waiting for him to finish with the last customer and lock the front door. First his nose, then his shoulder. The heat came up in cloying waves, and the sweat trickled from his armpits. Worst of all, the handkerchief kept slipping. To undo the knot and tie it tighter would take both hands, and that would have meant letting go of the gun.

(The storeroom was where he had actually hidden. Saturday night Baxter's man had a train to catch about half-past eight, and he knew that Baxter always let him away early. His plan was to wait till Baxter had locked the door and drawn the blinds, then walk in on him from the back just as he was putting away the cash. It had to be timed right—everything depended on surprise. For if the money was away it would mean opening the safe, and turning off the combination. Baxter might have time to get back his nerve. Might dare him, argue, try something—and in the event of a hitch to his plan, Chris didn't altogether trust his own nerve.)

A thunder-storm was coming up. Already he could see the lightning flicker through the doorway that opened onto the back alley. It brightened, grew steadier. Then it began to move towards him, not lightning now, but a powerful flashlight. He stood rooted, dripping sweat. He wanted to raise his gun and fire, but his arm had gone numb again. The door was open, right in front of him, but the rain was splashing in the street now, and he shrank from getting wet. And then, seizing him by the collar, Baxter said, "It's your turn—up on the table before I boot you."

(There had been a flash of lightning just as he ran out of the back door, so blinding and unexpected that he cowered a moment, thinking it was for him, that he was caught already; and a second later the whole street went down before the first clap of thunder. Others burst upon him in quick succession, jarring, hard, like the smash of stones. As he ran he had the feeling that he was dodging them, that he was it. Each one seemed to graze him; he seemed to be running in jerks and leaps. Yet mingled with his terror there had been a kind of exhilaration: they were such wild, long leaps, and he was making them so effortlessly, as if he had springs in his shoes.)

It was a heavy wooden table, like the block in the front shop where Baxter cut up his meat, and with a sudden sense of outrage Chris saw that it too was smeared with blood. But he said nothing, remembering that he was naked now, and that at least he wouldn't get it on his clothes.

There he was on the table, and at the same time he seemed to be standing back looking at himself, ashamed because he was so white and thin. His belly caved in; his thighs were shrivelled. He brought up his arms, trying to make his muscles stand out, but there was only a twitch of tendons beneath the flabby skin.

He lay still and passive now. As Baxter began feeling his arms he tried to tell him that ordinarily he had good muscles, that they had shrunk and softened only tonight, but his lips were heavy and unresponsive. And then he realized that it was Larson examining and feeling him, not Baxter. He tried frantically to struggle to a sitting position, remembering now what he was here for, but Larson pressed him back and said, "What's wrong, son? You look scared."

He screamed and woke. It was one of the times he was sure that he had actually screamed; he even imagined he heard footsteps outside his door. But when he listened the house was silent except for a faint night creak and a stir of breeze through the open window, and gradually he relaxed and began to breathe again.

But the dream was still real for him. He was awake, yet not quite awake, and somehow the substitution of Larson for Baxter didn't surprise him. There was a cruel streak—making North drink with a snaffle, for instance, and always slapping the pup down and calling it a no-good fool. He knew that he was safe in bed, that his muscles were as hard and firm as they ever were—he tried them—but he felt uneasy none the less, vaguely threatened. They were a queer pair anyway. Best maybe if he collected what was coming to him in the morning and cleared out.

But instead of leaving, he arrived again. This time Larson was at the station to meet him, and they went straight to the restaurant and sat at the counter and had chocolate sundaes. But Larson did not touch his. "I've got to go back to the station," he said, "so you'd better have both. I'll only be a few minutes, so wait right here for me."

(He couldn't have been more than seven, and his mother had said, "Be nice to him now, and tell him how much you miss him. It's all up to you—tell him you're frightened when I go to work and leave you alone, and this time maybe he'll stay."

(It was an enormous responsibility. When the tall stranger arrived, so much younger than he had expected, so much more like one of the big boys he sometimes watched playing baseball or riding motor-cycles, he could only sit waiting for the right opening, tongue-tied and fearful. "Give him a few days—he's just not used to you," he heard her say one night when he woke up and they were quarrelling. "If you'd only show more interest. He's scared you'll go away again."

(And the next afternoon they went for a sundae. "Just the two of us this time," he said. "It's about time we got acquainted."

(The girl behind the counter had pale blonde hair. As she served them she said, "That's a fine boy you've got there," and he answered, putting his hand on Chris's shoulder, "They don't come better." Then, pushing his own sundae away, he said there was a little business he had to attend to, but he would be gone only a few minutes.

(He waited outside the restaurant a long time after they put him out, afraid to go home, but to his surprise his mother didn't blame him. She only cried a little and then said, "Never mind, we'll be better off without him. Now we're going to have a real good supper and maybe if there's time take in a movie.")

But this time Larson returned. "Did no one else get off the freight?" Chris asked, and he replied, "Lots, but you're the one." And while Larson called the girl again he waited happily, the elected and approved.

The girl, when she came, was Sylvia, and instead of a sundae she brought him a glass of milk. It was an enormous glass. Standing on tiptoe, he could just put his lips to the rim. He was grateful at first, she had brought him so much; then as he began to drink he saw specks floating on the milk, and he turned away in disgust. But Sylvia, towering over him, a giantess now, said she would drown him in it if he didn't drink every drop, and he and Larson both began to run. They ran ducking and twisting round the stools, very small and agile now, until at last he tripped over her foot, screaming again, and woke as she bent down and seized him.

He lay thinking about this too a while. It didn't seem a particularly fantastic dream. Sylvia and the glass, of course, were both far too big, and the specks in the milk were really the pills she intended to give Larson. But it was true that she was a strong woman, stronger than he was. Without his knowing it, that had registered—and her strength both appealed to and threatened him. He didn't for a moment doubt that if ever it suited her she would put pills in his milk too with as little hesitation as she planned to put them in Larson's.

It wasn't strange either that both he and Larson should be trying to hide from her. She was the one who spoiled things, for both of them. He thought of all the times Larson had seemed about to confide in him, had touched his arm, then drawn back shyly, and suddenly it struck him that she was what stood between them. "You're the one," he had said. Farm, horses, Cadillac—without her, everything would be his.

Without her, or without him.

The thought slipped into his mind compact and ready-made, but he shied from it. It didn't make sense. Everything belonged to Larson. He and the farm went together. Whereas she had been waitressing somewhere and Larson had just picked her up. She didn't belong, wasn't part of things. The man at the gasoline shed had been right. She was the one that would be catching a train, just as soon as she had fleeced him.

He hadn't liked Potter. Too many questions, too friendly. The whole town, for that matter. All the eyes turned on him, looking for the best, the worst—it was like a cross-fire. Sooner or later someone would begin to suspect the truth.

For a few minutes he had seen it clearly, and then, even after warning himself, had forgotten again, pretended to himself that he was like other people, that he could date girls, learn to play the guitar. But he was on the run—on the run and wasting time. It was a dead-end. The situation was too much for him. A year from now, even though his pay was up a little, he would still be doing chores. Sylvia the same. She was interested in him only as a change, a relief from Larson. When it suited her, when she decided it was safe—a year from now he would still be her chore boy too.

He tossed angrily. Maybe she had more on her hands than she had bargained for. He'd come like a tramp, but maybe he wouldn't leave like one. Say he asked for a thousand, let her beat him down to five hundred. Come across or he'd tell Larson—once she realized he meant business she'd start digging fast.

Unless—suddenly he sharpened and lay still—unless he did it the other way round and put the screws on Larson. Supposing he *did* tell him; *he* might start digging fast too. He was an old man and he liked to show off his young wife. He liked to put the idea across that he was still a lot of use to her. He wouldn't want people to know she gave him pills so she could have a time across the hall with one of the hired men. Explain how easy it would be—in the poolroom, say, or at the dance—how they would all lap it up. But a couple of grand and not a word. No laughs, no trouble. He would go quietly, and Larson would have her to himself again.

And with two thousand he would be on his way. He could get clothes and a gun and take his time. He wouldn't have to go begging to Rickie like a broke kid and jump at the chance to do a little dirty work. Rickie would respect him, cut him in on something worth while.

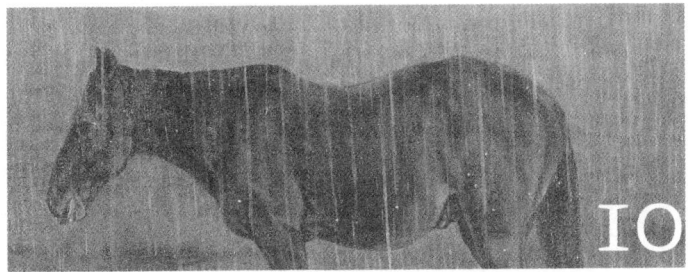

10

NOTHING REMAINED OF IT in the morning but an uneasy feeling that he would be wise not to stay much longer. Both Larson and Sylvia were too interested in him. Maybe they believed he was on his way home from the west coast, maybe they didn't; in any case he had to get lost again, trim himself down to anonymity. Another week—two weeks if there were no signs of trouble: he would risk it that long for the pay.

For it seemed that with a little reserve of cash even the freights would be easier. Just to know it was there—to feel, not to spend. Something to fall back on, the feeling of buying power. As always, his nerve and balance depended on it.

It was Saturday, and after supper Larson tried to persuade him to go to town with them to the dance, even offering to lend him trousers and a sports jacket. "Just hanging in the closet ever since we got married," he said. "Sylvia's idea; thought maybe if she spruced me up a little I'd look sort of like a young fellow." But there would still be shoes, Chris reflected, and when he was out he liked to spend. Besides, if Sylvia were really arranging things for tomorrow night, it would be as well to give Larson the impression that the prospect of an evening with her didn't particularly appeal to him.

He gave no thought to Elsie Grover whatever.

"You'll be the best-looking couple on the floor," Larson persisted. "She's crazy about dancing, and I play out fast. You've been working steady since you came. It just doesn't seem right, going off and leaving you."

Sylvia was waiting outside. She called impatiently, and Larson turned with a little shrug of resignation. Watching him go down the steps Chris wondered if he wanted him along as a kind of buffer, a protection from her contemptuous nagging. "Poor old bastard," he said to himself. "With a bitch like that a lot of good his money does him."

And again, just as in the night, it struck him that she was the intruder, the one who spoiled things. In his own time, his own way, Larson would get round to giving him a lot more than a pair of pants and a jacket. Play along with him, take it easy—without her he would have everything.

And again, a flick of the words that his mind could not resist—without her, or without him.

It was eight o'clock and dark already. He stood looking after the car a minute, then sat on the steps stroking the pup and listening to the plunk of Steve's guitar. He would have liked to join him, but was afraid that the others in the bunkhouse might freeze him out.

It was a long way from Boyle Street. He didn't even dare write to let anyone know where he was. The police always kept an eye on the gang anyway; now they were probably checking Helen and his mother too. Tapping their phones, watching their mail. For a while, perhaps only a few weeks, but he would never be sure. At that, they were probably just as well pleased to be out of touch with him. He had done a job, was on the run. It explained why Helen had been so anxious for him to leave town. She had taken things in fast, less than ten minutes. It was herself she had been concerned about, afraid he might be in her way. With sudden irrational bitterness he wondered about his watch and ring. "Leave them with me for now," she had said. "You don't want anything that might identify you. You don't seem to realize what a jam you're in." But they were worth at least two hundred dollars, and even in the excitement she had realized that he would probably be gone a long time. Rickie had given them to him when they first started working together, as a taste of what he could look forward to if he did what he was told and went all the way. Naturally he would want to know what had happened to them—he was touchy about such things—and he would despise him for having been so soft as to hand them over.

"Come in, why don't you, and have a glass of milk? You ought to be away enjoying yourself like the others, but it's nice to see a young man not crazy for drink and carrying on like most of them nowadays."

Mrs. Paynter had been lying down with a headache. She had wanted to go to town and come home early, and Sylvia had told her that she and Larson intended to stay till at least one or two o'clock. Now, her headache better, but her sense of slight undiminished, she seized on Chris in the hope that commiseration would be reciprocal. "There's liquor here—*she* keeps it—but I'm not offering you any. If it wouldn't make things worse for Larson, I'd pour it down the sink. He doesn't like it either. He just gives in for the sake of peace. Only like I keep trying to tell him, he doesn't get peace."

"A beer now and then's all right, but it's about my limit." He said this truthfully. It wasn't so much that he disliked liquor as that he was afraid of it. It meant loss of control, that he might expose himself. "But I'm not much for movies either, and I couldn't go to the dance in these clothes."

She sighed and motioned him to the table. "There's milk and pie. When a boy like you can see through her it really makes you think. I don't mind telling you I keep getting *my* eyes opened. You know how it is—with somebody in the family you keep trying not to see things—but I can't help asking myself sometimes where it's going to end."

She was busy at the stove a minute, lighting a quick fire of paper and kindling to make herself a cup of tea. Then, returning to the table, she continued, "She's deep, if you know what I mean. Those eyes of hers—you can't get *at* her somehow. You can never sit down and have a quiet talk."

"I don't know. Mostly I just see her at mealtimes."

"That's right, Chris—you're smart to keep clear of her. Smart and lucky. I wish she didn't mean any more to *me* than that."

As she talked she pottered drearily in and out of the pantry, fetching teapot, sugar bowl, cup. "One thing, though, for you to remember, like I already told you—Larson's not the fool she makes him out to be. Hear her raving away about the trains, right in front of people. It's queer all right, but it doesn't hurt anybody. Sometimes I wonder if she isn't trying to work up a case, so she can have him put away as crazy. Or maybe she just keeps saying someday he's going to catch a train because that's what she'd *like* him to do."

"All I know is it's a good place to work," Chris said tactfully. "Lucky I got off at Campkin instead of riding on a town or two like I nearly did."

"I know, Chris—he's taken to you." She looked at him meaningfully and spread her hands. "It's a shame things can't work out. Only for her, now ..."

He looked up. She set her cup in the saucer and kept her eyes lowered. "What I mean—well, I suppose you might say he's still looking for his own boy, and sometimes I see him watching you. Almost like he was wondering if you might do. But you mustn't, Chris. He's got a good farm and a little put away besides, but no matter what he wants you mustn't."

She leaned towards him across the table. "It'll just mean trouble for everybody. Bad trouble. Sometimes I catch her watching you too. She's against you now, but she could turn easy. He's an old man, remember, and you're just a boy."

He met her eyes innocently. As Larson's sister-in-law, he realized, she probably still had hopes of coming in for something herself, and a son in addition to a wife was the last thing she wanted. "He did say something about giving me a job for the winter, but I've got to get home. Just as soon as I get a little ahead. My mother's not very well—I promised her."

Her thin red nose twitched. She stirred her tea rapidly a moment, then bent over the little whirlpool as if she were trying to read their futures. "Don't stay too long—even if you've got to ride the freights again. Your mother would be glad if she knew what you were running away from."

Again he looked up innocently, and lapsing from the oracular to the dreary she resumed, "I know *I'll* be glad to get home. Doing my best to help her out and never a civil word. My legs are bad and I can't climb stairs, so I've got to sleep on the chesterfield in the front room. Nobody ever sets foot in the house—she hasn't a friend, but you ought to hear her if I so much as drop a hairpin."

"When are you going, Mrs. Paynter?" He was not without interest. Even though she slept downstairs—the floor might creak.

"Tomorrow. Now that the wheat's done they're taking the combine to Ole's place and Bell's going to need me. She's expecting soon and the boy's a worry with his heart. I offered to come back later and help Sylvia pickle, but she says it's just as cheap to buy them. That's the kind she is. And no pigs and all the fancy clothes—you can figure out for yourself how long poor Larson's going to stand it!"

Chris pushed back his chair and she went on quickly, "And two-faced. Tomorrow, now, she's asked Ole and Bell and young Chris for supper. Not a word till this morning, and then she phones she's been wanting to have them for weeks only it's so busy. Tell Ole she's got a little Scotch, she says, and they'll have a drink to the new crop before he starts harvesting. That sweet all at once, and if you knew the way she hates them."

"And they said they'd come?"

"What can they do? It would only hurt Larson."

He nodded. "You'd think, all right, she wouldn't have waited till this morning."

"Right after breakfast. Scared like as not I'll tell them the way she's been treating me and it'll get back to Larson. If you're around just listen to her being sweet to me too, so anything I say they won't believe me. Take my word for it, Chris, she's a sly one. She's got a way of getting what she goes after."

He was ready to agree. Last night, when telling him she would try to arrange things for Sunday, she had said that Ole and Bell were coming for supper. Evidently, then, she had planned the visit as she was talking to him—planned it and resolved upon it right then and there. And he smiled as he said good-night to Mrs. Paynter, gratified, restored. It was a lot of trouble to go to for the sake of an hour in bed with him. It showed him where he stood, what he could look forward to if he handled himself right. The same old Chris Rowe—Boyle Street or the middle of Saskatchewan. He wasn't slipping after all. Before he finished he'd be doing more than chores.

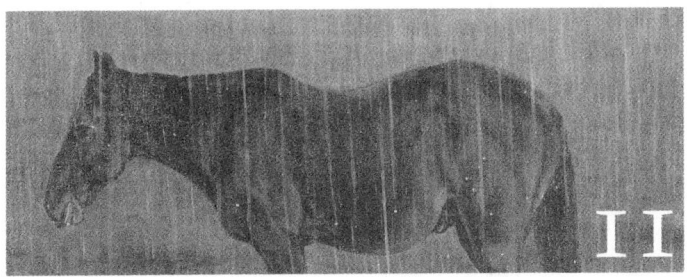

SUNDAY MORNING there was a mare for North, a young, wild-eyed bay that plunged across the yard with a whirr of wheels and a spatter of bloody foam. It had been five miles in the dust and heat; every step of the way the man in the buggy had braced himself and leaned back hard on the reins to hold her in.

But in front of the barn, when he drew her to a standstill and jumped down to unhitch, she stood spent and quiet. Her sides throbbed. Her coat was sopping. She mouthed the bit a moment, then let her head fall. Instinctively, her hind legs spread a little, she seemed to brace herself for what was to come. In his stall North was stamping and neighing furiously, but she seemed indifferent now, gave no sign she even heard him.

The rest of the barnyard, though—even the geldings, even the men—were caught up in the excitement. The horses in the barn snorted nervously. The two- and three-year-olds in the pasture crowded against the gate, ears pricked forward, nostrils flared. And the men wandered over slowly from the bunkhouse, scratching themselves and making jaded little jokes in an effort to appear casual.

Chris, too. He was the first to reach the barn, and leading North out he felt an almost proprietary sense of importance.

So many were there; when North reared they stood back so respectfully; even old Charlie, who had been a farm hand all his life. It was like an acknowledgement of his right to handle such a horse, of his skill and courage and their own incapacity.

But Larson was piqued, and when it was over, following Chris and North back into the barn, he said peevishly, "That fellow Jackson never pays. If you hadn't been so fast bringing North out I'd have told him to take his mare somewhere else. Seven or eight colts already—hasn't paid for more than two. Next time no matter who it is you ask me first."

"But you said you didn't care—you said there were never enough mares for him anyway."

"Never mind what I said. Next time just wait." His satisfaction in possessing North was being encroached upon; Chris had to be reminded of his place. "He cost too much. I'm not standing for a lot of deadbeats bringing their mares like they had a right to."

Chris bridled a little. "You said you didn't care," he repeated. "I asked you why not make them pay, and you said they'd only go somewhere else and then how would *he* like it. What's the sense keeping a stallion anyway, if you're not going to let him have the mares?"

"That's what I sometimes wonder myself, son." The resentment was gone. His voice was friendly and relaxed again. "Just eating his head off and getting older. It's no way to run a farm."

"You mean you might sell him?"

"I might. I've had him a few years though—I'd be lucky now if I got a thousand. Crazy anyway, paying what I did. One of those stock shows—they led him around and I sort of lost my head."

Without looking at Chris he began stroking North. "Actually, I guess, it was on account of the boy. Same as everything else, the lights and the buildings. He's a good horse, and I wanted him same as anybody would, but all the time the boy was back of it. Somebody in the business ought to have him—a real breeder. Me, I grow wheat. I just want work horses."

"But he's yours—that's worth something." The extravagance of the gesture appealed to Chris: twenty-five hundred dollars for a horse he hadn't needed, simply because it was a fine horse. As he went on his face was almost anxious. "You wouldn't feel right if you got rid of him; it wouldn't be the same farm."

"I told you—it was on account of the boy." He turned on Chris, and peered into his eyes. "Just supposing now that you were the boy—just supposing—would you want him or the money?"

Chris turned his face away and looked at North, as if considering. "I think I'd want him, so long as I didn't need the money."

"You talk like that because you're not the boy." Larson made a little movement of impatience, then spat. "If you were, you'd be a farmer, and you'd know there's no place on a farm for anything that doesn't earn its keep."

Perhaps he was aware both of Chris's admiration and of what had called it forth. Perhaps, defensively, he was stiffening his countryman's hard-headed instincts of thrift and caution against the soft, easy values that he imagined were the city's—values that appealed to him, but that he could not yield to self-respectingly. "On a farm whatever you get you've got to work for. There's no time for frills."

Perhaps, too, even as he scowled and rasped out the words, he was edging towards Chris. Chris was reality, the boy an illusion. Abandoning the one for the other wasn't easy; resistances were old and stubborn; and perhaps his sudden antagonism meant that the struggle had begun. Chris watched him in silence a moment, then said reasonably, "A thousand means you've lost most of your money anyway. Why not make the best of your deal and be a real breeder yourself? Do it right, start keeping books ..."

"I know myself—it wouldn't last." He stood shoulder to shoulder now with Chris, watching North and nodding patiently. "It would mean hiring a man to take him round the country, working out the route, finding the right man—fuss and trouble all the way. Then you go after your money and you get everybody sore at you. And I'm scared of that, like I've told you already. I'm sixty-six and I've got nobody. Horses don't count so much now anyway—it's all tractors."

"I know. You're thinking you could stand up to them all right if you had the boy."

Larson looked at him searchingly for a moment, then veered. "Sylvia's always after me to get rid of him. Doesn't like him on account of the mares. After there's been one she says she can hardly look the men in the face when they come in for a meal, because they've been watching and making jokes and she knows what's on their mind. Says it makes me worse too." He winked and gave a hitch to his overalls. "Says the day there's been a mare she knows what *she's* in for."

His boastfulness always repelled Chris a little. For a man his age it somehow wasn't right, wasn't what he expected of him. With a tight laugh he said, "I'd never have thought you needed a horse to give you ideas."

"Don't worry—I got plenty of my own. Enough to give even him some." Larson too laughed, but his answer didn't quite make a joke. It had a touchy promptness that revealed an old man's anxiety. "Take winter, when there's next to no mares—I don't just go to sleep on her then either."

Chris was silent, his distaste showing a little, and Larson veered again, "Just a funny streak she's got, same as all women. Farm girl herself once, knows things like that have got to be, but now she carries on about it. Worries what the neighbors'll say."

He caught the disbelief in Chris's face. "Sure, she worries. There's a lot of sides to her. When she first came people started in treating her all right—talking a lot naturally, but willing to fit her into things. She figured, though, they were just coming round on account of me, because we were all old neighbors, so straight off she started putting the idea across that she'd got along this far without them and was ready to keep right on. Scared a snub was coming, getting hers in first. And a new wife, that's never easy either. Some of the old ones remembered Cora."

He too stood remembering for a moment, then led the way out of the stall. "If you like," he said hesitantly when Chris had the door closed on North, "we'll go over now to the old place and I'll show you what I mean about her. Sunday's the only day I've got, and Ole and Bell are coming this afternoon."

Chris lit a cigarette without answering, frowning as he turned away from the wind. "It'll be a chance for you to try the Cadillac," Larson said. "We've nearly a couple of hours before dinner. It won't take us that long to look things over, so you can drive round afterwards and get the feel of it."

"I wouldn't mind." Chris had been thinking about the Cadillac ever since his first day, but he was careful now to control his eagerness. The value of indifference, how to suggest reserves of interest and intention—it was one of the lessons Boyle Street had taught him early. "I've been sort of hoping you'd let me try it. The time's going fast—first thing, I'll be on my way again."

"But you've only got here, Chris. Don't start talking already about leaving."

"It's a smart-looking car." He looked straight into the dismay that had spread over Larson's face without a sign that he had noticed. "You'd better not let me get used to it, or it may disappear the same time I do."

"But supposing I do let you get used to it—then maybe neither of you'll disappear." His smile was hurt, defenceless, as if already he had begun to count on Chris. "Wait a minute!" He put up his hand in urgent sign for him to stand right where he was. "I nearly forgot—there's something we've got to take with us."

He smiled again, eagerly and importantly this time, then shuffled off across the yard to the garden. When he returned he was carrying a watermelon about the size of a football. "Like I promised, " he said, patting it and beaming. "Just for you and me."

He held it up in front of him a moment on his outspread palms, then put it carefully on the back seat of the car. Under his breath Chris said, "Jesus!"

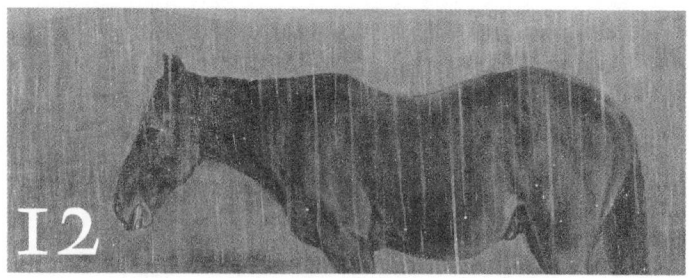

12

IT WAS ONLY ABOUT A MILE, but on a side road, in the opposite direction to town, and Chris had never passed that way before. The house, little better than a shack, was unpainted and weather-greyed, with boarded-up windows and a leaning chimney. Weeds grew in a wild tangle right to the old broken steps. The old sod stable had a lurch to its walls as if they were made of rubber and starting to soften in the sun. On its roof grew a knee-high crop of yellow mustard. Half-way between house and stable the grey cribbing of a well projected two or three feet above the ground, with uprights and a cross-piece like a make-shift gallows. Enclosing it all, in bright trim contrast, was a fence of stout new cedar posts and freshly-strung barbed wire.

"Just put it up last spring, right after seeding." They left the car at the side of the road and crawled carefully through the close strands of wire. "Got tired fixing the old one. All the strays in the country seemed to get the idea there was something special to eat inside. Every time I'd go by there'd be another post down and cow clats right on the step. Cora wouldn't have liked it."

His face and voice were humorless. He put his hand on one of the cedar posts and tested its solidity with satisfaction. "Weeds are bad." As they started across the yard towards the sod stable he kicked at them resentfully. "Never thought, when I wired up the gate. Used to bring the mower over two or three weeks a summer, but now I've fenced myself out."

He picked up a piece of half-rotten board a few steps off the overgrown path and began taken swipes at the thistles and wild oats. "Soon as I get some spare time I've got to come over with the scythe. And all that mustard on the roof—scared, though, if I try climbing up I'll bring the whole thing down. My old man put it up over sixty years ago—the first summer we were here. I put a new roof on, but they're the same walls."

Inside it was cool, with a dry clean smell of musty straw. There were no windows; the only light came from the door and a few chinks in the roof where the rain had eaten away the sod. The floor was bare, hard-packed earth; the litter on it fluffed around their feet like chaff. The mangers were worn and gnawed; some of the axe-squared poplar poles of which the stall partitions were built had cracked and fallen. In a corner stood three or four bottles that once had probably held liniment or creolin, all swathed in cobwebs now like giant cocoons.

"This was Ned's stall, and Fanny's over there. They're the only two that are left. You see there was another stable after this one, but when I moved to the new place I tore it down for lumber. People say I ought to take everything down, fill in the well and seed right over. But they'll do it fast enough when I'm out of the way, so I figure I'll hang on."

He stood nodding absently a moment, then turned to Ned's manger. "See," he said, pointing to the gnawed wood, "always was a great one for chewing. Couldn't cure him—what they call a cribber. Now he's cured all right—got no teeth."

Alongside the stable was a patch of dense, breast-high pigweed. "Good to eat when it's young," Larson said. "Vinegar and salt—just like spinach. In the spring, when I was little, my old lady used to send me to pick a pot two or three times a week. First green stuff—good for the blood. Ready long before the garden. You take them when they're young, not all seeds and up to your chin like these. In those days we used to get a bag of oranges once a month. If we were lucky."

He broke off a stalk and stripped the leaves reminiscently. "Right here where it's growing so good, this is where the other stable stood. Before I tore it down on account of Minnie— thinking maybe I could forget. That was the real reason. It wasn't for the lumber."

He took two or three steps into the pigweed, then turned and faced Chris. "It was right here where I'm standing now. As pretty a little mare as you ever set eyes on. It wasn't coming to her."

"You mean this is where you shot her?"

"Climbed into the manger and let her have it square between the eyes. Plain murder. She just got scared and started kicking—didn't know she was hurting him. I'd got her for him so he could ride to school. They were both that proud."

He stood a moment staring vacantly out from the pigweed, then set off towards the house. He walked round it two or three times circumspectly, Chris following him. It was almost as if he were making sure no one was inside. At last, halting and feeling for his keys, he said, "Never got round to painting it. Promised her I would the first chance I got, but just kept putting it off. Next year, though—just watch me. Next year for sure."

"You don't mean you'd waste paint on it now?" It struck him that maybe Larson was crazy after all, crazier even than Sylvia thought. "Old and empty—what would be the sense?"

"White with green trim, like I promised her."

"But she wouldn't know. It wouldn't do her any good."

"Makes me that wild, though, every time I look at it and start thinking the way I let them stop me." The impatience in his voice was directed against himself, not Chris. He gave no sign of having even heard him. "Worrying what they'll say—and they say I'm crazy anyway, so what's the difference? It's my house and my paint. I've got a right to put it on. But I don't. I let them beat me."

He broke off and nudged Chris knowingly. "Six gallons of white and one of green. Sure, I've got it—up in the loft, at the far end under the sheaves. Three years now, trying to get up my nerve."

Chris laughed guardedly, humoring him. "Go ahead then, put it on. Supposing they do talk, who cares?"

"That's me for you. Once I get something in my head nothing can stop me." He squirmed and rubbed his hands together, then broke off with a dejected shrug. "Nothing but her and them. Paint's for painting with, not for hiding under the sheaves. I'm not so sure of things. I get the feeling she's watching me—waiting for something. I mean if I did it she'd have me. She'd say that proves it—he's crazy, sure. Listen today when Ole and Bell come if she doesn't start on about the trains."

He looked at Chris with a little gesture of appeal. "You put up a stone with some fancy words on it and everybody says that's fine—you're showing your respect. But me, I'd rather paint the house where she used to live, like she always wanted. What's the difference? She wouldn't know about a stone either."

He took out his keys, and after unlocking the door stepped aside with a shy, slightly formal bow. "It's a long time now since I asked anybody in. Cora'd be ashamed—she was a great one for curtains and things. Had it fixed up just like a house in town."

Two rooms, a lean-to kitchen and an attic. Small, dark, low-ceilinged, overpowering with dense, still heat. As they moved across the creaking floors Larson's lips moved silently. The boarded-up windows and the walls with their peeling, faded paper—he seemed trying helplessly to explain to Chris their importance, the difference between appearance and reality. His face took on a faint look of embarrassment; every few steps he brought his hands up, then let them fall again. Finally he said, blinking as they stepped outside again into the bright sunshine, "Can't get used to it yet—all these years seeing him little, and now telling myself he'd be a way older than you. Over there, just about where the car is, that's where the saddle turned."

Feeling his soft streak threaten again, Chris stretched and yawned—the appropriate response, what Boyle Street would have expected of him—then began impatiently drawing Larson towards the Cadillac.

But when they were through the fence Larson pulled up short. "Thinking too much. Forgot what I brought you for. Forgot the watermelon too."

Heedless of the exasperation on Chris's face, he gave him the melon to hold while he crawled back through the fence, then took it from him again and carried it before him admiringly. At the well he set it a little to one side in a clump of thistles, then brought out his keys again and unlocked the padlock that secured the cover.

"I keep it locked," he said, "in case somebody might come round and leave it open. Don't want anybody falling in, dogs or gophers either. The least I can do is keep it clean."

He lifted the cover, and resting his hands on the sides breathed in the dankness that drifted up from the moldy, half-rotten cribbing. "Over sixty feet—all by hand." He spoke the words into the well, almost shouting them, then like a child turned his head and listened. "Cora and a horse—all one summer. Cora and old Ned."

He straightened, found a pebble and wiped it carefully on his overalls, then leaned over again and dropped it in. "Now it's steady again—I can see it shining." He glanced round after a moment and gave a pleased little nod. "Drop something in and you lose it for a while. Always comes back all right, but you've got to give it some time. One day last spring when I was putting up the fence something went wrong—thought I'd lost it sure. You can see it shining and you can see yourself. You don't know it's you till you move, and then it moves too."

Then, with the same old-fashioned little bow as when he ushered Chris into the house, he straightened and stepped aside. "Now it's your turn—everybody likes looking down a well. Here's a stone for you too. Just wipe it to be sure it's clean."

To please him, still thinking of the Cadillac, Chris took the pebble and wiped it on his overalls just as Larson had done, then leaned over solemn-faced and dropped it in. But Larson had been hasty. It was one thing to talk about the well, another to share it—and seizing the cover he unceremoniously thrust him aside. "Must be getting on to noon anyway," he said, "and we've still got to eat our watermelon. About the only chance we'll have, just the two of us. I told you before, I'm not letting *her* in on it."

He sat down stiffly, his back to the well, and then, with a bland, important look, like a host about to carve, brought out his jackknife and motioned Chris to hand him the melon. Chris obeyed listlessly. He was hot and bored now, and at the sight of Larson giving the knife a preliminary whetting on his thigh he felt a kind of revulsion. When had he last washed it? For that matter, when had he last washed his hands? Revulsion, then anger—did the dirty old bastard really think he was going to *eat* the goddammed thing? Jesus! Was it supposed to be a treat? "Here you are, it's all yours," he said, not even picking up the melon, but pushing it with his foot. "Looks about right for a good bellyache."

Larson glanced up reproachfully, but kept silent till he had cut through the melon. Then, snapping the halves apart, he held them up with a look of triumph. "Look at that, will you. What have you got to say about a bellyache now? Nice and pink, just like the ones you buy."

The pink center was a very pale pink, and only about an inch in diameter, but Larson cut off a slice and held it up with a flourish. "Go on, you can have all you want," he said. "That's what I grew it for, just you and me."

"It's not ready—it's green. You should have left it."

"Not in the middle. Go ahead! Tastes fine."

"I'm telling you, it'll double you up." He was glad it was green. He shrank from putting his lips to anything the knife had touched, and in his sudden hostile mood—as if the little upsurge of fastidiousness were a disguise—he welcomed the chance to reject and disappoint.

"It's pretty green all right." Larson munched disconsolately a moment, then brightened and snapped the knife shut. "It shows you just the same. Wait till next year. I'm going to start them inside and plant a whole acre. I'll show you what a real watermelon looks like."

"Not me—you won't be showing me." Chris didn't so much as glance down. Head back, thumbs hooked in his pockets, he stood looking across the prairie as if he were already on his way. "It's hard to say where I'll be this time next year. Not around here, though, that's for sure."

"I was hoping once you got used to things you'd feel like settling in. Harvest's as good as over. I'll have more time for you."

Having scored, Chris was sorry. The way Larson turned his face up, then let his slice of melon fall—his impulse now was to make amends. "It's nothing to do with you. I know I could be a lot worse off. But I've got things to do. I can't explain exactly—"

Departure and after—his own words suddenly brought home to him again what lay ahead. Larson too was looking straight out across the prairie now. "You're safe here," he said hesitantly after a moment, "whatever it is you're running away from. Just try and not worry too much. Stay as long as it suits you ..."

It was what he wanted—someone older and stronger than himself to lean on, someone to take over, assume responsibility. For a moment his sense of relief was so deep that he failed to realize the implications of what Larson had just said. And then he wavered. He was still relieved, but he was also resentful. It meant that Larson had the upper hand, that the moment there was trouble he could crack the whip. It meant living under a perpetual obligation, owing him perpetual gratitude. There was one impulse to respond, and another to flare up and ask him what he meant. They neutralized each other. He flushed, then half-smiled, then stood silent and abashed.

"Ought to have filled it in long ago." Larson struggled to his feet and abruptly changed the subject. "Never going to need it—lots of water in the new well—but all that work. Me at the bottom filling the bucket and Cora leading the horse."

He leaned over and stroked the cover gently. "For a bucket we had an old boiler—held as much as five or six buckets ordinary size. And a pulley and a horse hitched to the rope. I'd yell when I was ready and she'd lead him away till the bucket was at the top; then she'd whoa and leave him standing and come back and empty it. Hotter than it is now—worked right through July. I'd dig a few feet and then crib, and while I was doing that she'd get a meal or do what she could in the stable. Every few buckets I'd come up and shovel back the dirt. Couldn't afford any help, and the first well that the old man had dug was going dry. Started in right after we were married, always called it our honeymoon well. Little joke, just between ourselves."

"You've come a long way."

"Best time of our lives, doing it together. That's why I can't fill it in. That's why I want to paint the house for her, white with green trim."

"Go ahead then, paint it." It was genuine sympathy now, even though diluted with the realization that, considering what Larson suspected, it would be prudent to keep on the right side of him. "There's nothing Sylvia can do to you. Just don't be scared of her."

"That's right, we can stand up to her." He stood smiling and lost a moment, then with a glance at the sun started back briskly towards the car. "There's still time for a little run—out on the highway if you like. We'll just see what she can do."

On the highway Chris opened up to eighty. For a mile or two Larson sat tense, clutching his knees. Then, beginning to enjoy himself, he leaned back expansively and smiled. "You sure handle her nice, Chris," he said. "Me, I keep her down round thirty-five; wasting her, you might say, scared I won't be able to think fast enough if anything goes wrong. But you've got her right where you want her. She'd never dare try anything with you."

And when they were home and walking towards the house he added, "Always wanted to show the boy what she could do and never had the nerve. Now here you are, showing me. You'd better stay, Chris. You'd better think over what I've been telling you."

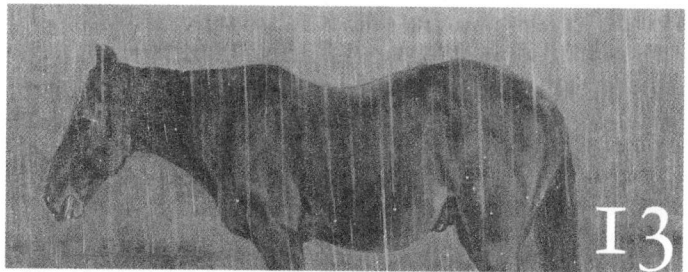

13

CHRIS WAS IN HIS ROOM, stretched out on the bed with a magazine, when the visitors arrived. He closed the door at the sound of their voices, but the next minute Larson shouted up for him to come down.

"Here he is, Bell—the new fellow I've been telling you about. Chris, this is Mrs. Paynter's daughter." They weren't even sitting down yet. It was exactly as if he were a relative or an old friend of the family. "You know Ole, and this is the boy. Another Chris—growing up fast. Going to be eight around Christmas."

Bell was pregnant. Pale, tired, mouse-haired, wearing a shapeless maternity dress, she made no other impression. She acknowledged the introduction with a soft, sprawling smile, extended her hand country-fashion but kept her body rigid, seeming to fear that a step would make her condition more noticeable. Then, still without moving her feet, she reached out and drew the boy towards her, and with one hand on his shoulder held him in front of her like a screen.

Embarrassed in turn, Chris shook hands quickly and dropped his eyes to the boy. Stepping back and letting his voice boom a little, he said, "Hello, Chris. So you're the young fellow who's been stealing my name."

Young Chris had bright blond hair, round china-blue eyes and a way of holding his head back and his lips slightly

/ 103

parted as if steeling himself to ask a difficult question. He stood still a moment, his expression blank; then, thinking perhaps that this stranger with the big voice really was accusing him, he slipped away from his mother and sat down quietly on the chesterfield.

But along with shyness there was a show of independence. Watching him, Chris sensed a wish to escape identification with the fussy, overwhelming softness of his mother; sensed, too, that it was himself who was responsible.

"He makes shy, "Bell said apologetically. "Shame on you, Chris. Why don't you speak to the man? He'll think you've got no manners."

Distressed at finding herself alone and exposed, she put her handkerchief to her mouth, then stood hesitating between the chesterfield, which would mean crossing the room, and an armchair, which was right beside her. Quickly, before she could decide, Chris took the chesterfield himself. "But we're not going to be shy long," he said, giving young Chris's shoulder a companionable slap. "Chris to Chris—there should be lots to talk about."

Young Chris sat rigid a minute, his thin legs sticking out straight from the chesterfield. Then, after a quick glance round the room for signs of disapproval, he fished in his pocket and brought out a piece of strap with a rusty buckle.

Bell was still standing. "Put that dirty thing away and say how-do-you-do to the man like I tell you. And look at your tie—all crooked again. Next time if you don't learn to behave I'll leave you home."

Again she estimated the distance to the chesterfield, afraid of making herself still more conspicuous and at the same time itching to assert her authority. Ole, whose attitude towards Chris had been suspicious and aloof from the first day, stood glaring in the doorway, with his big shoulders hunched and his brows knit painfully, angry at the way she was nagging the boy and at the same time sharing her disapproval. Chris looked at them coolly. Somehow their resentment stimulated and pleased him. Turning again, deliberately shutting them out, he said, "It's too hot for ties anyway.

That's a woman for you, always trying to make a man's life miserable."

Bell remained standing a moment longer, tight-lipped, her hands clenched. Then, as Sylvia hurried in from the kitchen with a tray of glasses, she eased herself carefully into the chair beside her.

Sylvia went to Ole first and winked broadly. "Take this one," she said, "before I get mixed up and give it to somebody else. Spiked it a little. I know how you like grape juice."

Ole and Larson took chairs too now, while Mrs. Paynter, ostentatiously sabbath-minded, however godless the others might be, funerary and severe in black silk and jet beads, sat down on the chesterfield between the two Chris's.

Sylvia's color was high, her eyes bright, and as she went round with the tray Chris felt a little twinge of excitement and admiration. There was one glass short: he admired her for that, too, for the contemptuous impatience in her voice as she said, "Oh—you're here too. Well, if you want some you'll have to get it yourself. The bottle's in the pantry. Just see you *don't* spike yours." Right in there, not missing a trick. They all knew now what *she* thought of hired men who sat in the parlor with the company.

Something in her smile, the little bursts of bright false laughter—he knew now that it was to be tonight. For a moment or two the excitement was almost unbearable, almost a fear. Then, with a wrench of will, reminding himself that it was only four o'clock, he shut it off. She was the kind of woman that couldn't be thought about that way for six or seven hours.

He turned to young Chris. "What do you say we go and see the horses? There's one called Minnie. You can go for a little ride if you like. I'll lift you up and lead her round."

"He wants to hear the piano." Bell's voice fell like a sledge across the room. She fixed her eyes on young Chris warningly, and made a beckoning movement with her head. "Do you mind putting in a roll, Sylvia? He's always asking when are we going to get a piano that plays by itself like Uncle Larson's. Aren't you, Chris? If you sit over here by me you'll be able to see the keys better. That's what he's so crazy about, seeing the keys go up and down."

Young Chris sat still, industriously scratching at the rust on his buckle.

"Just a minute, Bell, till I rest my feet." Sylvia sat down on the piano bench, facing the room, and took a dubious sip of grape juice. "He'd be better out looking at the horses and working up an appetite. There'll be time for the piano after supper."

"Sure, Chris'll take good care of him," Larson said. "A ride on Minnie's just what he needs."

Ole frowned. A look of protest on his big face remained inarticulate.

"I'll play for him then," Mrs. Paynter said, rising from the chesterfield with a grimace, one hand clutching her beads as if she were pulling herself up by them. "As usual, of course, I've done nothing all day but sit with my hands in my lap, so my feet aren't tired. It's little enough—What would you like to hear, Chris?"

But young Chris, still scratching at his buckle, said flatly, "I don't want to hear anything—I want to go and see the horses."

Chris had him out of the kitchen door and down the back steps before there was so much as a stir of protest. But Mrs. Paynter was not far behind. As they started across the yard she called, "You, Chris—big Chris—there's something I've got to tell you," and in response to the urgency in her voice, motioning young Chris to stay where he was, he turned and went up the steps again.

"Remember," she said in a hoarse whisper, the cords of her neck jerking beneath the dry yellow skin, "he's not going to be with us long. Promise you'll be careful."

He glanced round uneasily, then nodded. "All right. I won't let him ride Minnie, and I'll see nothing scares him. We'll just walk round a while."

"It's not that, Chris. Naturally we want to keep him with us as long as we can, but it's only a few months or a year anyway. I mean what goes on in the barn—he's not to see or find out about it. We keep him away from things like that. He's innocent, and we want him still innocent when he goes to meet his Maker. You understand? Don't let him see things. If he asks questions, get round them."

He stared at her a moment, then went down the steps without answering. Everything was spoiled. Setting off for the barn again with young Chris, he felt a vague sense of guilt, as if Mrs. Paynter's high-pitched anxiety had suddenly made him aware of the remoteness of his own innocence. It wouldn't be enough to keep him away from North and Fanny, to forestall questions. What he himself was—had become— it seemed beyond him now to keep at least a little of it from seeping through.

"First we'll look in and say hello to Ned. Your Uncle Larson says he's the oldest one he's got—nearly thirty."

"And I'm only seven and a half. That makes him four times older."

He spoke in a precise, quick voice, like the bright boy in the class, then with an old man's sigh put his hand on Ned's shoulder. "But I'll get to be that old. They say maybe I won't get to even eight."

Not quite sure of himself, Chris forced a laugh. "I bet it'll end up the other way round—you'll be four times as old as Ned. With a bald head and white whiskers."

Young Chris too laughed, tickled at the picture of himself that Chris's words had conjured up. But the next moment, the corners of his mouth down, he persisted, "I know— that's what she called you back for just now. She said you're not to let me ride Minnie."

"That's just it. You're not very strong now, so you're careful. You'll grow up and last far longer than the ones that tear around and do what they want to. I've seen it happen myself—lots of times."

"Not me!" His voice shot up almost gaily, as if it were a game between them, and he were showing Chris that he was too smart to be fooled. "Eight's the most. One day I was supposed to be upstairs and I heard my mother tell all about me on the phone."

Chris swatted a fly on Ned's flank. "Doctors make mistakes—everybody knows that." He hesitated, looking for another fly. "Look at me—when I was seven my mother was just the same. Worrying because I was so skinny, always after me to drink milk and cod-liver oil."

When he was seven she was still working in the bakery. She would bring him home left-over tarts and cakes, and then explode in tired anger because he filled up on sweet stuff instead of eating the things that would be good for him.

The fault-finding was incessant: why didn't he go out and play more? Why didn't he get a job delivering after school? But all the time he knew that none of it was important, that on the contrary it was a source of pride and satisfaction to her that he was different from the other boys.

It was before the quarrel with his Aunt Rosemary—the day she called his mother a street-walker, the first ever to disgrace their name, and then slammed out, erect and self-righteous, never to return. And she, too, worried and fussed about his health, even accusing his mother of not looking after him properly. But at the same time she took a spinsterish delight in his clean, well-brushed good looks and polite bright answers, as if she saw in him, even at that age, the family's hope, had already elected him to redeem their mediocrity.

"The real little gentleman and scholar he is—just listen to this now, will you?"—and she would sit back, her head tilted proudly, while he read aloud from a book she had brought him. "And the hands on him, will you, and the long fingers—that shows he'll be good at music when he gets older. One of these days you'll have to be getting him a piano."

Then, as a reward, she would treat him to ice-cream or a soda, always coming with him and having one herself instead of just giving him the money. And when she was gone at last and he was back upstairs, his mother would go round with thin lips muttering incomprehensibly about dried-up, interfering old maids. So that her visits became a signal for jealousy and resentment, and he began to dread and even avoid them. Her final departure would have been a relief had it not been part of the general ruin, one of the many things robbed of meaning or importance by the betrayal that preceded them.

"Where's Fanny? Once Uncle Larson let me sit on her."

"She's got a stomach ache, so we'd better not bother her. Too many oats. Instead, let's go and see Minnie."

It wasn't so strange. With surprise, forcing back his memory, he realized that at seven he had known nothing either. So long had he made a point of not remembering such a time, the humiliation of it, that he no longer believed in it. For it wasn't until they moved to Boyle Street, when he was at least eleven, that Rickie and the others had set him straight on the real facts of life, jeering him for his backwardness, displaying him as a kind of oddity or freak; and it was the shame of that backwardness, the determination to live it down, that had helped him, once through the first bewilderment of understanding, to accept with cynicism and a shrug the significance of a room of his own and a liberal allowance of pocket money.

"They say Uncle Larson has had four or five Minnies—all like this one, with white front feet and a star. Have you heard that too, Chris?"

Chris nodded.

"The first Minnie killed his boy, and then he turned round and killed her." It was plain, even though his voice rose a little, questioningly, that he knew the story inside out. "He was sorry afterwards, so he got another Minnie and pretended it was the same one. Do you think he's still pretending?"

"Sometimes, maybe. Here's the old saddle. After she kicked it to pieces he put it together again, just like new. But over on this side is the one we always use."

Young Chris touched one of the stirrups of the old saddle with his fingertip, almost experimentally, as if half afraid some of its old fatal potency might still be alive within it. Then, looking up at Chris, he asked, "When you ride her, which one do you use?"

"The old one just sits there—nobody uses it."

"I thought maybe you did. They say Uncle Larson acts just like you were his own boy come back. Sylvia tells everybody—she thinks it's because he's going crazy."

"Your uncle's not crazy." His voice was sharp, as if some secret loyalty were at work within him. "He told me about the boy and how he got killed. So he knows all right. He couldn't get him mixed up with me."

"He could if he's crazy. Sometimes he could."

Then, politely forestalling further argument, he turned back to Minnie. "Is she fast?" he asked. "When you ride her does she ever buck?"

"She doesn't buck, but she's fast all right. The wind sometimes just about blows your hair out."

"Why don't you wear a hat? A big one, like a cowboy?"

"I'm afraid I'd make a pretty poor cowboy anyway. Minnie's the first horse I've ever been on."

"I'd like to see you just the same. I bet you're better than a cowboy."

"Maybe I could take her out now for you and ride round the yard for a while." He had to force himself; if they looked out they would think him a show-off fool, trying to make an impression on a boy. "I'm warning you, though, I'm not very good. If she shies or starts acting up I'll like as not fall off."

Young Chris considered a moment, then—disinclined perhaps to put him to the test, preferring him intact for future use—shook his head. "Just round the yard wouldn't be much good anyway. What I mean, I'd like to see you when you're going *fast*." He drew back a little, pressing close to Chris, and with an involuntary movement that had in it something of apology, Chris put a hand on his shoulder.

As if on cue, Minnie raised her head and neighed, eyes shining, a glint of sunlight on her sorrel mane. At that moment she *was* going fast; under his hand Chris felt young Chris's shoulder quiver. Again there was a feeling of guilt—unfittedness, this time—and he stood silent, easing the pressure of his hand, trying to withdraw, efface himself. Again she neighed; again the shoulder quivered; and then from the doorway Mrs. Paynter's voice broke in on them, shrill and anxious. "Chris," she called, "what are you doing there? Chris, do you hear me? Where are you?"

And they answered in unison, "Here—in here with Minnie."

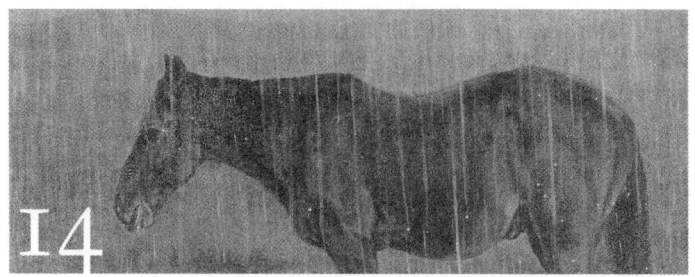

14

AFTER THE MEN HAD BEEN SERVED as usual in the kitchen, the family sat down in the seldom-used dining-room. Chris, at Larson's insistence, ate with the family.

Sylvia put on a good show of annoyance, but Mrs. Paynter whispered, "Don't mind her, Larson's the one that's running things. When she said you belonged with the first sitting, he told her you belonged where he wanted you. I wish you could have seen the look she gave him."

At the table Sylvia continued to act well. For at least a quarter of the meal she was silent, breathing hard, working her lips in an obvious effort to control her indignation—such a good performance that even Chris felt uncomfortable. He had to keep reminding himself that it was all for the benefit of the others, a ruse to throw them off the scent. As a performance it was just a little too good—it gave him a glimpse of her capabilities. He had won, had become important to her, but as he ate he kept glancing furtively from her face to the others with an uneasy feeling of commitment.

"Come on, Chris, you can do better than that." As an excuse to break the silence, Larson leaned over and tapped the boy on the shoulder. "Chicken's good for you—just what you need to make you grow. You can't fill up on pie."

"Oh—you're talking to *that* Chris!" Sylvia threw up her head with a snorting little laugh. "For a minute I thought you were starting to worry about the big one's appetite. The last couple of weeks that's all we've heard around here: Chris this, Chris that, till I want to scream. I don't know why he doesn't see a lawyer—draw up the adoption papers and get it over with."

For a moment there was not even the clink of a fork. Then, her voice climbing hysterically, Sylvia went on, "I can't help it. It's driving me out of my mind. First it was the trains, now it's Chris. At night they stand out in the yard and listen together. They're both that way. Chris came on a freight, and just watch if they don't disappear on one."

This, Chris realized, was running far ahead of her plans for tonight. It meant that both Larson and Mrs. Paynter were right—she was scheming to have him put away. And he watched her uneasily again. Larson was an old man. It wasn't coming to him. He had been old when she married him—she had known what to expect. In any case, there was another room. She could always lock the door.

But in almost the same instant, sharpening, he wondered what it might mean for him if she succeeded. According to Larson and Mrs. Paynter, her plans had begun long before his arrival, but perhaps, now that he was here, he might fit into them. Handle himself right, encourage her—she might make it worth his while to stay. She was thirty and no fool. Just on the border; another five years and she would be starting to sag. And from the way he had sized her up, she would take it straight, wouldn't try to deceive herself. If he was what she wanted, she would be willing to make sacrifices. No fool, in more ways than one. She wouldn't plan to have Larson put away without also planning to get her hands on everything he owned. There would be lawyers; as his wife, she would naturally be appointed to look after things. It would be her farm—everything—and if he stayed on, making himself useful ...

"I'm sorry. I don't know what came over me. Eat up your dinner everybody, and don't pay any attention." She smiled round the table, then turned to Bell. "Try my pickles. It's your own recipe that I got from your mother—she's always after me. Be honest now, and tell me what you think."

Bell munched a piece of cucumber a moment, stolidly conscientious. "Very nice, Sylvia," she said. "Too sour for me, but that's just a matter of taste."

Only he wasn't crazy. Chris watched him reach for young Chris's plate, and with a wink push aside the dark meat and dressing that was left on it, then replace it with small pieces of white, and he wondered how she thought she would ever get away with it. Gossip wasn't enough; there would have to be doctors as well. He worked hard, he drove a Cadillac—she would never get insanity out of that. Besides, Larson himself suspected what she was up to. Already he was stepping carefully.

And then with a little jerk he brought his head up and looked straight in front of him. His eyes narrowed; the skin on his shoulders twitched. What would it be worth to her, he wondered, to know that Larson kept the paint for the old house hidden in the loft?

But when the meal was finished and he returned to the barn—alone, this time, for as he rose from the table Bell caught young Chris's eye—he decided it would be wiser to get away. Already, suspecting what he did, Larson was dangerous. Dangerous and unpredictable; even if he wasn't crazy, he had a funny slant on things. Sylvia could mean trouble too. For while there were no moral issues for Chris, he was none the less aware that even a sane, well-balanced husband is likely to react violently to the discovery that someone has been substituting for him with his wife. It didn't occur to him that he wasn't involved yet with Sylvia, and that he need never be. His vanity—even his self-respect—was too deeply engaged for that. The humiliation he had suffered the first day still rankled. Tonight was not to be so much a matter of indulgence as the settling of a score.

He wasn't concerned about tonight. After watching and listening to her he was satisfied that everything would go smoothly. But there would probably be other times, and Larson was no fool either. You always relaxed after a while, grew careless—it was only human. "Never crowd your luck,"

Rickie used to say. "Whatever it is, fade while you've still got good pickings."

Two or three weeks at the longest; by then he should have well over a hundred dollars, enough at least for clothes. If he didn't pick up another job he could thumb rides as far as the mountains, and from there on there would always be the freights. In the meantime, though, he might as well accept what came his way. Not to take advantage of her willingness would be like refusing food when he was hungry. And he wasn't made that way. There was nothing of the ascetic about him, either by discipline or nature.

"Chris, they're ready to leave now. You'd better come and say good-bye."

It was the kind of invitation that ordinarily he would have pretended not to hear, but now, thinking of the boy, he obeyed promptly. By the time he reached the house Sylvia was serving drinks. They were all in the kitchen, Bell, Ole, Larson, young Chris and Mrs. Paynter, ranged in a stiff semi-circle, watching Sylvia as she filled the glasses. Mrs. Paynter, her help no longer needed now that the harvest was finished, was going home with Ole and Bell. Despite the heat, she wore hat, coat and gloves, all black. With one hand she clutched young Chris, with the other an old suitcase.

"No, Sylvia, there's no use pouring any for me. I won't put my lips to it."

"A drop of good Scotch never hurt anybody. Just a small one—to celebrate the crop."

"If you want to show your heart's grateful for a good crop, the right way's to get down on your knees. On the Lord's day, in front of the child, it's a disgrace."

"We've had this bottle since last spring—I'm tired of looking at it. Just a little send-off—to show my appreciation for all the help you've been."

"I've got my check—that's all the appreciation I need. With me it's not the last day that counts anyway."

"Well, at least it's not going to be wasted. Here's Chris, right on time." She knit her brows, then pointed to his glass without looking at him. "The big help he's been he ought to have a bottle to himself. If Larson hadn't picked him up, I don't supposed we'd have got the crop harvested at all."

"He does his share, and I don't hear Larson complaining." As the others sipped their drinks, Mrs. Paynter took a fresh grip of young Chris's hand. "It's always the same round here—the more you do the less thanks you get."

Aunt Bessie too. If Sylvia could fool a bitter, sharp old woman, intent on adding to her store of grievances, he had nothing to worry about the way she would handle Larson.

"We'd better go." Ole drained his glass with a little smack of relish, and then, looking guilty, set it back on the table. "I've still got to see to the stable, and I don't want Chris up late."

Sylvia filled his glass again. "Just a small one for the road. You're a big man—you hold more than the others."

He drank it expressionlessly and they all filed out to the car. As Chris followed he tried to catch up with young Chris, but Mrs. Paynter strode ahead, eager to display her relief at getting away, and her grip of his hand remained firm. Chris pressed close to the window as they started off, but there was no response.

As the car went through the gate he raised his hand, let it fall. The tail light disappeared, and still he stood looking after them. Then behind him the screen door slammed, and Larson called, "Come on, Chris, it's nearly half-past nine. Seems like it's been a long day—I'm just about played out. Sylvia's going to make us an eggnog, and then we're going straight to bed."

But as Chris entered the kitchen Sylvia came out of the pantry with a glass that held two inches of Scotch neat. "This is what you need more than an eggnog," she said good-humoredly. "A man's drink for a change, instead of that mess of milk and eggs. And this time Aunt Bessie's not watching, so you can relax and enjoy it."

"Just about half that, Sylvia. You and Chris have some too. Make it three."

"There's plenty left for all of us. You've had a hard summer. It's coming to you."

He took the glass from her and held it up to the light, his furtive expression revealing that while Aunt Bessie was gone, Cora now was standing in for her. "I'll have a big head in the morning," he said, puckering his mouth dubiously, "and I've got to get started early."

"You'll have a good sleep for a change. Lately you've been kicking and moaning so I can't sleep either. Hold it a minute—maybe you'll feel more like it if we all drink together."

She brought two more glasses, each containing about half as much as Larson's. He looked at Chris doubtfully, seeming to seek sanction for such indulgence, then gave a reckless shrug and winked. They clinked and drank, their faces grave, their eyes fixed on their glasses with an almost ritual-like solemnity. For a moment Chris felt chilled—it was so smooth and deft, she was carrying it off with such competence; then, as the glow of the liquor spread through him, his desire returned, and he watched her with an impatience in which was mingled an almost childlike confidence. She was so strong, so much older. And suddenly resentful of Larson, he scowled, wishing he would go, so she could devote herself to him entirely.

"Upstairs to bed now. As soon as you hit the pillow you'll be dead till morning. You too, Chris—out of my way. I've still got work to do."

"I'm not finished at the barn yet either. I'll be a while."

"See you come up quiet then. There's warm water if you want to wash, but keep things clean. If you're still hungry you'll find plenty in the pantry."

"See Chris, she growls a lot, but she's not so bad as she lets on. We're going to be a happy family yet." The Scotch was beginning to work on him; his voice had already taken on a mooning, sentimental lilt. "Sure, she likes you—don't you, Sylvia? Treat him right and he'll maybe stay all winter. Just the three of us—that's what I'm trying to talk him into."

They stood motionless a minute, listening again as Larson's step receded into the hall and up the stairs. Then he turned to go, and she whispered, "In about an hour."

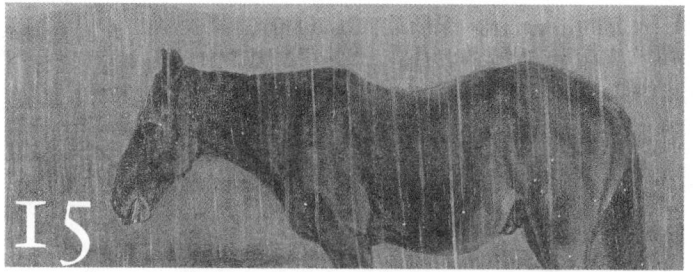

15

FOR CHRIS, TOO, IT HAD BEEN A LONG DAY. He lay awake a while, listening intently, afraid, despite her promise, that she might not come; then gradually a drowsiness crept over him, and his thoughts began to drift. The events of the day hovered round, shifted confusedly into dreams. Once it was the well: he was peering into its dark, moldy depths, with the water gleaming up at him like a bright coin, and then he began to fall, the black air rushing past his ears, clogging his nostrils, and he wakened struggling frantically with sheets, his face buried in the pillows.

Another time Larson was holding the melon on his knee. He had the blade of his knife sunk in up to the handle, was slowly cutting round. Then it was himself on Larson's knee, with the big horny hands feeling him over lightly, indifferent to his discomfort and precarious balance, as if he were something inanimate laid across a trestle.

Slowly, like an insect, the fingers came up his side and across his chest. Then, as they crept higher, he was seized with a fear that instead of stopping at his throat they would continue towards his eyes. They reached his throat, lingered there a minute, pressing on his windpipe, pinching the skin, and he steeled himself, afraid of the pain, yet thankful it was to be no worse. But after a pause, almost like a parley among themselves, they crept on over his chin and mouth, halted at his nose a moment, as if surprised at finding it there, not quite sure now of the way, and then, making a careful detour, moved on again purposefully towards his eyes.

Again he woke with a feeling that he had just screamed, and sitting up in bed, his hands locked around his knees, trembling, he waited for Larson or Sylvia to come running. But the house was still; a little breeze had sprung up and he could see the curtains on his window swell out and sink listlessly against the dark; and with an overwhelming sense of relief and safety, some part of his mind still convinced that he had just escaped a great danger, he sank back sleepily onto the pillows.

He wondered if Sylvia would come. It all seemed unreal now, like something he had wished for, imagined—and then he drifted off again. The curtains fluttered and fell; young Chris was waving to him now, waving and running. He followed. In his great haste to overtake him he had somehow got into the Cadillac. "Let it out, you can handle it all right," Larson kept saying. The wind was rushing past his ears again, as if it were Minnie he was riding. Young Chris was headed for the old place—he could see the sod stable with the mustard waving on the roof, the bright new cedar posts and the close strands of wire—and suddenly he cried, laughing in his excitement, "Now I've got you, now you can't get away from me."

But young Chris, instead of struggling through the strands of wire, bobbed under effortlessly like a rabbit and kept on running towards the well. Then as he himself struggled through the wire the door of the old house opened and a woman appeared. She was in a long white robe, and she came towards him silently, her hair shining and golden. The fence between them vanished. He forgot young Chris, and settling peacefully among the pillows again, he waited.

The three or four steps from the door to his bed—it could have only been that—but it seemed he lay a long time watching her come towards him. He was awake, and not quite awake. He knew now that it was really Sylvia, but still it seemed that she was coming from a long way off, floating rather than walking down a long corridor. Sylvia and not quite Sylvia—a white, draped figure, scarcely more than a white shadow against the darkness, and yet smiling, shining, mysterious.

"Chris? Are you awake, Chris?"

She drew near, touched the bed, spoke his name in a husky whisper. Pretending not to hear, he turned a little, as if stirring in his sleep. It was not a deceitful pretense, not intended to ignore or evade her, but simply to prolong the half-waking, dreamlike state in which the expectancy of pleasure was mingled with a sensation of childlike peace, as if he too were floating, disembodied and free.

"It's me, Chris—Sylvia. Don't you hear me?"

She bent over him, put her lips tentatively on his forehead, after a moment slipped a hand under the sheet and let it lie cool and heavy on his chest.

He shivered slightly, then drew a deep breath and lay still again, his senses intent on the coolness, following it almost analytically as it melted and flowed into his own warmth. Her lips moved to his mouth and he submitted to them passively. He lay with one arm flung out limp beside him, the other under the sheet, crooked across his belly. A little tremor ran up his thigh and side, but he made no move to embrace or draw her to him. She raised her head and listened a moment, peering at him in the dim light for a sign, then stood up and gently drew away the sheet.

There was no pretense of sleep now, only limp, passive silence. She lay down and he hitched his body a little, making place for her beside him on the narrow bed. For a while she lay motionless and tense, still waiting for his response, then raised herself and turned so that as she kissed him again he could feel the pendent heaviness of her breasts.

They too were cool a moment, a fine, silky coolness; then gradually as they lay on him it seemed they began to throb and glow. He resisted the impulse to raise his hand and stroke and hold them. There would be time for that later. He still wanted to prolong the spell of her coming, cool, floating apparition-like, to yield to her, to lie passive and receptive.

Her hair fell round his face and throat; he liked that. It tingled his skin, enclosed him so that he could open his eyes without her knowing, without committing himself to response or initiative. Her hands and lips moved with gentle insistence, caressing, rousing, exploring, and as the rich, big-breasted warmth of her body enveloped him he felt small and childlike again, infinitely at peace.

It went on like that a long time. Her hair slipped away from his face, its silky prickle first on his chest, then slowly along his arm, and closing his eyes, following it with the same sensuously analytical intentness as he had followed the coolness of her hand, he waited for it to return.

Presently it did. Then he waited for it to begin moving over his body again, and presently it did. Opening his eyes, he watched the curtains waving, no longer beckoned by them, no longer needing to pursue, and then, looking calmly into the darkness over him—a blank soothing darkness now, on which was written neither the dangers from which he had fled, nor the dangers still to come—he sighed contentedly and smiled.

A long time like that. When at last he roused himself and turned upon her to perform as a man, it was almost with a reluctance, a feeling that now he could not do less.

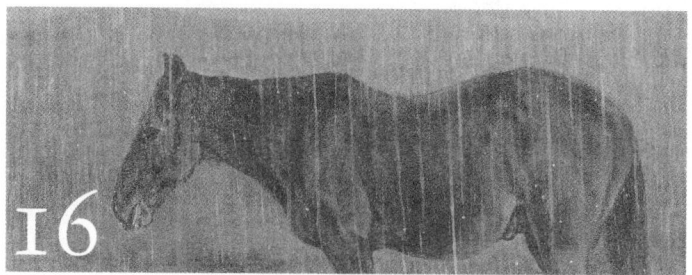

16

NONE THE LESS it was a performance to her satisfaction. Tuesday afternoon she called him from his work, and again on Thursday.

They finished the wheat late Monday afternoon. Tuesday morning the combine, the grain teams and the men, all but Charlie, moved on to Ole's place to start the harvest there. Larson was happy to see them go. He resented the combine; it was a concession to modern farming methods that he made grudgingly; and he still argued—not to convince anyone, not even himself, but simply in loyalty to the old days, a kind of gesture—that what you saved in time and labor you more than lost in wheat. For the wheat, before you could start on it with the combine, had to be dead ripe, and since all the fields usually ripened together, the last to be done suffered heavy shelling from the wind; whereas with the binder you could start cutting early, a little on the green side, and let it harden in the stook.

And now, with the binder out for the oats—and an intelligent, responsive four-horse team hitched to it instead of the blind, chugging tractor—he was in high spirits. It restored his sense of importance. For with Ole running the tractor and Charlie on the combine he felt out of things. He came and went busily, asserted himself, gave orders, but still he didn't count. And Chris, watching him climb stiffly onto the binder seat and click up the horses, began to understand how the size of the farm and the need to hire men frustrated his enjoyment of it, made possession more nominal than real. "That's why he doesn't keep anybody in winter," he told himself. "So he can feel it's all his. His idea of a good time—forking feed to a lot of goddam cows."

He paused a moment, nodding at the neatness of his interpretation. "That's why he wants me to stay. He's getting too old himself, but at least he'll be keeping it in the family. Sure—practically the boy. That's what he can pretend anyway so long as it suits him. Except that instead of coming in for everything like the boy, I'll be drawing my hired man's pay."

He brought this in quickly, scoffing aside advantages and possibilities, stiffening himself in his determination to get away. "Not so crazy after all. She'd see to it anyway that he didn't cut me in on anything that might be hers."

Charlie worked that morning with Chris, repairing the pasture fence. In the afternoon, Larson having had a few hours start on him, he went out to the oat field to stook. Chris took Minnie out as usual, and when he returned Sylvia waved him to the house. "It's as good a chance as any," she said, direct and businesslike. "I've got things fixed, just in case."

No preliminaries, no hesitancy, not so much as a smile or glance to sound him out, discover if it was what he wanted too. He crossed quickly to where she was standing at the window and drew her to him. Not so much because he was roused yet as because he felt such an occasion, however casual, did call for preliminaries. When he went with a girl it was because he wanted her, because she excited or challenged him, even though, as often happened, he might not want her again. He prided himself too much on playing his role well, on being unique in this as in everything else, to begin coldly. At such times, moreover, there was often a cruel vanity at work, a desire to be remembered and regretted, to cast a blight of inadequacy on whoever might come after him.

But responding with only a perfunctory kiss, turning to the window again, she said, "You can see them both from here. Charlie's at the far end of the field, and Larson can't leave the horses, so we don't need to worry. There's no use thinking about it at night again for a while. He feels that stuff too much in the morning, just like a hangover, and I've got to have an excuse to give him a drink. Now here's how I've got it planned in case somebody else comes ..."

As practical and undemonstrative as ever, she led the way into the living-room and nodded towards the chesterfield. "Upstairs it would take too long getting down. We'd be trapped. Nobody ever comes to the front door, but I've locked it anyway, just to be sure."

As she spoke she tried it again, to reassure him, then returned to the kitchen and opened the door on to the basement stairs. "I'll hook the screen door—fly time that's what you expect—so nobody can walk in. If a car drives up or somebody knocks all you do is get down here fast while I see who it is. I've tried it—anybody standing outside couldn't see you making tracks downstairs. And when you get down, here's what you do. Nobody's going to come, but just in case."

He followed her down, and she pointed to a bucket and a broom. "I've got you cleaning the basement. First thing you slosh some water around, get your boots wet so it'll look natural. Then while I'm talking to whoever it is you put on these old overalls. I've dragged them round the floor so they're dusty. That'll look natural too. And do like this." She went to the furnace, ran her finger along a ledge on the door where a film of dust had collected, and made a little smear on her face and forehead. "Dirty yourself up. Slosh the water round like I say, but start sweeping on the dry side too and raise a dust. Just keep your head. People fool easy."

He looked at her dubiously, disquieted somehow by the thoroughness with which she had gone about things. "Jesus," he said with a short laugh, "you must have been lying awake nights figuring it all out."

"Just do like I say. If you keep your head there's not much you can't get away with."

He laughed again, guardedly. "You sound like you know what you're talking about. Like you've had experience."

"Maybe I have." With a corner of her apron she wiped the smear of dust off her face and started towards the stairs. "But don't go nosing into my experiences, Chris, and I won't go nosing into yours."

He flinched, wondering again how much she guessed or suspected, then shut his mind to it. But the uneasiness was still there—he had denied, not overcome it—and now, its way blocked, it made a swift detour, and reappeared with a different face. What they were doing was too dangerous, too many things could happen. He saw himself running downstairs, stumbling, dropping something, even running full tilt into Larson. Perhaps it was less the actual danger that concerned him—she had made her plans carefully, and Larson, in any case, was hard at work in the field—than the furtiveness, the sudden picture of Chris Rowe from Boyle Street hitching up his pants and running down cellar like a scared little boy caught doing something dirty; just as in his nightmares, even in his bad moments during the day, it was less his actual crime which haunted him, than the ignominy and misery of flight, the beard and filthy shirt and the smell of his own sweaty body.

But at the same time he wanted her—his uneasiness served to sharpen his desire, to make the consoling warmth of her body and the male pride of possession a need—and all that stood in his way was the scrambling descent to the basement. Eliminate the possibility of that, give a little twist to her plan, and he would be able to have his satisfaction and at the same time retain his self-respect. "What's wrong with down here? Look—it'll just take a minute to clear it."

He pointed to a big, old-fashioned couch at the other end of the basement on which a few bundles and boxes had been thrown. "If he comes down before I put the things back it'll just be part of the cleaning—like the dust and the broom."

She turned, two or three steps up the stairs, and looked at him coldly. "You've got to get a few things straight, Chris. The other night it was the loft, up in the hay—like I was somebody you could take anywhere, somebody you'd just picked up ..."

"I still don't see what's wrong with the loft—or down here." The glare in her eyes made him falter. He glanced at the couch again, then shrugged appeasingly. "All right, maybe it's dusty. We can throw something over it."

"Somebody I like I'll go all out for—somebody that knows how to treat me right. But no smart ideas, Chris. I don't just play around."

It was as if she too were concerned with self-respect. Meeting her eyes, he had an uneasy feeling that she had read him, knew how, the day of his arrival, he had determined to even the score, humiliate her in turn. "I've got no ideas," he said quietly, swallowing and wetting his lips. "I just thought down here it might be safer."

"I've got a lot more to lose than you have. You can leave the worrying to me." She started up the stairs again, then half-turned and put out her hand. "Just the same we haven't got so much time we can stand here talking. It's getting on to four."

She began, though, as she had the first night, letting him lie passive a while, seeming to understand that this was where his need lay, to feel her lips and hands and breasts on him, to yield the initiative, to open his eyes within the obscurity of her hair and lie unseen and irresponsible. But when presently he turned it was as if in the daylight he were aware of his submission as he had not been in the dark, and to give it the lie, to make up for his lack of male aggressiveness, he closed upon her with a flare of passion that spent itself quickly.

"Never mind, there'll be other times," she said, stroking the back of his head as he lay resting a minute. "All winter if you want to. Larson says I'm to talk to you and try to make you stay."

"Sure, winter'll be fine. We'll have a lot of times together." He released himself and sat on the edge of the chesterfield a minute with his head in his hands. His voice was sullen and accusing, as if she were to blame that their pleasure could not be had or lingered over at will. "In December, I suppose, he'll still be cutting oats."

"No, but as soon as it turns cold his rheumatism's going to be bad again. It always is. He'll be taking his pills regular, and any time I want to I can slip him a couple of extras."

As she spoke she reached out and stroked his arm, her touch now soft and placating. "Leave it to me—I'll fix things. In the meantime he *is* cutting oats, so tomorrow again if you like, or the day after. Let me know—you don't always have to wait for me."

And it was then, as he left her and started back to the barn, that he remembered the woman called Flanders. He had forgotten her first name, wasn't even sure she had told him. For she had been efficient too, and he had not returned. The advantages notwithstanding—the good time and the drinks and the ten dollars, the possibility later on of being able to insist on more.

It was three years ago, when he was nineteen. She could have been anywhere from thirty to forty-five. For there had been a hard, dark brilliance about her, something lacquer-like, almost a glaze, that in their few hours together he had not penetrated; something assured and worldly, a certain stamp that had impressed him, made it impossible to see her accurately.

"Can I drive you somewhere?" she had said, and dropping his eyes, unaccountably embarrassed, he had got in sheepishly without a word.

It was a quiet street. She had come out of a store just as he was passing. Their eyes met a moment, a kind of recognition, a hypodermic dare, and then, instead of walking straight to her car, she turned and pretended to see something that interested her in the window. There were shoes in the window, women's shoes. He went over and stood looking at them too.

Four or five feet separated them. They studied and posed for each other by turn. She raised her head, as if to look up at something in the window, and her tilted chin lifted her breasts, showed to advantage her profile and the curve of her throat. Then he took out his comb and ran it through his hair, bending springily at the knees. Now she too used the window as a mirror, and watching her preen and turn her head he wondered if it might be mimicry. He hesitated a second, on the point of anger; then, in caricature of the performance she had just given, not expecting to be taken seriously now in any case, he thrust out his chest, brought his arms up, fingertips to the back of his neck, and took a few strutting steps like a muscle man before the judges.

But a moment later when she spoke all his insolence and bravado deserted him, and with a sudden feeling of awkwardness beside her trim elegance, not just cynically willing now, but deferential, eager to let her see there was more to him than Boyle Street, that he could rise to a woman such as she was, he had smiled ineptly and gone home with her for a drink.

The first drink was a short one, and for a moment he had been anxious. Not because he wanted more—or, for that matter, needed more to give him courage—but because a hint of meanness, a thrifty eye, would have shaken the pedestal of style and distinction on which he had already placed her. (The pedestal was important. Watching and listening to her, admiring the apartment with its handsome grand piano and well-stocked bar, he had begun to hope, furtively still, not quite daring to believe it, that the world to which he rightly belonged was at last about to acknowledge and make place for him. For Boyle Street was an accident. He never for a moment doubted that to right it, bring him into his own, he needed only a lucky break, the magic of a good contact.) But then it occurred to him that she didn't know how much he could handle, was simply concerned about keeping him in good form, and raising his glass he smiled complacently. Things were looking up for both of them. She had chosen better than she knew.

Emptying her own glass quickly, she said, "My husband's in his office, but just to be on the safe side I think I'll phone."

As she dialled she gave him his instructions. "His secretary knows my voice so you'd better ask for him. Just say 'Is Mr. Flanders in?' Wait till he takes it and then hang up. We want to be sure—there you are, it's ringing now."

Mr. Flanders was in. Brisk and shrewd as he cradled the telephone she said, "Even so, it won't do any harm to look around. Something might bring him home. He works too hard and his pressure's high. His doctor's always warning him."

But from the telephone he had had a good view of the piano, and now, instead of following her, he took a few steps towards it. "Do you play?" he asked, halting respectfully at the edge of the rug. "Maybe you could take a few minutes—I'd like to hear you."

"The piano—*now*?" Her amazement ran into a shrill laugh. "Oh no—not *you*! Those arms and shoulders. I thought ..."

"Skip it—it doesn't matter. It's just the way it looks there."

"*He* plays, and one of his friends has a fiddle. When they get tired they put on records."

But it was a denial, and even with her two hands clasping his arm—to span such an arm it took both hands: that was what she succeeded in conveying—she could not quite make it up to him. A Boyle Street pick-up, an afternoon's diversion. He could not quite escape the realization now that to her he meant nothing more.

"Now pay attention. It's the maid's day off, but there's always a chance she might come back early. She has a key to the front door, so I'll put the chain on. At least she won't be able to walk right in. I get nervous when I'm alone in the apartment—the chain won't be a surprise. I've gone to bed with a bad headache—that's happened before too. I'll put some aspirin and a glass of water beside the bed. Now the back door. Nobody's got a key to it—you can only open it from the inside. I just want you to try it so you won't lose time."

In the main, the afternoon had gone successfully. Now, though, as he went about his chores, it was not the gratifications he remembered, but the telephone call, the details of the chain and doors, the instructions that had paralleled so closely those of Sylvia. He didn't reflect on the parallel. He only wondered again why, when everything had been there waiting for him, he had not returned.

Tuesday, the Flanders woman. Thursday, Elsie Grover.

He had almost forgotten her. Their encounter had left scarcely an imprint. Indifference, dismissal, capitulation—

the game was too old, the pattern too familiar. He had been shrugging off better for the last six or seven years.

But now suddenly she was vivid before him—the freckles and the short, untidy hair, the touchy independence, the look of concern as she warned him they played crap in Campkin too. He felt no surprise. He didn't ask himself why, after a two weeks' eclipse, she should step into his thoughts so insistently. (At that, he had got along better with Sylvia than the time before. There had been no arguments, no briefing in the basement, and their hour together had consequently seemed less furtive.) Nor did he remind himself that in contrast to Sylvia she was a green girl, that in any case he was leaving soon and that nothing mattered in the meantime but to save his money. Instead, absorbed in the prospect of seeing her again, he began to think about the dance. The time dragged. He grew restless and impatient, began to itch for excitement or distraction. He told himself that Larson was right—he needed a change, was sticking too close to home.

"Sure, we've got room for you. You don't have to ask." Larson's eyes brightened. If Chris started going out a little and enjoying himself, meeting other young people, he mightn't be in such a hurry to get away. "Dances aren't bad—real nice little orchestra. Real nice girls too—just waiting for somebody like you to come along and make them happy. Me, I'm out of things now, but I hear stories. Always lots going on."

"Last week you said you wouldn't mind helping me out with some clothes—a pair of pants and a jacket. I'm going to take you up on your offer."

"Sure, Chris. There's a couple of sport shirts too. Way too young for me. Sylvia got them for me the first year we were married, thinking they might help." He looked Chris over approvingly, then added, "You might as well have them to keep. She's got it through their head I'm sixty-six. She's stopped fighting it."

Blue shirt and trousers and a light grey jacket. A little wrinkle on the shoulders; still, it wasn't bad. He had always liked clothes, and now, after a few weeks of work shirt and overalls, he looked at himself in the mirror with the same sense of gratitude and re-discovery as the day of his arrival. Nothing had changed—still Chris Rowe from Boyle Street. Better, if anything: browner, harder, the gauntness gone.

"But these'll hardly do for the dance," he said, looking down at his shoes. "I'll have to draw on my pay and get a pair." Then he straightened and looked in the mirror again, touching his hair and frowning critically in an effort to conceal his satisfaction. "If there's time I'd better have a haircut too. It doesn't show so much till you take off the overalls."

"Haircut or not, you and Sylvia are going to be the best-looking couple on the floor. People are just going to stand and watch you."

"Sylvia? Oh no—I'm not in her class." Still looking at himself, he gave a little hitch to his shoulders and smiled wryly. "She'll want something better than one of the hired men."

"She's had it a lot harder, Chris, than you've any idea. You just don't understand her. Used to work out on farms herself when she was young, then got this job waitressing in Regina."

He glanced at Chris guiltily, as if telling such things to a stranger was a kind of betrayal. "It's made her a great one for keeping people in their place. Not so sure of herself—scared they'll maybe start pushing in on hers."

"She does a good job—I'm not likely to forget for a while." Pulling at the lapels of the jacket, he assumed an injured look. His voice had a nicely gauged touch of bitterness. "Anyway, she's got nothing to worry about. I'll keep my distance—I won't embarrass her."

"No, Chris. You're thinking about the first day when she let fly at you, but that was on account of me more than you." He hesitated, drew closer. "You see, you're not the first one. I've done it a couple of times. Thinking it might be the boy—broke and needing help—maybe hungry. I just can't stand it."

He, too, was dressed for town: a dark blue suit with vest and watch chain, stiff white collar, bright red tie. "And Sylvia, she's smart. There's not much misses her. When she first came I told her everything—thinking she'd make me forget about the boy anyway. Now if I bring somebody home she's scared I've got ideas. But that's all. She'll get used to you."

He circled Chris proudly. "If you stay I'll be able to let all the men go, Charlie too. Soon as we finish the oats and alfalfa. After that if I need somebody extra there's always Ole. Just the three of us—just like a family."

Was it a trap? Chris wondered. Had he become suspicious of what was going on? Did he think that with a little encouragement they might go too far and give themselves away?

But no—suspicious himself, seeing deceit and guile all round him, he still couldn't doubt the old man's shy affection. What then? Had it never occurred to him that Sylvia might have eyes for someone younger? More than twice her age—could he be such a fool? Or was identification complete? Had he accepted Chris as the boy and forgotten the boy had grown up? Resuming the relationship where it had been broken off thirty years ago, was he unable to see him now as man and rival?

Something like this, swift and confused, went through Chris's mind—including the other, even stranger possibility, that the old man's trust was the answer, that it simply hadn't occurred to him to be on guard against someone he liked and had befriended. With a feeling of rudimentary shame, taking a last quick look at himself in the mirror, he followed him out and downstairs to the car.

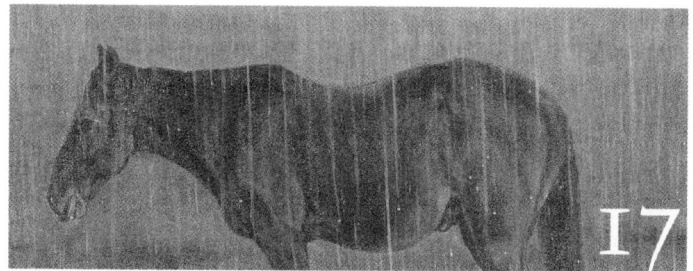

17

THEY ARRIVED JUST A MINUTE OR TWO BEFORE the lights went out, and as they went up the centre aisle, slowly, looking for three seats together, Chris was aware that they were making something of an entrance. Heads turned, chatter trailed off into stares and whispers. "The Larsons," he heard once, "they've got their new man with them."

It pleased him. He liked to be looked at, and remembering what the barber shop mirror had shown him a few minutes before, he felt at ease and confident. Remembering too what he had seen in Elsie Grover's face when he told her he was from the east, he glanced round the hall indulgently, with the condescension of a visitor from the outside world. It wasn't distasteful to him, either, to imagine what they were thinking as they looked at Sylvia and then made the inevitable comparisons between himself and Larson. Another time, another mood, he would have felt exposed. So many eyes would have reminded him that he was wanted. But tonight something had to be defeated, something reasserted, and when they found their seats he remained standing just a moment longer than was necessary, giving himself as much time as possible to be seen. A glimpse of him now, then two hours of darkness—all that time to think of him sitting attentive beside another woman. In his unconscious, wily arrogance he didn't for a moment doubt that if Elsie did catch a glimpse of him she would see little of the picture.

It was an old gangster film that he remembered seeing two or three years before. He sat through it irritated and bored. Knowledgeably bored: a good boy from the wrong street getting mixed up with the wrong crowd and gradually drifting into big-time crime—the real thing wasn't like that at all. His own experience hadn't taken him very far into the big-time, but he did know Rickie. And Rickie had the goods. If they caught up with him on a quarter of his jobs he'd be in for fifty years. He'd maybe swing. But he didn't go round shooting cops and falling for slinky blondes. He was tough but natural. Just human, just smart. And when they teamed up there'd be a lot more smart things going on. Rickie always said they needed each other. Just wait—together they'd make movies look like kid stuff.

Larson, on the other side of Sylvia, kept offering him candy across her lap, rattling the bag and hissing, "Chris!" The seats were folding chairs with slats. There was no slope to the floor, and the couple in front of him obscured his view. He wasn't interested in the picture—he had even set his mind, disdainfully, to ignore it—but it increased his irritation no to be able to see easily and well. The youngsters, crowded together in front at half price, whistled and burst paper bags.

Forgetful even of Elsie, he fumed at himself for coming, for spending fifteen dollars on shoes. Nothing mattered but to find Rickie. Now. He was wasting too much time. Forking manure, digging potatoes, laying the old man's wife—what a laugh for Rickie if he knew!

But when it was over his mood changed again. The lights came on and he began purposefully to scan the crowd.

They filed out, around and in again—it was the management's way of collecting second admissions for the dance. The folding chairs were gathered and stacked outside. A muddy-looking old piano was pushed onto the stage and the musicians appeared, all four in skin-tight jeans and scarlet shirts. "Go on, take her," Larson said as the first dance began. "She's crazy about it, and I'm better looking on. Good a way as any to get on the right side of her. She hates sitting out and a lot of the fellows are sort of scared of her—on account of me."

She danced well, with a grace and lightness that surprised him. There was something in her smile too that he had never seen before, something young and relaxed, as if she were caught up in the music, had for a moment escaped herself. But even at the press of her body he remained detached, withholding, as if within him there were a secret prohibition, and as they danced he said, plausibly discreet, "We'd better not overdo it. Like as not he's keeping an eye on us—making it easy, maybe, just to see how far we'll go."

At that moment he caught sight of Elsie standing near the door with two or three other girls, all watching him intently. "After this dance," he said, "I'll look around and get interested in someone else. We'll have a couple more later on."

"Just don't get too interested." Her light, half-laughing tone didn't quite conceal her anxiety. "Remember I'll be keeping an eye on you, too."

When the dance was finished he escorted her back to Larson, reserved and deferential, then made his way through the crowd to Elsie. "Remember me?" he began, drawing her away from the other girls. "I'm the one that tried to date you a couple of weeks ago and didn't get very far."

She braced herself, swallowing hard like a cornered child. She had make-up on—the rouge was on her cheeks in two bright hasty daubs—but he saw the sudden color at her throat. She nodded, silent a moment, then said impulsively, "I even went home and dressed up for you—special, I mean. Soon as I saw you. I came in slacks. Missed the show and wasted half a dollar—just like that."

Not very convincingly, with what seemed half-hearted loyalty to the carefree independence on which she had no doubt always prided herself, she shrugged and snapped her fingers. "I know I look terrible. I tried on three dresses, and I couldn't do anything with my hair."

"You look fine to me. I'd still like to keep that date."

She didn't look fine to him at all. Her pert, tomboy air had suited her, had detracted from the soft big mouth and turned-up nose. Now, with her organdy ruffles, she looked insignificant and outlandish. Her short, dishevelled hair had added something, had been just the right last touch. Now it exposed her features, made futile her attempts to appear feminine and appealing.

But still, for tonight at least, she was what he wanted. Unknown to himself, he had taken her measure accurately, and when, fresh from his experience with Sylvia, he had felt the need of someone with whom he could play the role of aggressive male again, who would restore his threatened equilibrium—for such was his nature and development that equilibrium could be maintained only by satisfying both child and man—at that moment, with a kind of instinct, it was to her he had turned. As they danced her eyes were soft and admiring; the slow gentle hands were on his sleeve now; and he felt excited, eager, all at once determined.

For until now it had been less definite than that. He had wanted someone on whom he could impose himself, who would wait for and yield to his initiative, but such acknowledgement and response would not necessarily be conditional to physical satisfaction. That would come, but his meeting with her tonight, could he have sorted out the confusion of intention and desire, would have emerged as a preliminary. In part because he expected her to be fearful and evasive; in part because her resistance—and ultimate submission—would be a protracted satisfaction, a more complete restoration than an easy victory.

Now, though, he wanted her tonight. It was her nearness, perhaps, or the realization as he looked into her face that it could be tonight; or the face itself, its plainness, an impatience that it roused in him, a feeling that for him, Chris Rowe, one night was all she rated.

"You've been on my mind a lot," he told her blandly. "Ever since that day you sold me the magazines. And even tonight when I saw you I wasn't sure. The time before, you remember, you sort of brushed me off. And after all, I'm just Larson's hired man."

She smiled ecstatically. These, no doubt, were the things she had imagined and hoped he would say. "I've been thinking a lot about you too, Chris. I didn't mean to brush you off.

Maybe it was because I was scared. Afterwards I kept going over everything we'd said, wishing I'd been nicer. And then last Saturday you *didn't* come—"

Her voice trembled with the remnants of an accusation. Her disappointment had been acute; she had raged at him probably all night. "I got dressed up for you—proper, I mean, took plenty of time—and then when you didn't come I said I'd never make a fool of myself like that again. You think I'm crazy? The girl's supposed to play hard to get, like in stories—but I don't know how. Not with you, Chris—I just don't know how."

The hall was hot and crowded. They danced again, then went outside and sauntered slowly up one of the little side streets. They followed it to the end of the sidewalk, the edge of town, and stood arm in arm watching the moon rise. It was an enormous, yellow moon that left the prairie dark and yet lit it he felt misty glow. He kissed her, crushing her to him till he felt her body set defensively—like Minnie, he thought, when he was tightening the saddle girths. When he released her she snuggled her face into his jacket with a little shudder. "Oh, Chris—I just can't stand it. Don't you think we'd better go back to the dance now?"

"Already?" He lifted her face and laughed. "And leave the moon? I thought you liked it?"

"I do, Chris, I do." It was such a supreme moment for her she could not respond to his laughter. "It's just that I think we ought to. We don't know each other yet—not enough."

It would have been easy to persuade her now, but he took her arm and started back compliantly. It was still early. The moon had barely cleared the horizon.

They danced again, and then he returned to Sylvia. "You're getting interested all right," she said as the music started and they stepped onto the floor, her smile bright and angry. "She's a little on the young side, isn't she?"

"And what's wrong with being on the young side?" he countered, selecting his words brutally, keeping his smile soft and innocent. "I'm not bald or shaky at the knees myself yet."

Then, having reminded her of the realities, he added artlessly, "I'll admit, though, another couple of years wouldn't do her any harm. She took me for a walk just now to see the moon. Like a picture, she says—she *loves* to watch it come up."

He could afford to give her this much, and moreover, the realities notwithstanding, there was something about her anger that made him flinch a little, made him willing to come to terms.

She smiled again, acting well. "Whatever she said, it's made you look pretty pleased with yourself. Anyway, I'm making the most of it with *him*. As a matter of fact, he thinks you should be able to do a lot better. Chris, he says, ought to have a girl who knows how to put make-up on and comb her hair."

He stiffened a little. "If it makes him think my taste runs away from blondes who do know how so much the better. See to it he keeps on noticing."

He watched with satisfaction as the anger seeped into her smile. It was not a new experience, leaving a trail of jealousy and frustration. It created, temporarily at least, an illusion of distinction, defeated whatever feelings of worthlessness or failure which happened at the time to be working on him. Tonight there was especial need of it because, however successful he might be in forgetting his predicament, in blinkering himself with here and now, the fact was still there that he had shot a man, was on the run. He knew, even while refusing to admit that he knew. The old gangster film had had its effect too: the memories of Boyle Street and Rickie that it had roused had left their sediment of fear.

When the dance finished he left her and went straight back to Elsie. "There's a square dance coming up and I don't know how—suppose we sit it out. Not in here—it's about time to see how the moon's doing anyway."

She nodded, and heedless of who might be watching, kept her eyes fixed on him. "You know where we were before. Just a little farther, over to the side, there's a hill. Not much of a hill, but you can look down and see the town and the lights. I go there alone and pretend things—somebody like you coming along, living happily ever—crazy things like that."

They started up the street, arm in arm; then he said, "You can't sit on a hill, not in that dress. I think there's a rug in the car."

Larson's car was parked on the next street. As they walked he tightened his grip on her arm protectively. "I've got the keys, he let me drive in," he said, "but he mightn't like it if I took you for a drive. He's queer about a lot of things. She mightn't either."

"I know—there's a different story every week. She tells things herself, funny things, that you'd think she'd want hushed up."

"You don't like her very well."

"She comes in the store sometimes. We have to order things for her, like special perfume. Never says much, just looks the place over like it's not what she's been used to. But likely she knows people talk, so you can't blame her. Here—I'll hold it."

They had reached the car and taken out the rug, and now he was trying to light a cigarette. "I used to think they were just jealous and that she'd be all right if they'd give her a chance. But just now I was worse than any of them. I could have scratched her eyes out."

"Anyway, I left her and came back to you."

"But you see and talk to her every day—I can't help thinking about it. She's the best-looking woman there tonight. She's got the best clothes."

"Right now, maybe. But another five years she's going to be the size of all outdoors."

"All right—let's forget her. Here's the end of the sidewalk. It's uphill now, but not far."

As they stepped off the sidewalk onto the prairie and the scuffed, wind-blown grass she drew away from him and walked on in shy silence. And yet it was somehow a dogged, purposeful silence. She was shy and frightened, and she was also unwavering. Sensing the sudden tension, he smiled complacently.

The Well / 139

He thought of the mares that came to North, sweating and exhausted, in torment, and then, when North was led out and they heard his neigh and snuffle, the way they braced themselves and waited, as if it were something imposed upon them, their lot, against which there was no appeal. The comparison amused and pleased him. It also touched a deeper level and gave him a sense of mastery, of right, such as he would not have derived from mere consent.

She was still carrying the rug—now that they that had separated and she was a few steps ahead he noticed—but he checked the impulse to take it from her. It made him think of a squaw. Sometime, probably as a child, he had read or heard that the squaw always did the work and carried the bundles—and again the comparison pleased him. There was no implication of contempt. It was just that the primitive simplicity of her submission impressed him as an acknowledgement, a recognition of his due. That was what he had come for, to be yielded to and restored.

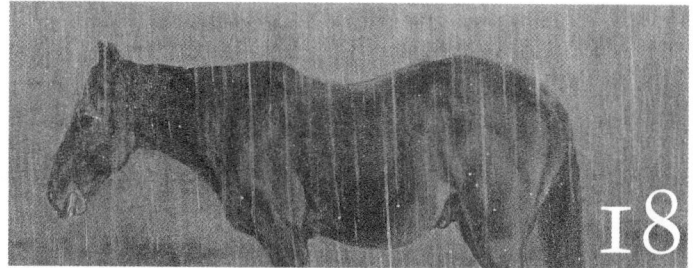

18

THAT NIGHT, when finally he reached bed, he slept badly again.

Everything had elated him, his success with Elsie, Sylvia's ill-concealed anger when he returned to the dance, and finally, driving home, the speed and power and luxury of the car, the illusion of possession in which he indulged himself; but as if his high spirits had been only a defense against recognition of his real state of mind—a defense which in sleep could not be maintained—he woke repeatedly, struggling and in a sweat, from dreams of flight and capture.

It was the picture he had seen that evening, and it was Boyle Street. The melodrama of gangland, with bullets and sirens and grim-jawed, slit-eyed desperation, and the little schemes hatched up and wrangled over in the poolroom and tavern, the safe little fifty and a hundred dollar jobs split four or five ways, the boredom, the scrounging, the pretense.

Tonight, for the first time, he saw where he stood in relation to Boyle Street, what it had offered, what it had denied, how he had tried to fit into it and failed. He saw it clearly, with something like serenity, the insight bringing relief and thankfulness, a feeling of being set down safe on earth again after a long, labored flight.

He had hated Boyle Street. Hated and been afraid of it. Always. He got out of bed at last and stood at the window remembering, staring out across the moonlit yard at the barn and windmill and seeing the dingy, poster-spattered street with its petty traffic of bread wagons and ice-trucks, bargain-hunting housewives and boys on bicycles delivering beer and groceries; remembering the glare of cement and dirty glass on summer afternoons, smelling and entering again the places where the gang had hung out, the bars and taverns and poolroom, the grubby little cafe where they picked up easy dates, played the juke box and made a drink last; where despite their listless contempt for one another they always returned, drawn by a need of companionship and support, where they bragged and lied and idled away their existences, envious, jaded, lonely.

That was the real Boyle Street. He had moved there a timid boy, and for the first few weeks the other boys had made his life a torment. It was not very different from the street where he had lived before, but there he had been known, taken for what he was, jeered at briefly or ignored, while here he was pounced on as a newcomer, a diversion.

Then there was the day he learned to spend, to buy—the sudden awaking to what the world was really like, the determination never to be helpless or exposed again. But it was more than that. With time something was added. He not only wanted to be safe, to have money in his pocket as a kind of street and playground insurance; because of the bullying and humiliation he had already endured—perhaps because of the money itself, what it implied—he also wanted to stand out and dominate. An itch to get even developed, a taste for power.

But spending, as time went on, was not enough. He could buy the boys, but he could not buy himself. For that matter, he could never quite sell himself either. They knuckled down to his spending power, not to him. Leadership was more than that, and something within him—a surviving streak of honesty, perhaps—protested, refused to let him get away with it.

So he learned to do things he would rather not have done. Good and bad both—nearly always with Boyle Street as his standard. The others stole from the neighborhood stores:

fruit, biscuits, candy; he stole from stores where more nerve was required, where a get-away was more difficult.

The others played baseball. A fumbler and blind striker at first, he bought their tolerance until he was their star. In addition, a gesture, he donated a ball and fielder's glove, the ball paid for in cash in a downtown sporting goods store, the glove admired and tried on forlornly under the eye of an indulgent clerk and then just walked off with.

They also played hockey, a rough, dirty game, and he learned to play the roughest, dirtiest game of them all. Most of the time it was just scrub hockey among themselves, but occasionally there would be a more or less official game, played under the auspices of a police club. He still played rough and dirty; usually his team won. Sometimes it was worth a penalty to eliminate a good player from the other side. He had a way of looking sorry and crestfallen afterwards, making what he had done seem just a fit of boyish temper, retaliation for something done to him, and the referee was usually less severe than admonishing. Even when there were boos and catcalls he didn't mind, so long as his own team knew what he had done and why. Prestige was what mattered most, and to win for his side under a cloud, to draw abuse upon himself, had a distinction about it greater than that of merely winning to applause. It was in the nature of a sacrifice—a bid, perhaps as much for devotion as leadership.

Then Rickie came home—only nineteen he had been serving two years—and again everything was changed. Chris, broadening out and a good six feet already, had an easy smile with a steel-hard, wise-to-the-lowdown twist which to Rickie spelled good material. They played pool and drank beer and talked. Rickie bought a car, and sometimes they went away together for a few days, to the mountains or across the border. Rickie was an ugly, old youth, hook-nosed, gap-toothed, with black shaggy eyebrows running all the way across—not the sort that Chris cared to be seen with everywhere. But there was something about him nevertheless to which he responded, something fearless, deadly and completely unpretentious which, in contrast to the noisy, gang-brave toughness of the

Boyle Street boys, impressed him as the stamp of the professional.

Himself he was a determined amateur. He had no intention of slipping into a life of full-time crime. Partly because it was important to him to be approved and admired, partly because his ambitions ran in socially acceptable channels. But Rickie was a name and a power on Boyle Street, and Boyle Street was where Chris still belonged. For the time being, at any rate, his offer of friendship could not be prudently ignored.

Rickie, into the bargain, always had money, always seemed to be able to get his hands on more, and Chris's financial problems were increasing every year. Dimes and quarters didn't do at seventeen what they had done at twelve. He had discovered his looks, was taking an interest in his clothes. His looks were good; it was only right and fair that his clothes should correspond. (Not pure vanity: rather the awareness of his appearance as an instrument, a means of getting what he wanted, satisfying his needs. His needs were urgent: to stand out and shine, to be liked, looked up to—and because his sense of validity and purpose was involved it was as necessary to satisfy them, as much a duty to himself, as to satisfy his hunger.)

And there were other things. He liked to be seen with a girl who had the air, not of virtue, but of discrimination; he wanted a car, an apartment of his own, to ski, to fly to Florida; and the cool, blinkless competence of Rickie's eyes was infinite in promise.

Rickie's way of spending, moreover, was faintly humiliating. (Deliberate, perhaps, an attempt to goad him over the hump, needle him into an active partnership.) When they were out he always took the check, but there was often a resigned sigh, an unspoken, "Jesus—me again!" The same with the car. His brusque "Get out and see," sometimes gave Chris the feeling that he was flunkying for the ride.

And while Rickie didn't mind a touch, five or ten at a time, he kept careful count. The total mounted, and he jabbed with it steady and hard. "So how, then? You got a big shot uncle somewhere? Or maybe you figure putting the screws on your old lady's boy friends? So how then? You got guts, or you just a bum? Sure, Chris—Rickie knows—you got lots of guts. You just got to start *using* them."

At seventeen he was helping Rickie with his dope deliveries. At eighteen he was waiting in the lane with the motor running, and afterwards, when the haul was loaded, making contact with the fences. Sometimes, when it was a good haul—jewelry, clothes, several times furs—there were three or four fences. They had to be met, sounded out, haggled with. When delivery was made, they had to be held to their bargain. It took nerve, a hard eye and some discreet gun rattling—Rickie's gun, not his own, just in case somebody got smart ideas. That was his role, and he was satisfactory. The set of his jaw, the twitch of his lips, all the gradations of scorn and amusement, impatience, anger and ultimatum that the role demanded—he practised and was good. Perhaps it was not quite so important a role as he liked to think: all that he had to do was make it clear that Rickie was behind him. But Rickie never rubbed that in. On the contrary, he was enthusiastic, encouraging. Now that his boy was doing what he wanted him to do, he could afford to be generous with his praise. Generous with his cuts, too. From ten per cent they jumped to twenty-five; sometimes, in a burst of exuberance and good fellowship, to fifty.

But all the way, oranges to muskrat, he had been scared. He had forced himself, bit down the panic that welled up sometimes like nausea, squeezed in his belly till he couldn't feel it squirm. At the end, even Rickie had known. A yellow phony, he had called him—a two-bit yellow phony—and a few days later he left for the west coast alone.

Although, in fairness to himself, phony wasn't quite the right word. Rickie, who claimed to have connections in Vancouver and San Francisco both, always said that the really big money was to be made in narcotics. But there, for Chris, lay a special fear, that he could scarcely have explained to himself, much less to Rickie. It wasn't only the risk of getting caught and jailed; it was the dread of committing himself to an organization that would henceforth have power over him. Once you were in, you stayed in. Rickie himself said so, admiringly. You quit only if they agreed, only if you were not particularly useful. You never walked out when you felt like it, of your own free will. Once and for all it cut you down to crook size. Taped you, slammed all the doors.

And with Rickie gone, it was cheap, small-time Boyle Street jobs again—back-street stick-ups with a switch-knife, the take often as not a couple of dollars and a watch; breaking into cars for rugs and radios. Alone, that was his size.

Sometimes, trading on his looks, he would even go to a bar and get picked up by a woman, and then, back in her apartment or hotel, take whatever he could lay his hands on: money, watches, rings. (Usually afterwards: partly because in the jaded ebb of his desire, projecting onto her his own disgust and self-contempt, it was easier to insist, if necessary be rough; partly because there was a twisted streak of probity still uneasily alive within him to which he could reply, having performed, that his take was coming to him.) Goon stuff, safe stuff. Crap and poker games for piddling stakes; pool in poolrooms where his game wasn't known and he could take unwary strangers.

Then Helen—and there were two brothers; he couldn't just walk off and say he wasn't interested—told him she was going to have a baby. From his good days with Rickie he had put away seven hundred dollars, a little reserve that he had made up his mind was the minimum, to be forgotten about and drawn on only in an emergency. Bail or a lawyer or a fast get-away—something serious like that. Now he had to draw on it for an operation. The woman who accepted her charged a hundred, but something went wrong and she had to call in a doctor. Because of the risk, he wanted five hundred cash. When it was over and everybody paid he was down to a few dollars, and a lean month later, in desperation, because money was so important to him, he was screwing up his courage to walk in on Baxter. He had been scared then, too. Nervous, jumpy, sick—before starting out he had had to go to the bathroom to vomit. That was the reason he had bungled it. To fire once when the handkerchief slipped and Baxter recognized him, then not to have the guts to fire a second time and finish the job—that was his size when he was alone. Dropping the gun and taking to his heels without the money: Rickie would be proud of him when he heard. Somebody the police were after—maybe a murder rap—that was just the kind of partner he'd been looking for.

He saw it clearly. It brought at feeling of collapse and shame and worthlessness, and it also brought a feeling of relief. It was his fear and arrogance that had fallen. He himself was still standing.

He saw it all clearly—what was in store for him if he caught up with Rickie, the advantages of staying where he was. Lie low, make himself useful, fit into things. At least it was better than doing time. Help Larson and Sylvia to forget how he had come. Once they forgot, the town and neighbors would soon forget too.

His fear all at once seemed childish and hysterical. The search hadn't come this far—either that, or it had gone straight through. People were friendly, ready to accept him. Working for Larson, being trusted by him, was a kind of guarantee. He was safe so long as he made no enemies.

A rival could be an enemy. Fortunately it seemed that no one else was interested in Elsie Grover. But he should have thought about it earlier. The little things were what he had to watch; he couldn't afford to take chances. It gave him a feeling of slackness, and his shoulder twitched uneasily.

As it was, he had to think about her father. A cheerful, mild man, he remembered, with old-fashioned steel-rimmed glasses and suspenders—it shouldn't be too hard to get around him. The next time he was in town he would try to start a conversation. Make a good impression; usually he could if he took the trouble.

Turning up broke and dirty was a strike against him. Living it down, getting a job and holding it, that was half a dozen in his favor. It was the sort of thing the little fellows liked, could understand. Tell him what a fine fellow Larson was—show he was appreciative. Say the big places weren't all they were supposed to be. Make him think how smart he'd been to stay put all his life in a godforsaken hole like Campkin. He was the kind to lap it up and want more.

And as Rickie used to say, there was nothing like time. Already it was getting on to two months. There had probably been a dozen hold-ups, another shooting or two. Already there were a lot of new names on the page. Another two months and they'd have turned the page over.

They weren't chasing him this far. Old Baxter wasn't that important, even supposing he was dead. They might have sent his description out, to the big places, but what little time they were spending on him they were spending it in the east. That was were he belonged, where his gang and girl and old lady hung out. They were so smart, the cops. They always had you figured out, knew exactly what you were going to do. Working on a farm—oh no, they'd never fall for that one. "Not him," they'd say, "not our boy." Up at half-past four and to bed again at nine—they'd never believe he had it in him.

He smiled a little and folded his arms. It didn't occur to him that his satisfaction sprang not so much from a feeling of having outsmarted the police, slipped a fast one over them, as from the realization that he did have it in him. He would have been ashamed for Boyle Street to know he was working, had sunk to the level of a job. By himself, unaware of the change, he was beginning to take pride in his ability to work. On Boyle Street a job was something for the dopes. Here, still so dim that he would have scoffed at the suggestion, it had something to do with being a man.

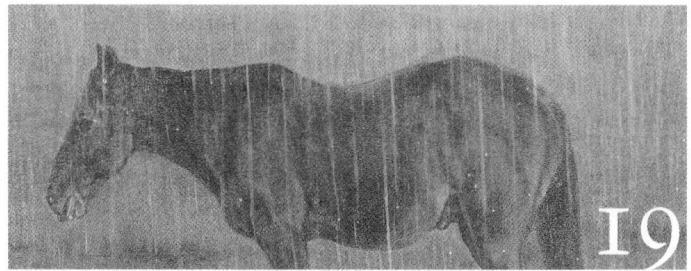

19

FOR THE NEXT FEW DAYS, concealing her anger behind a front of indifference so successfully that Chris was almost convinced by it, Sylvia ignored him. Then, Thursday afternoon again, she waved him from the back steps as he rode past on Minnie. "Take a few minutes and pull up a chair," she said genially. "I've just made coffee and I feel like company."

She poured herself a cup, then sat down at the kitchen table opposite him. He noticed that she had put on a little make-up, and that her hair was arranged with as much care as if she were going to town. His courage rose. Smiling, with candid, wide eyes, he said, "Whatever it is, let's get it over with. Have I done something?"

"I'd just like to know why, Chris. Maybe you're scared on account of him and it's your way of getting out—or maybe you're just showing off, seeing how much I'll take from you. But it doesn't make sense, either way. Not you. I can't understand and I keep wondering."

He sipped his coffee and drew a faint puzzled smile. "But it's you. The last few days you've been looking right through me—like you were trying to put me in my place ..."

"I could understand if she had something over me—looks, or even clothes. I'd say it was all I could expect, and I'd take it. Lots of the younger ones have plenty. But her—throwing her in my face as much as to say I didn't mean anything to you at all—"

There was a rising tremble in her voice. He said quickly, "Sure, she's got nothing over you, so you ought to be satisfied. You ought to know what she means to me. And with him watching I still think it was a good idea to play up to somebody. We talked it over, while we were dancing."

"Talk straight, Chris. I do."

"We had a few dances and we went for a walk. They started doing square dances, and I didn't feel like trying to learn how."

"I know—you were out looking at the moon."

"You followed us, I suppose." He lit a cigarette and tossed her the package irritably. "Jesus! You think I can't look at a girl without getting ideas about scoring."

"When you came back it was written all over you. It still is—right now."

"All right—it wasn't just a walk." He finished his coffee and rested his arms on the table defiantly. "But dancing with you was what got me started. That shouldn't be too hard to believe, the way things have been between us lately. And what was I supposed to do?" He drew hard on his cigarette. His voice rose accusingly. "Get it out of my system like I did, or come back and lie listening to you have a time with Larson?"

"What am I supposed to do? He says that's what a wife's for."

"An old fellow his age? You could keep him in line if you wanted to."

"A lot you know. It's easier to give in and get it over with."

"That's tough." He watched her through the smoke with narrowed eyes. His voice took on a hurt, slightly bitter edge. "Ever stop to think, though, that it's tough sometimes for me too? Sure, when he's out of the way and everything's safe you don't mind giving me a turn, but it's just a turn. You're married to him and I'm the hired man. Maybe I'd like to take you serious, but what good's it going to do me? What do I do between turns? Hang around like the last week, wondering if you've had enough and it's time to hit the road?"

Her lips twitched. "But if I meant anything to you at all I don't see how you could *want* to go with her. Just like it didn't make any difference—like one of us was as good as another."

He went to the stove for the coffee pot and filled both their cups. He was puzzled—one was as good as another. In different ways they both satisfied him, were both necessary. The one dominated, the other clung. The one took the initiative, the other left it to him. The one restored to him a sense of cared-for peace, the other filled him with the urges of a man.

"Sure, it makes a difference," he said, sitting down and stirring his coffee thoughtfully. "But sometimes when we can't have what we want we take the next best. Saturday night I took her. I guess maybe that's why you took him."

"If you knew how I hate him!" A sudden savage look came over her face. For a moment, shoulders hunched, she seemed crouched for a spring. "I lie thinking what I'd like to do to him—so it would hurt—so I'd see him twist and yell. Like the coffee pot; sometimes I come up behind when he's eating and I want to spill it over him. I've got to hold on to myself."

"He hasn't changed as much as all that since you married him." He felt his power over her. Her distress made him scornful. "I thought it was only four or five years? He couldn't have been much of a playboy then either."

"I was waitressing. My feet hurt."

She looked up, her eyes leaden and slow. "I come from a farm myself and I had a mean old man. It got so I couldn't stand it. I cleared out and got a job."

"Only waitressing turned out to be hard work too. Larson came along and you thought you'd try the farm again."

"Maybe he's told you—he was in on a little trip to see the fair. He came in for something to eat this day and got talking—wanted to take me out to the fair to see the midway. First I cut him down sharp, like who did the old fool think he was, and then all at once I started thinking wasn't it about time I got a little back. Because all along it had been the other way—everybody'd been taking me. And like they say in the movies, it's just a jungle anyway.

The Well / 151

"The trouble with me I never learned to pick them. Thinking about it now I figure it was the catalogue. Mail order, spring and fall—there's one over there on the shelf by the window now. Look at it sometime and you'll know what I mean. The women showing off the hats and dresses and the men the suits and shoes—the farmers' Bible. Up till I was seventeen the only men I knew were the neighbors and my old man, and they used to wear smocks an overalls and make a shave last a week. Maybe there was a young one now and then a little better, but not much. Like Larson and Charlie, only worse. Because round that part everybody was poorer.

"So I'd sit looking at the men in the catalogue in their suits and ties, and I'd pick one I liked and maybe give him a name and keep thinking about him and planning things. It used to help with the work. Haying or stooking or slopping round the barn—first thing it would be quitting time. Then I'd get tired of that one and pick another. You might say they kept me going.

"What I mean, I got in the way of picking them slicked-up and smooth, and when I got to the real ones that's the way I kept on. I always went straight. I never tired making money. It had to be somebody I really wanted, and that was the kind. But that's the worst kind, sometimes, and after you've been played round with and thrown over a few times you get tired. You turn mean and start working up a hate. Somebody like Larson comes along and you say now it's my turn.

"I stalled a while. I said I'll think it over, and maybe around Christmas if he was still interested we could talk about it again. But he had to get back to his crop, and he wanted me right away. Now that he'd found what he was looking for there was no sense waiting. I still hung back, so he said I could fix the house over any way I liked and he'd put in electric lights. And on top of that, since he knew he wasn't a young fellow any more, he'd be fair and give me a thousand dollars cash—for a wedding present—and every fall a couple of thousand more so long as the crop would stand it. All my own, no questions. And I've got to hand it to him—it's five years now, and he's stuck to his bargain."

As she talked her voice had had a sullen sincerity; now on the last words, she raised her hands to her temples and gave a light laugh. "He sticks to his part of the bargain, and he sees to it that I stick to mine."

He caught it on the fly. Two thousand a year for five years—ten or eleven thousand if she had saved it—and it was an offer.

He didn't know what kind of offer. He was the hired man and she was Larson's wife, so things between them couldn't change. But he was being sounded out—he was sure of that much. As she put her hands to her forehead again her eyes were birdlike and intent.

"So you're right, Chris. When I picked up with him he was exactly like he is now. Only there was a lot I didn't know. I thought anybody his age would be cooling down. His wife had been dead so long I thought he'd be over her too. But he's worse because he's old. He keeps trying to show me he's better than the young ones. And that's my part of the deal—that's what he got me for.

"That's *all* he got me for. It's Cora he's still thinking about. Cora and the boy, just like they were still alive. Nights I said no I've seen him get up and play the old gramophone in the bathroom—because it had been hers—just to show me. Now it's got so I don't trust myself. Something's got to happen soon."

He wasn't sure. Her voice rang true again, but unconsciously he was on Larson's side. He couldn't help feeling that if she meant only one thing to Larson it was because in everything else she had failed him. By instinct he was on the man's side anyway. He had listened to her story with interest: it satisfied not only his curiosity, but also the obscure vindictiveness that still persisted in his feelings for her. Revealing her origins and humiliations was to some extent delivering herself into his hands. But he hadn't been moved or softened. All the way he had sensed something predatory and cunning.

"It was easier before, just making up my mind to things. But now you're here I can't stand him to come near me. You said maybe if you let yourself go you could take me serious. I could too, Chris—if that was what you wanted."

She was pleading now, revealing herself, dropping all the little wiles and reticences on which he would he would expected her to depend, but even in her entreaty there was an insistence, something not far off anger.

"What I want doesn't make any difference. You're married to him." Screwing up his eyes as he lit another cigarette, he watched her carefully. "We've just go to play along a while—watch our chances."

"No—you'll get tired that way. You'll pick up and leave and I'll be left alone with him again." Her voice shook. She half rose, gripping the edge of the table as if about to overturn it. "And I want more than that. You hear me? I'm not going to sit back and lose you. Not now—I'll do something first. I'll kill him."

"Take it easy—I'm not leaving." He rose and went round the table to her quickly. "It's just the way things are—I don't like the set-up any better than you do. But it's no use losing our heads. We've got to be careful or he'll notice something."

As she sank back in her chair she seized his hand. "I'd do anything, Chris. I'm like that—you don't know me yet. I wouldn't care what it was. I'd take chances."

Ten thousand dollars was a lot of money, but she wasn't the kind that would just hand it over. She wasn't the kind it would be easy to get clear of, either, and with the police looking for him it would be safer on his own. "You're just sore now on account of Elsie, but a day or two and you'll be over it." He shrugged and laughed. "Jesus—I'm only the hired man anyway. What's all the fuss about? Remember what you thought of me the day I landed here—I haven't changed that much."

He couldn't resist this. He had already won, but he wanted a little topping for his victory. "Right now we're talking too much and wasting time. Next week he'll be around more. We won't have many chances."

"If only we could get rid of him. If he'd take a trip."

"We're rid of him right now—for the next couple of hours."

"If you really meant it, Chris, about being ready to take up with me—I mean to last, staying on here ..." She drew him towards her, her arms locked round his thighs, her face so tight against his body that he had to strain to hear her. "If you did, Chris, I wouldn't be scared. We could get rid of him for good."

"He's not that crazy." With a jerky laugh Chris drew back a little. "You'd never make them believe it. They don't lock a man up because he likes trains."

"I'd do more than that—if you wanted me to."

She gave a shudder, then clung to him tense and still. "I mean it, Chris. I'd do a real job. I lie awake, all night sometimes, thinking and planning."

"You're the one that's crazy." He took her face in his hands and forced her to look up at him. "I suppose you've got it all figured out some night when you're giving him his pills you'll slip him something extra, maybe a little arsenic. Smart girl—they'd never get wise to that one."

"Maybe I'm smarter than you think. Maybe we could if we did it together."

"Whatever you're planning, don't count me in. If you hate him as much as all that, why don't you put him down cellar—make him sleep on the floor?"

"It's a good farm; we could just carry on. The last few years he'd been clearing five or six thousand easy. Clearing that much, after everything."

"Stop it." He jerked his hand away and shook her roughly. "Talk like that and first thing you will try something. It'll grow on you. You're getting two thousand a year. Why don't you take a trip yourself? Play around a little; he's not going to last forever anyway."

"No, Chris—he's the one that's got to take a trip. I wasn't talking about arsenic."

She seized his hand again. "That's what he wants to do, isn't it? Supposing instead of just listening to the trains he gets on one—keeps travelling, forgets to come back?"

"But he never would. He thinks too much of the farm. If he ever did start out he'd be back inside a week. He'd be worrying about Ned and Fanny."

"Arsenic!" With a sudden scornful laugh she stood up and began to clear away their cups. "I'm a lot smarter than that, Chris. I thought you were smart enough to know."

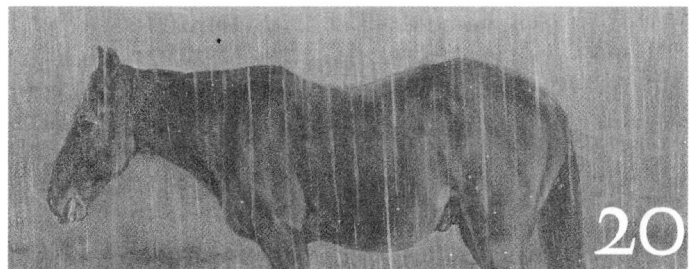

20

THE FOLLOWING SATURDAY, Larson caught Chris leading North out to water without a snaffle.

It was about four o'clock in the afternoon. The men, with the combine and tractor and grain teams, had just come back from Ole's place, where they had finished the wheat about noon. It was too late in the day to start working again; they were idling round the yard, in and out of the bunkhouse.

After a long, unbroken stretch of sunny weather the sky was overcast, and Larson, smelling rain, was irritable and impatient. He wanted to be rid of the men. There was a week's work for them: another fifty acres of oats to be combined, the last growth of alfalfa to be cut and gathered for ensilage; then he would have his farm to himself again. He was letting even Charlie go. After sounding Chris out, only that morning, he was satisfied that with a little persuasion he would stay. Just the two of them, they would manage fine. There was still fall plowing to be done, but Ole was always glad to earn a little extra. Larson preferred him to a stranger, just as he preferred Chris. The men—including Charlie, who had been with him three seasons—were intruders. They shared the farm with him, destroyed his sense of achievement.

This year he resented them more than ever because in his mind a compromise was being struck between the fantasies of the boy and the reality of Chris. He didn't understand what was taking place, didn't consciously grant him the status of a son. But he was convinced, none the less, that when they were alone, sharing the farm, something would be restored and fulfilled.

The harvest finished, the feed stored, just the two of them to meet and defeat the rigors of the winter, watch the stable, build up the fires—the thought of it carried an echo of the lean, anxious years with Cora, and he found it hard to wait.

But if the weather broke he might have to keep the men another month. And here they were, noisy and aggressive, taking over from him, making him feel unnecessary, unwanted. He watched them sullenly, feeding his resentment on every word and turn. There was an itch in his fingers. It was all he could do to keep from letting fly at them with a storm of orders and abuse.

And then, about an hour after they arrived, he saw Chris leading North out to water. For a moment his ill-humor vanished. The sight of the shining stallion and the handsome boy transfixed him. His face softened; his eyes lit with pride. But only for a second or two; then he noticed that Chris was leading North by the halter.

Something snapped. The rage seething within him suddenly found outlet. Forgetful of his stiff joints, he darted forward and tried to snatch away the halter shank. For a moment he was silent with effort; then in a fury he yelled, "Give it to me—give it to me, you goddam fool. If he gets away you're going to pay."

Chris might have let go of the halter shank had they been alone. But Charlie and Steve were standing just outside the barn, and conscious of their eyes on him, he took a fresh grip and squared himself. For a moment or two Larson tugged and jerked like a child in a tantrum; then he retreated a few steps, took a deep breath and came at Chris with his hands out as if to seize him round the middle. Chris swung in close to Larson, and in the same instant caught Larson in the chest with a thrust of his elbow. Larson staggered past clumsily, threw out his arms in an effort to keep his balance, and a few feet farther on came sprawling to his knees.

For a moment Chris was sorry—the old man looked so helpless and foolish in his rage. But Charlie and Steve were still watching, and unconsciously straightening a little for their benefit, with a shrug to show his unconcern, he started on with North towards the windmill.

Larson picked himself up slowly, glanced round as if he too were conscious of Charlie and Steve, then ran past them into the barn and a moment later reappeared with a pitchfork.

There was a shout from Charlie. Chris swung round, just as he reached the trough, and saw Larson coming for him at a lopsided run. He leaped aside, at the same time tried to seize the handle of the fork. But though slowed and turned a little, the force of Larson's lunge carried past him, and one of the tines caught North in the shoulder.

North gave a frightened snort. He reared and broke away from Chris, and then, with a look of pettish offense, dropping all his dramatics, lumbered straight back to the safety of his stall.

Larson sat down unsteadily on the edge of the trough. Ignoring him, Chris followed North into the barn. He was pleased that he had been so cool and steady, and it was gratifying that he had had Steve and Charlie as witnesses. But though there was a swing to his shoulders, he had to clench his hands to keep them from trembling. He felt a kind of bewilderment, a dismay which had nothing to do with the risk of being run through with a fork. He didn't want Larson this way. It was as if a support had been removed, almost as if he had been betrayed.

In the barn North was waiting for him, wanting to be petted and fussed over like a big spoiled baby. Chris rubbed noses with him and scratched between his ears a minute. Then, not knowing that the fork had more than pricked him, he saw with a start that the blood was running from his shoulder in a thick, dark stream.

It seemed a great deal of blood. The straw where North was standing was red and glistening. He took a step to look at the shoulder, and felt a wet squelch under his foot. Not knowing what else to do, he took out his handkerchief, rolled it into a tight ball and held it against the wound. But in a moment the handkerchief was sopping. The blood began to run from one of the corners as from a spout. He tried the straw with his foot again and there was another squelch. The tine probably had gone in deep; suddenly he was afraid that unless he did something North might bleed to death. He shrank from blood anyway. Only a few weeks before he had watched it running from a bullet wound with the same quiet persistence.

He wanted Larson now desperately. To take over, do what had to be done. But after what had just happened, he was ashamed to run out and call him. He felt that in any case he ought to be able to take care of North without help, the same as a few minutes ago, assured and capable, he had handled the situation in the yard.

Then North swung his head and nickered. Sensing someone at the door, Chris shifted his position slightly, and gave his undivided attention to the wound. A moment later when he looked round, quickly, pretending surprise, he faced Larson. There was a little silence, Chris illogically relieved, Larson haggard, his head sunk and his eyes upturned, seeming to present himself in an attitude of penitence.

"You'd better look at him," Chris said after a moment. "He's bleeding bad."

Larson examined the wound carefully, spreading it a little and wiping back the flow of blood to see if it was serious. "Nothing much," he said at last. "As good a place as any—plenty of room for it to go in without doing any harm."

Chris relaxed. "He seemed to be losing a lot of blood. The handkerchief was all I could think of."

"You were doing all right. A little bleeding's good though—washes out the dirt. Put the handkerchief back if you like. Pretty soon now it'll start clotting."

"The size of him," Chris said awkwardly as he pressed the sticky handkerchief against the wound, "I don't suppose it would hurt him if he did lose a few pints."

He held the handkerchief with exaggerated care, embarrassed, self-conscious, afraid of meeting Larson's eyes. Larson, for his part, watched the dribble of blood intently and kept his hand on North's shoulder, only an inch or two from the handkerchief, as if he too were helping. They stood like that five or ten minutes, in complete silence, breathing in unison, until the blood slowed gradually to a drip and at last stopped. From time to time North swung his head round and plucked gently at Chris's sleeve.

Then Larson said, "You'd better wash, son; you've got yourself all smeared," and as Chris turned from North he touched him lightly on the arm. Chris hesitated, expecting something more, something important that it seemed now he had been waiting for a long time—but Larson only added, his voice at once reproving and apologetic, "Just the same, I want you always to use the bit. He's a stallion—you never know what he'll do. And me, I'm crazy old Larson. You never know what I'll do either."

Neither the reproof nor the apology was what Chris wanted. The one made him seem hostile and repressive, the other weak, irresponsible, someone to be despised rather than trusted; and he went off to the trough to rinse his hands with a confused sense of disappointment, of having been cheated again.

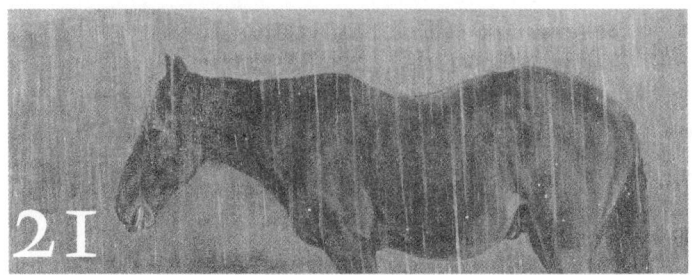

21

THE RAIN SET IN AT SUPPERTIME, a quiet, windless drizzle that Larson said would last all night and probably the next day. After a short discussion it was decided not to go to town.

Larson was stiffened up worse than ever on account of the rain—to Chris, his complaints sounded as if he were trying to make his rheumatism an excuse for the way he had behaved that afternoon—and with offhand generosity he suggested that Chris and Sylvia go without him. Sylvia said no, emphatically—no hired man was escorting *her* to the dance—and after a moment's hesitation, as if he were making his decision independently, Chris said he wasn't interested in going either.

He was calm again, just a little wily. Sylvia was right—they had to be careful, lean over backwards to keep Larson from suspecting. He had just given a good demonstration of what he might do. The pitchfork was a warning.

At the same time the prospect of another evening with Elsie Grover appealed to him. But it was raining, there would be no place to go, and he drew back at the thought of setting out to possess her and failing. For this afternoon he had won only superficially. On his inner consciousness were registered weakness and humiliation. Larson had sworn at him, called him a fool in front of Steve and Charlie—and without a word of protest he had gone quietly about his work. Everything had been satisfactorily settled between them as they stood by North, watching the blood drip from the handkerchief, but it was too subtle and shapeless a settlement to be grasped by the mind in retrospect and used in disposing of a sense of grievance. So that he needed to be confirmed in his strength, his irresistibility, not in the feelings of inadequacy which were now coming to the surface. He knew that, instinctively, and repeated, "No, I'd just as soon stay home. Unless there's something you need—groceries or something. I could drive in and come right back."

Larson considered. "Nothing I know of. You can take the truck in and go in for anything Sylvia wants on Monday."

But now suddenly his mind coiled, flickering and wary. If he went tonight with Sylvia he would take the Cadillac. Wasn't Larson just a little fast with his suggestion that instead he go on Monday with the truck? Because he had caught him taking North out without a bit had he decided he wasn't to be trusted with the car? Was this the thin edge? Was he on his way out?

They were crazy thoughts, he knew, yet despite his common sense he couldn't quite control them. Even later, up in his room, they persisted, as he tried to settle on the bed with a magazine. He smoked and stubbed and stared unseeing at the pages. The rain drummed on the window mournfully. All the wilderness of night and prairie was in it. The room was warm, but suddenly he shivered, and in the same instant sprang to his feet and closed the window. Then, leaning his head on the sash, he peered out. But there was not a light now even in the bunkhouse, and he looked into the darkness as thick and opaque as if a black curtain had been hung outside the glass. Only the raindrops were visible, white-rimmed scallops that dissolved even as they formed and slid down the pane in crooked rivulets.

But presently, faint and polarizing in the darkness, he made out the light of a neighbor's window a mile or more away. It drew him back sharply to the reality of night and distance. From here to the light—that was a measurable distance, and with a great grasshopper leap of his mind he reached it. Reached it, sickened, swayed. It was only the first leap. He could never gather himself for the next one, into the wet black void that lay beyond.

Wet city night was not the same. You ducked and ran and were there. Or you looked out and saw the cars sloshing past and the neon lights reflected in soft red and yellow splashes on the pavement. But here, earth and wet and darkness were all one, floodlike, engulfing. Step after step after step—train after train after train—and finally, somewhere at the end of it, supposing he got through, the streets and lights again. The streets behind him and the streets ahead; where he always had been, always would be, afraid. He had nowhere to go. Only here, in this close little cell of light and walls, was safety.

He drew back a step and closed his eyes, then threw himself on the bed and buried his face in the pillow. He was too tired now—he could never start out again. They could come and take him here. Take him, hang him, anything they wanted. Then they would be satisfied.

Presently the door opened. He sat up, dishevelled and wild-eyed.

"You look scared, son. Been asleep?" Larson set a glass on the bureau and turned away shyly. "It's not nine o'clock yet, but I'm on my way to bed. Just brought you an eggnog. Knee's bad—Sylvia's been doping me again, so I'll get a good night's sleep."

He turned to the door, then glanced back curiously. "How about you? You look beat. And it's hot in here. I'll open the window. You'll sleep better on the cool side."

"No—leave it alone." His voice was so sharp that Larson swung round and stared. Then with an embarrassed little shrug he added, "Whatever you like. I was cold, I guess, and then I fell asleep."

"You'd better undress and get into bed. You're maybe coming down with something." He went to Chris, and as simply as if he were talking to a child, put a hand on his forehead. "Feels hot, all right. Tomorrow's Sunday, so sleep in. Just lie around all day."

He drew back a step, faltering, concerned. Their eyes met a moment. Then, yielding to an unexpected impulse, Chris said, "I'm sorry about North. Next time I'll use the snaffle, whether you're there or not."

"Sure, Chris—I know. He's so friendly you forget sometimes there's a lot of meanness in him. At that maybe he'd never turn; you've got a way with him. But we can't take chances."

"I was just showing off in front of Steve and Charlie—showing how easy I could handle him."

He was frightened of himself as he spoke. Everything by which he had always lived, insolence, pride, defiance, he was abjectly throwing it away. But a sense of helplessness and dependency had seized him, and Larson now was someone to be appeased, won over. For a moment it cost him an effort not to put himself completely in his hands, break down and tell him everything.

"I'm the one to say I'm sorry. Never felt such a fool in my life—been too ashamed ever since to look you in the eye."

He sat down on the bed beside Chris and began picking at a little barbed-wire tear on the knee of his overalls. "Don't know what came over me. The way I'm aching maybe—and the way Sylvia's been carrying on lately, like she can't stand me touching her. You and North just happened to be there."

"I should have had more sense," Chris persisted. "You were always telling me."

But Larson wasn't listening. In a worried voice he continued, "What makes it bad is Sylvia. Sure, she saw us. Trust her—out on the back step watching. Just what she wants. She'll wait till it's time, and then say remember the day he took after Chris with the pitchfork. Something more to prove I ought to be locked up. A while ago she started carrying on about it in front of Charlie, making out she's scared what some day I'll maybe do to her. A good two years now she's been at it. Never misses a chance."

He stood up and brought the glass of eggnog from the bureau. "It'll be good for you. She put some pills in mine so I'll sleep. Says she needs some sleep herself, and she's not going to have me kicking and groaning. No feelings. It's nothing to her if I'm crippled up so I can hardly walk, just so long as *she's* not bothered."

His voice for a moment took on a old-man's tremble, then hardened bitterly. "I picked her up and gave her everything, and now she's trying to have me put away. So it'll all be hers. I'm crazy all right. She's the one I ought to be taking after with a pitchfork, chasing her right back where she came from."

He took the empty glass from Chris and shuffled away. When he was alone Chris sat motionless several minutes on the edge of the bed, bewildered by his sudden submission to Larson, trying painfully to understand what had come over him.

He had crawled. Got right down on his belly and crawled. Said he was sorry, promised to be good. It didn't make sense—not Chris Rowe. He had never said he was sorry in his life. He must have fallen asleep. When Larson came in he must have been still half-dreaming. That was it—it had to be. What could you expect anyway, living with a lunatic? Somebody for no reason at all trying to run a fork through you; your nerves couldn't stand it.

Then it struck him that the pills Sylvia had given Larson probably meant he could expect a visit from her. A little twitch of excitement ran along his nerves, as if it were to happen for the first time. He went to the bureau mirror, combed his hair carefully and took off his shirt. As yet he felt no physical desire. He was excited, not because she was coming to him, but because she was coming to him in preference to Larson. As he threw out his chest and tensed the muscles of his neck his smile was exultant. So far as his relationship with Sylvia was concerned, he had until this moment thought of Larson only as someone in the way, a nuisance, a threat. Now, for the first time, he was a defeated rival.

His smile deepened, became faintly cruel. Anybody that stupid was just asking for it. "Yes, son, no, son—oh no, *I'm* the one to be sorry, son!" Jesus, that little act had gone over easy. The silly old bastard had actually *believed* him. Work up something good and it was hard to say what he might get away with. Spend some time on it, practice—the old boy might even put him in his will.

It was something to think about. Three sections, five or six thousand profit a year. He hadn't sounded as if he would mind cutting down Sylvia's share. He was more likely to think it a good idea. So the smart thing would be to encourage her to treat him rough, keep things stirred up. Make him hate her, make him want to pay her back, get even.

He turned from the mirror and sat down on the bed again. Supposing he stayed, supposing after a while Larson died—it would be a lot easier handling Sylvia on a fifty-fifty basis. She liked her own way. If she wrote all the checks she would get it. Barn or bed, he would still be her chore boy. He remembered the night he had been with Elsie, the look in her eyes when he came back to the dance-hall. Fifty-fifty or better—it was something to work for. He liked his own way too. He wasn't made to sit up and beg.

Then her step sounded on the stairs. He slipped off his trousers quickly and put out the light and got into bed.

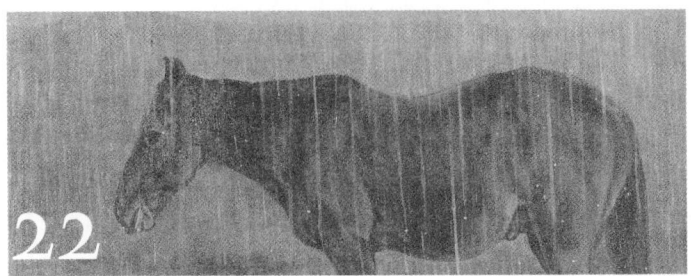

22

"What happened this afternoon?" she began abruptly, making room for herself beside him and then lying back on the pillow. "What got him started? You're lucky, you know, he didn't put that fork right through you."

The way she said it suggested that to her, looking on from the back steps, he had given an impression of helplessness and fright. He answered touchily, "It wasn't that bad. He went off his head a minute, just because he saw me take North out without a bit. He nearly got his face punched in, but I was glad afterwards I didn't."

"Glad?" He felt her body contract, as if she were raising her head in amazement and trying to look at him. "That's not what I'd be if he took a fork to me and I let him get away with it."

"But he's an old man—Jesus!" His irritation began to dissolve into a feeling of embarrassment. "As a matter of fact he was in here a while ago, saying he was sorry. If I had got rough with him I'd feel pretty stupid now."

"Just because he's old's no reason. Next time there maybe won't be a pitchfork handy, so he'll grab the axe."

"I tell you he got sore about North—nothing serious. He started coming for me and I just stepped out of the way. A couple of minutes and it was all over."

"I know. I saw you."

"What was I supposed to do? Take the pitchfork away and run it through him?"

"It would have been a good chance. Self-defense—Steve and Charlie for witnesses. Everybody knows he's crazy; they wouldn't have touched you."

He turned, resting on his elbow, and peered down at the blurred outline of her face. "What's got into you tonight? Anybody'd think you meant it."

"It's you, Chris—ever since you've been here." She drew him towards her and kissed him on the lips, then let her head fall back on the pillow. "I lie awake at night. I can't stand it when he puts his hands on me."

"If it's that bad lock him out—I told you before. He can't make you."

"You don't know what he can do. You just see one side."

"Maybe you just see one side. I'd say it's the other way round. He's scared you'll get sore some day and walk out on him."

"Once I did try locking him out. We'd had a row, not long after I came, and the next day at the table in front of the men he started talking how he met me—joking about it, saying how lucky he was to have picked such a good cook, but putting it across that I'd been waitressing in this cheap little joint and the minute he stepped through the door I grabbed him. Made out he was so high he didn't know what he was doing. Turned me into a whore right in front of them."

Her shoulders ground deeper into the pillow. "From then on every time they came in I'd wonder what they were thinking. I'd catch their eye, like as not meaning anything at all, but I'd get a feeling they were going over me, figuring to themselves the kind of time I could give them."

Her shoulders worked again. He was holding her hand, and her nails cut into his palm. "You'd think a man would want to say good things about his wife, show her off in front of people. But not him. I'm not his wife. He's still got Cora—Cora and the boy. I'm just for the meals and going to bed with. He's just paying me."

The Well / 169

In the dark her anger was somehow fiercer and more deadly than if she were striding round the room. With a forced lightness in his voice he said, "But people know he's crazy—they don't pay any attention. Even if they do, you're still his wife and he's not going to last forever. Everything'll be yours, and you'll still be young enough to enjoy it. In the meantime you're getting your two thousand a year."

He turned, trying to rouse her as other times she had roused him.

"The two thousand's on condition." Her voice was quick and impatient. She seized his hand and held it still. "He's not such a fool. Lock him out, and I'm working for my board. If I don't like it I can go back where I came from. Sure, back to waitressing—*he* knows. You get good meals here, better than most places, but it's on account of me. I made him. When I came he was eating salt pork and potatoes and prunes, giving it to his men three times a day. If he turned ugly he'd make us all go back to it tomorrow. He'd be happier. That's what he and Cora had. That's how he made his money, scraping and skimping, boiling the coffee over and saving the crusts. There's plenty he can still do—worse than talking in front of the men. That's why I want to get it over with."

He recoiled a moment, beginning to believe she meant it, then kissed her quickly to silence her. But thrusting him away she continued, "What's more, I'll not get everything. He holds that over me too. He hasn't made a will yet, and he'd just as soon put in Bell and Ole. We talked about it once. I said I was his wife and I had a right to know where I stood, and he just gave me one of those looks out of the corner of his eye. Treat him right, he says, and he'll treat me right. He plays fair—I've got nothing to worry about."

She rolled her head back and forth, like someone in a fever. "So if it suits him I'll get next to nothing. Just what I've got a right to by law. It'll be all wasted, everything I've taken from him."

He stopped breathing a moment. "Beat him to it, you mean—while he's still just talking."

"I'm his wife. If there's no will I get everything."

"You see where you're heading, though." He recoiled again, but this time more slowly. "What you're talking about—you can't do it. You can't—even if you were smart enough."

"I've got it all figured out. I've been working on it a couple of years. Not serious, not really thinking I'd ever get round to it. But with the two of us it would be easy."

He sat bolt upright a minute, his throat tight, then lay back again. "There's a lot more to it than figuring things out," he said quietly. "You don't know what you're talking about. He's an old man."

"Sure, he's old, so what's he got to lose? His money's no good to him. He doesn't know how to get any fun out of it. Like the Cadillac—it just sits there. He takes it to town two or three times a month. I want to learn to drive it and he's so miserable he won't let me. You come along and he says go ahead, take the wheel, just to show me where I stand. He's old and he's crazy—both. He's going to end up making trouble for himself and a lot of others. Like the pitchfork today. Where would you be now if you hadn't jumped in time? Where would *he* be?"

"But you can't do a job on him just because you think there's a chance he'll get sore some day and trying doing one on you." He laughed easily, and began stroking her breasts again. "It's like I keep telling you—you're crazier than he is."

He felt excited now, yet cool and self-possessed. His words seemed to come of themselves. Cool and reasonable, instinctive—just as the way he had stepped clear of the fork had been instinctive. It was as if some rapacious willingness within him had quickened at what she was suggesting, and he sensed the need of control. The laughter and the determined front of common sense, the sudden little flare of passion as he buried his face in her breasts—these were a kind of insulation, a screen to catch the sparks. "Crazier than he is," he repeated. "Forget him for a while and pay some attention to me. We don't get a chance like this every night."

"And there's his rheumatism." She released herself, and went on as if there had been no interruption. "At his age there's nothing they can do. Every year it'll just get worse."

Now he shook her. "You can't do a job on him either just because he's got stiff joints. Listen, it's getting late. First thing he'll be coming out of his pills. I don't want him in here looking for you."

"So all the time he's just suffering—and his money not doing him any good either. But it would do *us* some good. We'd know how. We could stay on a few years and then sell everything. Or rent it, have enough to live on coming in. Anywhere we liked, never lifting a hand."

"But how?"

For an instant the screen fell. His hand tightened on her breast. Then recovering himself, his voice severe, he said quickly, "You're just talking—you know that. But supposing you ever did try—how do you think you'd get away with it? Something like that happens and they turn a lot of smart boys loose on you. They ask a lot of tough questions. You don't just buy a coffin and send flowers. And you're not going to get much fun out of his money doing twenty years, or swinging."

"I'm smart too. You don't know me yet." She gave a quick, nervous hitch to her body. He felt a tremor run up her side and thigh. "My way there'll be no questions, not the kind anyway that I won't know how to answer. I don't want to swing any more than you do, and what's more I don't intend to. Now listen ..."

He wanted to laugh again, indulgently, but the quick, hard-breathing hiss of her voice forbade it. It was like being very small and listening to a horror story in the dark. He was repelled and fascinated. At the same time he rejected and believed. He wanted to break the spell and he wanted to remain possessed by it. He lay still and taut now, drawn back a little, scarcely touching her. Vaguely he was aware of his hand still on her breast, of the slight strain of keeping it there with his body withheld, but he let it stay.

"There'll be nothing to worry about. One of these days he just takes a trip."

"But you can't make him go. And he'd never stay more than a few days, anyway."

"He'll stay all right. Now just listen. You know how he's always talking about trains. And you know everybody *knows* he's always talking about trains. Well, then—who's going to be surprised?"

He stirred slightly, as if to protest. She went on, "Sure, everybody knows. It's got to be a joke. I realized that one day and started thinking why not play along and build it up? Joke about it too, sometimes. Other times make out I'm worried. The way he's always talking about trains, I'm scared some day he'll catch one. Like there's more to it than people realize. He was down watching the freight when he saw you get off. I've been working on that—scared you'll go off again one of these days and he'll go with you. Ole and Charlie and Aunt Bessie—last Saturday night I had a couple of chances at the dance. So when the time comes it'll fit in. Nobody's going to be surprised."

He stirred again uneasily. She expanded, "Anything he does that sounds sort of queer—I keep at it, tying it in with the trains. Today I phoned Bell after I saw him take after you with the pitchfork. Carried on, said he's been getting sore at everybody lately for no reason at all. Talking about trains is just talk, you can't prove anything. But a pitchfork and witnesses—that's going to set them thinking. I talked to Charlie too; played it up like I was just about crazy myself. And Charlie's an old woman—he'll spread it fast." She drew a deep breath and rubbed her cheek against his arm. "So nobody's going to be surprised. Nobody's going to ask those questions that are worrying you."

He shook her again. "Nobody's going to be surprised at what?"

"He just won't come back. He'll catch a train and that'll be the last of him. He says it's what he's been wanting to do as far back as he can remember."

"But how? Even supposing you talked him into it—he'd never stay."

"Here's how. We'll wait till the men are gone. Then some night you'll drive the truck to town—some night it's raining, if we're lucky, so there won't be much chance of meeting

The Well / 173

anybody. But you'll put his hat on and pull it down in case you do. At night when you meet another car you're never sure who's inside anyway. We'll spatter up the windshield to help. Then when you get there you leave the truck and walk back. Leave it near the station, as close as you think is safe."

"And where is he all this time?" He knew now—the knowledge was gathering in the pit of his stomach like a cold lead ball—but he wasn't ready yet for recognition. "We still haven't got him on the train."

"In the morning he's missing. I'm sort of worried, but not too much. Not right away. We had a set-to about something and he went off sore. I figure he's just sulking. But I phone Bell and ask her if she's seen him. In the afternoon I phone again, and then some of the neighbors. I put off getting real serious for a day or two, giving him plenty of time to get away. Sure, he's caught a train. No sign of him, the truck at the station—what else? Just like he's always wanted to do. It takes a while, though, to realize he's gone, a week before we get the police working on it. After all, he's got a right to go to Regina or some place for a few days if he wants to. You'd expect him to let his wife know, but he never does anything like other people anyway. So he's got a good start; they never catch up with him. It's just like one of those things you read about—a mystery. After a while people forget. After a while he's dead. That's according to law."

The words came in a harsh, breathless whisper, as if she were afraid he might interrupt and make her forget something. "In the meantime I go on running the farm and you keep on working for me. For the first year we'll take it easy, won't give people anything to talk about. In town I'll still be a good customer. Besides, there's always the chance that he'll be back. All the people that owe him will still owe me, and I won't be too keen on collecting either. They'll be glad to keep it that way. They won't want to rough me up. When I go to town I'll ease up on the clothes. Quiet and serious now—like it's been a real shock. It's changed me."

She paused for breath a moment. He could hear the faint sound of her lips gathering saliva. "You're just the hired man, but all the time you're getting friendly with people too. You're good at it when you want to—I've been watching you. They say to themselves it looks like one of these days he'll be stepping into everything, so they won't want to rough you up either. Even if they wonder sometimes. Neighbors are neighbors—it pays to get along."

"And in the meantime where have you got him stacked away?" With an effort he succeeded in breaking into a laugh. It was like struggling out of a dream in which a crushing weight lay on his chest. "In the loft, I suppose, under the sheaves?"

"The well."

He lay cold a minute, then laughed again. It was easier that way, to keep it at the level of a game, a sort of fantasy in which, like a child, she was giving rein to her imagination, to take his turn in a make-believe dialogue. "How do you plan doing it? Just say, let's go for a walk some night, and then when you get there, tip him in?"

"We'll have to do it first."

"*We'll* have to do it first! Hold on a minute—"

"It's fenced off. Nobody ever goes there. I don't suppose hardly anybody knows there is a well."

"You've been reading too many stories." His laugh trailed off uncertainly. He lay still a moment, seeing the possibilities. "In a way it's a smart idea. It just might work—after all the talk about trains people might believe it. But you're forgetting ..."

"Sure, they'll believe it. It's more or less what they expect. I've been getting them used to the idea. And they won't think it's something I schemed up because it's been going on for years. He was talking about trains and they were laughing at him behind his back long before my time."

"You've got it all worked out fine—except you're forgetting that first you've got to do it."

"We'll do it all right—when it's time. There's no use thinking and worrying about it too soon. That's the way you lose your nerve."

"You sound like an old hand. Do you plan to do the little job first, or just give him some extra pills and then load him in the truck and dump him?"

"Not the truck. We can sling him over a horse and cut though the field."

He forced another laugh. "Wouldn't it be easier to drive him over, and then run the pitchfork through him when we get there?"

"The pitchfork wouldn't be fast enough. It'll be better with a gun."

"And I suppose you've got a gun? Or maybe you plan going to town some day and buying one, just like a pound of coffee?"

"There's one here—don't worry. He keeps it locked up, but I know where."

"And afterwards, where do I come in? After I've played along and done your dirty work, what's in it for me?" He reached over and rumpled her hair good-humoredly. He wanted to keep it at a safe remove, to go on treating it as a game of make-believe, but he also wanted to make it clear that he was nobody's fool, that the only schemes he lent himself to were profitable ones. "If they don't ask questions I stay on as your hired man. And if they do, you say there he is—he's the one. There's been trouble between them, ever since that day with the pitchfork."

"Grow up! If I tried anything like that then you'd talk too, and you're the one they'd believe. I'm his wife—I get everything. There's a lot more reason for me to want him out of the way than there is for you."

"So we're in it together—and then what?" He tried to keep the tone of raillery in his voice, but despite himself his mind ran on, exploratory and intent. Even though it was an imaginary situation, one to which he had no intention whatever of committing himself, still he had to sound it out—all the angles. How much was in it for him? Even more important, were there any weak spots, any traps or tricks? Fear made it compulsive—fear lest he be outsmarted. Not so much fear of the actual consequences, what they might do to him, what he might suffer, as fear of the inner collapse should the situation prove too much for him, should he, Chris Rowe, have to admit his stupidity or ineptness. Even in an imaginary situation he dared not see himself vulnerable. He went on, a wily softness in his voice, "Sure, you can't talk; neither can I. When the job's done I can stay on chopping wood or forking manure, or if I don't like it I can catch another freight. You might like it better that way. There wouldn't be so much for people to talk about."

"I'm nearly thirty-one, Chris. Somebody like you's worth hanging on to." She took his hand and pressed closer to him. "That's how I'd feel if I was twenty, but besides, I know what my chances are of finding anybody else. You're my last chance, and a good one. I'm even ready to take a lot from you. I know it's coming—I've got to make up my mind to it. Like the night you had the Grover girl. I didn't take it easy, but I took it. You're a lot younger—I've no right to expect too much. Another ten years you'll be just about where I am now, and I'll be forty. So things are going to slow down between us, and the kind you are you're going to keep on playing round. But I've been watching you, Chris, and I figure that's all it'll be, just playing round. You won't want to break it up. In a lot of ways I'll still be more use to you than the young ones."

"That's all right for now, but what about this time next year? After you've got sore a few times ..."

"And I won't mind so much because for a while anyway I'll have had it right. You get over wanting things, but you like to be able to look back. Like when I was just a crazy kid—there'd be all the fancy dolls in the catalogue, real hair and dresses, but all I ever had was a homemade one, with fur over it like an Eskimo. What I mean, I got over wanting dolls, but I never got over the feeling that I'd been done out of something because I didn't get a fancy one. Finding somebody to team up with, the same—it's never been right. Until now, Chris—there's always been something missing. I always picked the wrong kind, trying to steer clear of the old Eskimos. Money didn't mean anything till I got tired at last and tried him. It hasn't worked out, so now I want to start over. I feel I've got it coming to me."

He still pretended not to believe her. The possessiveness in her voice made him uneasy. "You just think I'm what you've been waiting for. One of these days you'll take a good look at me and I'll be another old Eskimo too."

"I know—you're thinking what's your share going to be." She said it without disappointment. There was no indication that it humiliated her to realize she was not enough, that he wanted to strike a bargain. Her voice was as matter-of-fact and unresentful as if she were hiring a girl to help with the housework and it had suddenly occurred to her that they had discussed everything but wages. "You don't need to worry about that either. You'll get a good share. We'll work the farm together, and besides there's ten thousand of my own that we won't have to wait for. It'll be as good as yours. I can't turn anything over to you right away because it would look bad, but you'll have plenty for spending. And there's the Cadillac, and you'll be running the farm and giving the orders. Then in a few years we can get married. That's what I want, what I'm working for."

He ran his fingers through her hair again. "But supposing next summer there's another new man and you take a shine to him? What happens to me? Down the well too?"

She pressed closer, took his hand again. "The first year he used to talk about another boy, but I was scared I'd never be able to take him—scared he'd just be his. But yours would be different. I keep thinking what we could do for them: two or three, maybe, you all over. There's still plenty of time. I wasn't going to say for a while, but maybe it'll show you. The first time I thought about it was the day Ole and Bell were here. I kept saying to myself what a sight she is, and then I saw him look at her, and all at once I was wishing it was you and me. It was so crazy I made myself stop, but first thing I was at it again. So now maybe you'll believe me. You know how much chance there is I'll get sore and tell you to clear out."

Something jarred. He seemed to see Larson standing before him, the soft, half-believing look on his face as he told how everything had been for the boy, how each time he installed or built or bought something he still imagined himself showing it to him, asking him if he liked it; and at the thought of this gentle foolishness giving way to the reality of a stranger's son—his son and Sylvia's—he shrank back with a feeling that it would be double murder. "No," he said again, his voice slow and final. "You've got it all worked out except that first you've got to do the job. You're running away with yourself. You don't know what killing a man means."

She said coldly, "And you do?"

The muscles of his throat contracted. He raised himself on his elbow and his forearm trembled. "You don't have to kill a man to know what it would be like, to know you couldn't go through with it."

She laughed through her teeth, wriggling her head and neck and shoulders into the pillow like a cat rolling on its back. "What's wrong, Chris? You're shaking. Anybody'd think you'd done a little job yourself somewhere sure. I was only asking. He's the one that thinks maybe that's why you're hiding here."

"Who says I'm hiding?" He was in control again. His voice rose, scoffing and incredulous. "I'm on my way home. I'd have been there long ago only he keeps asking me to stay."

"*He* says you're hiding." She, too, was in control. Her voice, for all its needling emphasis, sounded indifferent, faintly bored. "It's nothing to me; I'm just trying to tell you. This nice friendly old man—he's the one that's got the idea you're on the run. Killed a man or something—I don't know."

He drew away from her, afraid he might tremble again. "But it's crazy. If he believes anything like that then what does he want me to stay for?"

"Maybe he's sorry—I don't know. Or maybe he thinks if he's got something on you he can make you work cheap."

"But he can't know anything; there's nothing to know." His voice faded as he remembered the day Larson told him he would be safe here. But even so, if he suspected something why would he go to Sylvia with it? When he wanted him to stay, and was afraid she was trying to get rid of him?

"Look, Sylvia—you're just wasting your time." He rose on one elbow and gripped her arm. "You're trying to scare me into it, but I don't scare easy. He's got nothing on me, neither have you. It's the other way round. He's scared already you're scheming to have him locked up as crazy. Suppose I tell him what's really on your mind? Which one is he going to believe, you or me?"

She laughed again, and reaching up ran her fingers over his lips. "You sure do scare easy, Chris. I only said he figured you must be out here lying low for a while, and you're jumping right out of your skin. All right. You say I'm just making it up. Then tell me, do you know a girl called Helen?"

He relaxed his grip on her arm and breathed carefully. "Helen? Why, sure—there's a girl at home called Helen, Helen Norbert. I used to date her. As a matter of fact it was serious for a while."

"You never told me about her. If I'm making things up how do you suppose I know her name?"

"I don't know. What's Helen got to do with it anyway?"

"Ask him. He's the one that told me. And if you're going home and just stopped off to earn a few dollars why do you never write to her? You say your old lady's sick; why do you never write to her either?"

"How do you know I never write? Do you think I've got to come and ask you how to spell?"

"No, but I think you'd have to come to me for paper and envelopes. You haven't got any of your own. Maybe when you were in town you sent a postcard—I don't know and I don't care. *He's* the one that says it's funny. He's the one that keeps adding things up and wondering what they want you for."

"First let's finish with Helen. I want to know what you're driving at." He spoke harshly, trying to conceal behind a front of anger the fear and sickness that had gripped him. "Like as not I mentioned her name to him; there's nothing wrong with that. As a matter of fact I think I did. Sure, after the dance—I remember now. He asked me if I'd really fallen for this Grover girl, and I said I had somebody back home. That's right—I know I did ..."

The words came in a sputter. He was positive he hadn't mentioned her name. How then had Larson found out? Even if he had heard something in town—say somebody had come across a paper with his picture—even so, why Helen? Even if she'd talked, told the police he'd skipped town and was headed west ...

"Chris." Again her voice had a soft, swift hiss. There was a deadliness about it, a hint of cat-and-mouse reserve that froze him. "Chris—there's somebody else. What about a man you used to know called Baxter? I've never heard you mention his name either."

"Baxter!" Unexpectedly he spoke in a faint whisper. The command of his will to keep steady and controlled exhausted itself against the numb tight muscles of his throat like the power of a motor against a hard-packed snowdrift. "Baxter—Baxter—" The sound was still sick and thin. Each time after pronouncing the name he hesitated, as if searching his memory. "Baxter—let me think—it sounds familiar ..."

"Yes, Chris—Baxter. Was he a friend of yours? Why don't you relax and tell me more?"

He struggled a moment to speak, to force a laugh, and then, unable to control himself, leaped out of bed. It was too much. The darkness round him was beginning to reel. He went to the window and pressed his forehead against the glass. In the sudden silence he heard first the thudding of his heart, then the soft steady beat of the rain. His mind raced again, not in conjectures now as to how she knew, but in a frantic effort to make plans, decide on his next move. Escape—but where, how? In a big place you had a chance. There were always so many—you could catch a train or bus and nobody would notice. But here it was just telephone poles and prairie. Even pass a farm and the dog barked. In town the train was the big event of the day: everybody was watching. For a moment he felt cornered, trapped. An impulse to thresh out and break the window seized him. His nails scratched on the glass. And then her voice reached him, gentle, craftily amused. "Don't be so scared—nobody's got anything on you. Helen and this man Baxter—they're just a couple of names. How he knows them, you have bad dreams sometimes. You do a lot of talking in your sleep."

He stood motionless a moment, biting down the desire to break into a laugh. Then, in an extremity of relief, sagging and limp, he stumbled back into bed and put his head against her breast. And she responded as if he were a frightened child, stroking his hair soothingly, until gradually he realized that yielding to her this way, abandoning his defenses, was in itself a confession, and that henceforth, even though he had spoken only Baxter's name in his sleep and revealed nothing of what had happened, he would to some degree be in her power.

But he didn't know he had only spoken Baxter's *name*, had no right to assume it. After a few minutes, tense and wary again, he sat up and laughed. "You started to get my nerve— like you'd turned out to be a mind reader or something. This Helen, she used to mean quite a lot to me. A redhead—gave me the run around for a while, about the only one that ever did."

Encouraged by the ease with which he was finding words, he laughed again, successfully. "It's news to me, though, that I talk in my sleep. I hope I haven't been giving away all my secrets."

"I don't know. According to him you've given away plenty."

He steeled himself, kept his voice even. "Jesus—as bad as that. Let's hear more."

"This fellow Baxter, he's got it figured out you must have shot him."

"*Shot* him! Jesus—he's the one that's been having dreams. Poor old Baxter! Why, we used to get our meat from him. He's a butcher, a couple of streets over."

"You shot him, but you didn't mean to. Something went wrong—you got scared and ran."

"Go on. Jesus! Tell me everything."

"I didn't hear you. He's the one that comes and listens. You were bad when you first came. You used to yell sometimes, right in the middle of the night, when everything was quiet. Like you were getting your throat cut."

"That's right—I remember—especially the first week. Real nightmares. But it's just because everything's different."

He paused a moment, thinking of the nights he had dreamed about Baxter, then lied quickly, "Like the horses—sometimes I dream they're running me down, or I'm falling off Minnie. Sometimes I wake up with a feeling I've just let out a yell, but I listen and it's all quiet, so I figure it's part of the dream. Why didn't you tell me? At least I could keep the door closed. He's the one that says leave it open, so there'll be a little draft."

"Sure—he's the one—and I wanted to tell you, he's the one that wouldn't let me. So he could get things out of you. You see, Chris, you don't always wake up after you yell. Sometimes you go on talking, and that's when he comes and listens. He says he's even talked back to you and asked questions, standing right here beside you, and you've answered so it made sense."

He didn't consciously disbelieve her. He simply made a substitution—in his mind's eye saw her standing beside him, not Larson. Somehow it was right that way. The substitution was involuntary. From what he knew of them, Larson wouldn't come to listen and worm out secrets, whereas she would. Just as she had noticed he wrote no letters, had bought no writing paper.

"He says this one night you were raving away you hadn't meant to do it, and he asked you what it was you hadn't meant to do, and you said you'd only taken the gun along to make it look good, like you meant business. Most of the time he says he can just make out a few words here and there, but that night everything was clear. Another time you wanted a bath. You weren't going to stay if you couldn't have one regular—on account of so much blood."

"Supposing I did? What of it?" His voice was unconcerned now, slightly scornful. Pretending a yawn, he lay back on the pillow. "Dreaming you've done something doesn't mean you've actually done it. That's the craziest yet. The first night I was here, as a matter of fact, I had a dream about you. Sure—the works—and up to then you hadn't got much further than calling me a dirty bum."

"You don't need to try an act with me, Chris. Talking in your sleep doesn't prove anything; we know that. But whatever you said, it's given him ideas. Maybe you're not on the run, but it looks like you might be. You know who Baxter is, and you know what happened. It's your business. I'm only trying to warn you."

She was quiet a moment. He could hear her lips gathering saliva again. "Maybe you don't care if he starts making phone calls—tipping them off there's a new man here that's got him wondering. Maybe what you say is true and you've got nothing to be scared of. But remember he's against you now, just in case there is something. Just the wrong look on your face some morning—that'll be enough to start him."

"But he's not against me. He was in here tonight, friendly, just like he's always been."

"What about the pitchfork? Five minutes before you'd have said he wasn't against you then either. And suppose he gets some of the smart boys asking *you* questions—are you going to be able to give the right answers? Don't you see: as long as he knows as much as he does he's in the way. One of these days, supposing he gets it into his head there's something between us?"

"So we get in there first—drop him down the well and live happily ever after."

She raised herself and pressed down upon him gently. Her arms enclosed him. Her lips and the soft fine prickle of her hair began moving slowly over his body. Then, pausing a moment, pressing her cheek against his shoulder, she said, "Don't you think we could be happy? Wouldn't it be worth it?"

The rain beat with a small, crinkling sound on the window, and he lay tranquil, his eyes closed, blanking his mind and abandoning himself to the return and fulfilment of his desire. But later, when she had gone, he told himself again that it was time to ask for his wages and move on. He was frightened—frightened of them both, as a child is frightened of a nightmare that may return. And mingled with his fear was a faint feeling of nausea.

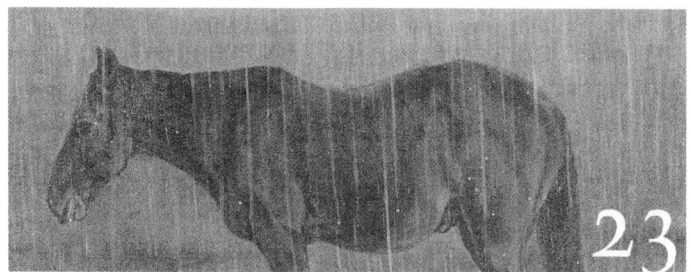

23

BUT HE DELAYED. His fears in the morning seemed groundless. Larson was limping painfully; he looked tired and shrunken; after breakfast he made conversation with Chris as if afraid of being left alone. His smile was friendly and anxious, still a little apologetic. "Maybe you think if I'm crippled up like this in winter you'll have to do everything yourself," he said. "But I'm fine again as soon as the snow comes and it's dry and frosty. It's the damp. I get a spell about this time every year. The sun's going to be out by noon. Tomorrow I'll be just like a young fellow again."

And Sylvia—no, it was just talk. She would never go through with it. You did a job by accident, the way he had done his, because you got jumpy, lost your nerve. You didn't sit down and make your plans and then do it in cold blood to somebody you knew. Not unless there was something wrong with you, a twist somewhere so you couldn't help yourself.

She was too smart. That little scheme of hers, to make people think he'd jumped a freight, gone for a trip—she had sense enough to know she'd never get away with it. In a way it was a good scheme, something you just might put over. But even supposing you were lucky and everything went right— even so, first of all you had to do the job.

It wouldn't do itself. Just like a woman, that was what she wouldn't face. From hating him to being rid of him, her mind jumped it. She skipped the fifteen minutes in between.

Just talk—a way of working some of the hate out of her system. If she thought he was starting to take her seriously, she'd like as not panic, go straight to Larson and tell him everything.

But his real reason for staying was dread of starting out again. He was safe here. He could draw breath and look around. On the move, the run—he knew now what it was like. Worst of all, he had admitted to himself that Rickie wouldn't want him, had faced his future for what it was. Freights and more freights, towns and more towns—always the fear of what was waiting round the corner.

He seldom thought it out as straight as that. The days went by, and he was busy. The men were finishing the oats, cutting the last crop of alfalfa and filling the loft and silo. He worked with them part of the time in addition to his usual chores. Then, when the alfalfa field was cleared, the cattle were turned in to feed on the stubble and aftergrowth, and for a few days he and Larson repaired fences. He felt less of a chore boy. The other men, even though Larson's interest in him made complete acceptance impossible, seemed friendlier. He repeated to himself that it wasn't such a bad life, and began mentally to settle in. Five dollars a day and saving practically all of it: he would be a fool to leave now. Where nearly everybody went wrong was rushing things. Lying low another six months—even when you were sure two was plenty—that was what kept you on the outside.

To make it easier, Sylvia was pleasantly aloof. All that week he was never once alone with her. Sometimes she would contrive to touch his sleeve as he was filing out with the others after a meal, or give him a glance that he knew was meant as an assurance that nothing had changed, that she was simply biding her time; and sometimes, because they seemed to assume his commitment, touch and glance filled him with uneasiness. There were even times when she loomed over him ominously, seemed darkened and inflated by what she had just revealed, just as to a child an ugly old man who has been pointed out as wicked or unclean takes on a new dimension of horror. But he never let his mind dwell on it. He went outside. He worked and rode. He even took pride in his strength, in matching himself against Steve and Charlie. He discussed crops and cattle and pests with Larson, asked questions, sometimes ventured an opinion. Larson's friendship was important now. It meant that he was safe and Sylvia was wrong. So long as he could count on it there was no need to listen to her, no need to leave.

He even began to think of Baxter more calmly, with what seemed sane detachment. All along, partly perhaps because of seeing it so many times through his nightmares, he had magnified and distorted what he had done. Now there lay behind him nothing but a piece of stupid bungling. Often, trying to quiet his sense of guilt, he had insisted on as much before; now it was not necessary to insist. He couldn't see it any other way. It was as if his conscience, like a circuit judge, had finished with that particular piece of business and moved on.

For all along, unknown to himself, his conscience had been involved. It was conscience even more than fear for his safety that had been responsible for the moments of panic that sometimes overtook him—the black moments of the day when he told himself that Baxter was dead, that if they caught him he would hang. But now he was no longer concerned with Baxter, only his predicament. (This, perhaps, because his conscience was so little accustomed to being deferred to that it made only modest claims, and accepted what he had already suffered as settlement in full; or because its mechanism and functioning were of so rudimentary a nature that the slight counterweight of rejecting Sylvia's scheme had been sufficient to restore its equilibrium.) He no longer felt guilty, only pursued. He had made a mistake; his problem was to escape the consequences. For the present, at least, he was probably as safe here as he could hope to be anywhere. Therefore he would stay. Sylvia and Larson both had their suspicions about him. Therefore he would do his best to keep on the right side of them.

So he demonstrated to Larson that he was capable of a good day's work, and dropped casual hints that the prospect of staying for the winter was beginning to appeal to him. Before, if Larson were sharp or impatient, he would sulk, keeping it up, as a kind of punishment, long after Larson was ready to forget. But now he maintained an even front of good humor. He always used a snaffle on North. When the pup leaped up he obediently cuffed it down. And he began slipping offhand compliments into his conversation, the difference between Larson's buildings and the neighbors', something he had heard one of the men say about the meals here compared with the salt pork and prunes you got most places.

There was no embarrassment, no sense of deceit. He was doing it as a means to an end, and consequently chalked up against himself no feelings of compromise or cowardice.

He did his best to keep on good terms with Sylvia too. Saturday night, for instance, he wanted to go to town. But from her look and tone he knew she didn't want him to go, was afraid he would see Elsie Grover again, and after a brief hesitation, yawning wearily, he said he didn't care one way or another. "As a matter of fact I'd forgotten it was Saturday," he answered Larson. "Whatever you and Sylvia want to do."

He was a little concerned now about Elsie. He had no particular desire to resume their relationship. The challenge of her innocence disposed of, there was little left; his experiences with Sylvia were more satisfying. But a number of times the last few days, almost reproachfully, he had found himself remembering Elsie's face as they danced together, its look of bright yet cautious happiness, as if she dared not yet believe in it.

Now it was two weeks. On Wednesday he had been to town with the truck again, but when he went to the drug store she was not in sight, and not knowing her father's attitude, he had been afraid to ask for her. Yesterday he had slipped in and telephoned while Sylvia was in the garden, but it was her father again who answered, and he pretended to have called the wrong number. So that it was two weeks of complete silence. He couldn't get her off his mind; his concern was genuine. Something that he had never done with any other girl, that he scarcely realized he was doing now—he began to imagine her feelings as she counted the days.

But he couldn't afford to offend Sylvia. Not right now. Elsie wouldn't have much use for him in handcuffs anyway.

He shivered and laughed. Sylvia couldn't do that to him—she didn't know enough. But still, if ever he rubbed her the wrong way, she might start making telephone calls herself. It was just one of those things—Elsie would have to get over it. The sooner the easier. Dragging it out would only hurt her more. He was sorry, but maybe a lesson like this was what she needed. The next stranger that came to town she would take her time and look him over.

Besides (which made the decision easier) the rain in the air had crippled up Larson again, and it was likely that Sylvia would see to it he had another good night's sleep. It was a more appealing prospect than an evening with Elsie, pretending what he didn't feel. Pretence would be difficult. There was something about her, at once helpless and unflinching, against which his most practiced voice and smile might fail.

And later that night, he continued to keep on good terms with Sylvia. It was almost exactly the same as the time before: what Larson suspected, how easy it would be to get rid of him now. But Chris was prepared, and instead of making protests or denials he went with her, sympathizing, agreeing, delaying. He didn't commit himself. He expressed just enough resentment of Larson, just enough uneasiness about the future, to convince her that he was coming round.

It was a good night. It make him look forward to others like it. He was doing all right, handling both of them. Just watch himself, take things smooth and easy—there was nothing to worry about unless he fumbled, lost his nerve.

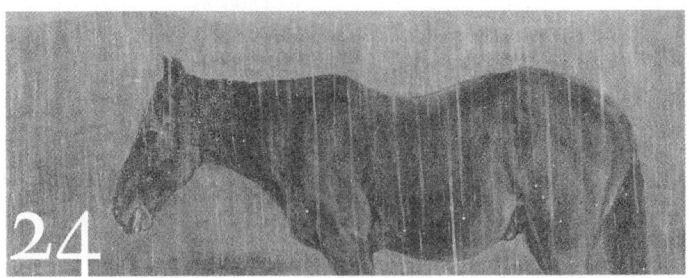

24

THEN THE MEN LEFT, and the three of them were alone. Larson was like a boy. He wandered pridefully around the farm as if he had just acquired it and were indulging himself in the new sensations of ownership. Several times he had Chris drive him in the Cadillac, and every so often, when the view was right, he would put up his hand for him to stop. For a while he would sit staring across the land, towards the buildings, a faint, half-furtive smile on his lips, and then glance round at Chris and nod, as if to make him feel that it was all his too, that this was the moment he had been working and waiting for all his life.

There was a great deal still to be done before freeze-up: fall plowing, wheat to be hauled, repairs to the cattle shed. But he told Chris that for a day or two they were going to take things easy. It had been a hard fall; a little time off was coming to them. Even though the weather was good again, and at this time of year mightn't last. There was a worried look on his face as he squinted up into the hazy, coppery sunlight—after all, he was a farmer, and the seasons were to be respected and taken advantage of, not flouted or defied—but the next moment he shrugged stiffly, a caricature of recklessness, and pursed his lips on his decision.

Then, always keeping Chris in tow, he set off on another tour of the farmyard: to lay a hand on the warm, silvery metal of the silo, to stand just inside the door of the barn, snapping on and off the lights, to walk in and admire North and Minnie. Often in his eyes there was less pride of possession than wonder. It was all his, but he couldn't quite understand how it had come about. He was checking, making sure. Somewhere along the way there had been a miracle.

But for Chris they were tiring days. He was never alone. He had a feeling that each time Larson turned to him it was with a look first of expectancy, then of disappointment. Some expression of enthusiasm or comradeship—that was what he wanted—some sign of right and worthiness to share in what was being offered. But Chris felt constrained, impatient. The eager, gentle look in Larson's eyes embarrassed him. It was a relief when, on the third day, early in the afternoon, Larson drove off in the truck alone, and he was left to exercise Minnie and go about his work as usual.

Minnie was fresh and keen, and he rode nearly all the way to town. When he returned, about four o'clock, Fanny was having her colt.

For a minute or two he stood well back, his lips curled, his eyes narrowed with disgust. It was the most loathsome thing he had ever seen. The colt was half-born; entangled in the placenta, it seemed lifeless. But recognizably a colt—that was what sickened him. Not just a slimy mass of flesh and skin, some kind of growth or mutilation, but Minnie and North in miniature. He could see an eye, the small neat teeth bared in a grimace of ancient, deathlike strain. It was as if life itself, by such a revelation of itself, were affronting him. It was an intrusion of something elemental and ugly that he shrank from, protested. He felt no concern or excitement, only revulsion, a vague sense of outrage.

Then Fanny groaned and heaved, and in response the colt moved too. Slightly, ineffectually, not so much an effort as a twitch or spasm, like the tremor of something dying rather than being born. Fanny tried again, then seemed to collapse. With a loud, rubbery snort she let the wind out of her lungs and lay still. Her teeth too were bared. Her coat was as wet as if she had been doused.

After a minute she raised her head again weakly, with another groan let it fall, and now he noticed that she was tied too short. Exhausted from this last effort, she was stretched out limp and motionless, but her nose was an inch or two off the floor. He knew he should go in and untie her, help her that much, but the impulse failed against his aversion and disgust.

The colt seemed to be making no progress. It struck him that before it was born she would be split right open.

Then there was another heave, another collapse. The way she began to gasp and groan made him think she must be dying.

Something was wrong. The realization forced its way through his other feelings slowly, then seized him with desperate urgency. Something was wrong, something had to be done. She threshed feebly with her forelegs again, as if drowning, trying to swim, and all at once, with a weak, sucked-out feeling at the knees, he realized it was up to him.

He spun round, ran to the door. Then, coming to his senses and remembering that Larson was away, he turned and ran back. It was a double stall, intended for a team, but lying on her side, her legs extended, she practically filled it. He hesitated a moment, wondering if he should go round into the feed alley and come over the manger—it was less her hooves he was afraid of than that with a sudden shift or lunge she might bring him into contact with the wet mass of colt and placenta. Then, scarcely aware what he was doing, all in a breath, he sprang forward over her legs and untied the halter shank.

It didn't make much difference. As if encouraged by his presence and the realization that he was trying to help her, she gathered herself and forced again, then with a long wheezing sigh sank back and lay still.

He went back out of the stall and looked at the colt. It had not moved, but it was still alive. The dog came in and ran up sniffing curiously. He jerked it back by the tail, struck it so hard across the nose it yelped and vanished. He stood still a moment, worried and helpless, not knowing what to do, then like a child wheeled away and ran to the house to tell Sylvia.

But when he burst into the kitchen she only laughed. "Don't ask me—I'm no vet. If you like I'll give you an apron."

"It's not coming right. I don't think she'll last much longer."

Sylvia poured him a cup of coffee. "Take a minute—it's fresh. I was just going to call you anyway."

"Later maybe. I thought maybe you could help."

"Fanny's twenty-five if she's a day, so supposing she doesn't make it? He's got more colts and horses already than he knows what to do with. Sit down and stop fussing."

"But we can't just let her lie there. Try and get him on the phone—didn't he say where he was going?"

"Maybe to see Ole—maybe to town to watch another freight come in. Chances are he'll land home with somebody else—put your nose out of joint."

"You could look at her anyway—tell me what to do?"

"Me tell you? If he can't stay home and look after things that's up to him. Go on, drink your coffee."

"It's just about half-way. Will it do any harm if I pull?"

"Go ahead—pull. If she's not going to make it anyway, what's the difference?"

He met her eyes angrily a moment, then sprang down the steps and ran back to the barn. Nothing had happened since he left. Through the transparent sac that partly concealed the colt, he could see that it was still alive and making what seemed slight, gasping efforts to breathe. At the sound of his step Fanny raised her head a little, and then, seeming to lack the strength to contract and force again, lay back with a groan.

Just for a moment as he stood over the colt he wished he hadn't seen it, that he could go back to the house and have coffee with Sylvia and pretend it wasn't there. Then his responsibility pressed on him again, and screwing up his face he bent quickly and took hold of the head.

It was easier than he had expected. Once his hands had actually touched it, felt its wet, slimy warmth, the worst was over. But it was hard to get a good grip, and he was afraid of dislocating the neck. Fanny heaved and strained again, as if doing her utmost to co-operate. To take advantage of her effort he dropped to one knee, seized the body with both arms in a kind of hug, and then, bracing his foot against the slight elevation of the stall floor, leaned back with all his strength.

It came slowly, but with smooth, surprising ease. He released his hold of it gently, bent over again and cleared away the placenta. The next moment a wave of nausea swept him. He stumbled into the adjoining stall and was sick.

He was there, still retching when Larson returned. For a few minutes neither spoke. Larson examined Fanny and the colt attentively, swore at Fanny for waiting till his back was turned, brought gunny sacks from the feed alley and gave her a light rubdown. At last—his look of surprise, perhaps, a little feigned—he turned to Chris. "What's wrong with you?" he said. "Just look at you, your knees and your belly—you've even got it round the eyes."

Chris assumed a slightly shamefaced nonchalance. He wanted to wipe his mouth, but his hands still felt sticky and he shrank from going into his pockets for a handkerchief. "It got stuck. I had to take hold and pull. Do you think they're going to be all right?"

"It'll take more than a colt to kill Fanny. But what happened? You look like you've been playing in it. I'd better bring some clothes to the bunkhouse so you can wash and change."

"I'm telling you—I had to pull." Chris took some straw from the manger and wiped his hands strenuously. "I didn't know what else to do. Do you think I hurt it?"

Larson hitched his overalls. "This is sixteen she's had, and I think he's going to be about the best yet. Let's get him on his feet and see."

"You mean, though, she'd have got along all right by herself?" For a moment he stood staring down at the colt, vaguely disappointed. "I'd never seen it happen before. I got sort of scared—thought she wasn't going to make it."

"Fanny's tough. So long as its head was coming first there's a good chance she'd have managed. But I'd rather see you try and help her than not care. Even if you did something wrong."

He hitched his overalls again. "You've got a way with horses—natural—better than lots that grow up with them."

Chris felt his face burn. He took more straw and began wiping his hands again, while Larson returned to the colt and squatted beside it.

And now, as unconcerned as if she had just been resting, Fanny staggered to her feet. She turned round, almost toppling Larson over with a bunt of her head, and began licking the colt. Larson edged back a little out of the way, but remained squatted on his hunkers. It was incredible. The wobbly little head was already held high; the white star on its forehead gave it a look of poise and self-sufficiency, just the right finishing touch. As he watched, the filmy eyes seemed to brighten, to show awareness and curiosity.

He crept closer, squatted beside Larson, and reaching out with his finger tip touched the star and ears. Fanny ignored him and went on licking. For a minute or two there was no sound but the faint, slobbery swish of her tongue. Then seeming satisfied with her job, she gave the colt a nudge in the shoulder, almost like a first intimation that legs were meant for standing on, and began to eat the placenta.

Chris felt his stomach turn. He stood up, ready to strike her in the face and make her leave it, but Larson touched his arm. "Doesn't look very nice, but it's good for her. Helps close her up—she knows. You'll find more gunny sacks at the far end of the feed alley, maybe we can wipe him off a little. Then we'll see about getting him on his feet."

It was more incredible than ever. The long, stick-like little legs buckled at first; then, when Larson had straightened them out and spaced them properly, they steadied and adjusted themselves to the weight of the body. One of them buckled again. A moment later it straightened itself out without help. Supporting and pushing at the same time, Larson persuaded it to take another step. Another, then another, right out into the aisle; round and back again. Just like that—it was walking.

Its coat was a rough dull black. One of the forelegs was white to the knee, as if it had stepped into a pot of paint. Possessive and admiring, Chris steadied it on the other side. Then like a child he suddenly laughed, and dropping to his knees put his arms round it. It was his—no matter what Larson said. Only for him it would never have been born.

As he clasped it, it felt small and frail. He noticed with concern that its sides were clapping together. Fanny swung round to see what was going on and to give the colt a proprietary lick between the ears. He noticed that she, too, was gaunt and shapeless, her ribs showing, her hip-bones high. Before she had just been a mare with foal—a bloated belly that had blocked his vision. But now he saw her as part of the farm community, the essence of its growth and strength, just as he had already learned to see old Ned. As she turned away she brushed her nose amicably on his sleeve, and he felt accepted, that he now was part of the community too.

"We'd better find out if he feels like supper." Larson began gently stroking Fanny's belly, then tried her udder to see if the milk was flowing. "Bring him over—a couple of good meals inside him and he'll be ready to race Minnie."

"You think he's going to be all right? I mean, he looks so small and skinny ..."

"Just wait a week or two—he won't look so skinny. There he goes. Between them, North and Fanny always do a pretty good job."

"You think he'll look like North?"

To Chris he already did. The question was for form's sake. Enthusiastic, he saw the stiff, toy-horse neck tower up and arch imperiously, the rough, scrubby coat take on a rippling sheen. "Maybe not quite the same," Larson said, screwing up his eyes. "There's his white leg for one thing. North's going to sniff when he sees that. But even so, I don't think either of you'll have anything to be ashamed of. I've been raising colts a long time. He'll do."

Then, as they stood a moment longer admiring them, there was a halloo from Sylvia. Ole was on the phone to tell them that young Chris had just died.

25

IT HADN'T OCCURRED TO CHRIS that he would be expected to attend the funeral, but Larson was emphatic—young Chris would have wanted him there. Half a dozen times, Ole said, he had asked when big Chris was coming to visit them, or when he could go back to visit him. And ordinarily he was a shy boy. They had never known him to make friends with a stranger before.

Larson, moreover, decided that it would be safer for Chris to drive, although Chris was inclined to think he was more concerned about style than safety. To find a parking place himself, perhaps on the next street, and then arrive inconspicuously on foot—hurrying stiff-jointedly to keep pace with Sylvia, who in public always seemed trying to give the impression that he didn't belong to her—would not be the same thing at all as to step out of the Cadillac at the church door and leave parking problems to his man. On the road he kept Chris to a prudent thirty-five, then at the outskirts of town said transparently, "It's just about time, so you'd better drop us at the steps. We'll be with the family up in front, and we'll keep a place for you."

Chris saw through him, and was illogically reassured. It made him simply a childish old man, harmless and absurd and human, not insane or sinister. And that, without his knowing it, was what he wanted. (So that he could stay, so that he could ignore Sylvia's warnings of what Larson already suspected, of what he might do if there was another quarrel. Yesterday, while Larson was in town making final arrangements for the funeral, she had pressed hard again, and because, under the spell of her urging, it had seemed that consent was the only alternative to the danger hanging over him, he had lain awake most of the night telling himself that this time he must really go, looking ahead with a feeling of helplessness and foreboding.) As he walked back to the church after parking the car he felt elated and carefree. His relief was so great he wanted to whistle or run. In the car, he had been thinking uncomfortably about walking into church in the old wrinkled raincoat that at the last minute Larson had hunted up for him, less on account of the weather (although that morning there had been rain again) than to conceal the light grey sport jacket which was all he had to wear, and which Larson thought unsuitable; but now he ran up the steps indifferent to the glances of the other late arrivals. It was all he could do not to smile back in friendly greeting. He felt expansive, eager to be on good terms with everybody.

The church was filled, townspeople as well as neighbors. Larson had evidently spoken to one of the ushers: as soon as Chris stepped inside he was led to the second front pew where Larson was keeping a place for him, directly behind Ole and Bell and Mrs. Paynter.

Someone was playing a voluntary on the organ, and there was a heavy, sweet smell of flowers. Ole had his arm over Bell's shoulder; after a moment Chris realized she was sobbing quietly. Then he glanced sidewise and saw that Larson was sitting with his head dropped forward and his shoulders slumped, his hands flat and heavy on his knees. And with a little flash of pity, contrasting this old, exhausted look with his jauntiness as he stepped out of the car, Chris said to himself, "It's his own boy. Coming into the church and seeing the coffin, it's made him remember."

All at once he felt drawn in. His impulse for a moment was to edge closer to Larson. He felt tired and despondent too now, and behind his first impulse was another—the same that already he had had to suppress several times—to turn to him for help, tell him everything, let him take over.

The organ droned on mournfully. Ole kept patting Bell's shoulder with his big, dirt-grained hand. Then the minister came into the pulpit and announced a hymn. When he stood up with the congregation Chris had a better view of the organ. A girl was playing; she turned her head slightly between the verses, and he saw that it was Elsie Grover.

At first he felt only relief that it was unlikely she would see him. But as the sermon began he found himself imagining another meeting, the angry, accusing things she would probably say, and what he would reply. It wasn't his fault. He hadn't dragged her up the hill. Naturally he hadn't meant all he said—at a time like that who ever did—and naturally he had no intention of marrying her. She had no right to expect it. She wasn't his type. She had no looks; she didn't even know how to make up her face. A couple of months and they would hate the sight of each other.

Then the brutality of what he was thinking struck him, and he sat shamed and mortified. That wasn't the way he felt at all. He was sorry. He wished he could do something to make up for it. Before there had always been satisfaction in the thought that a girl would find it hard to forget him, that his successors would suffer by comparison. Often, behind the immediate physical insistence, it had been the motive for conquest, food for his vanity. But now, self-effacingly, almost with a kind of charity, he wished there were some way he could drop from her life quickly and easily, leaving not a single memory.

"Sometimes, dear friends, it is hard to accept the will of God."

For a minute or two he listened. The slow, rhythmic sonorities from the pulpit became coherent.

"Sometimes we rebel, cry out in protest, harden our hearts. If He is really a loving God, why should He snuff out a young life that has scarcely begun? What wrong can a child have done? Why might not one of the sinful and old have been taken in his place?

"Friends, has it ever occurred to you that He may *want* someone innocent and undefiled? That He wearies of our sins? That He looks down on the fragrant, fresh-blown roses in His garden and is saddened that such loveliness should fade and be corrupted by the worm? ... And so today, to those whose hearts are heavy and grieving, I would say that we have only further proof of that great and all-embracing love ..."

Mrs. Paynter's nose was red. She blew it into a very white, stiff handkerchief, and with her head held high, the tight, screwed-up knot of grey hair suggesting the strain with which she maintained her composure, looked fixedly at the flower-heaped coffin.

Something like that was what she had said too—she wanted him to meet his Maker pure.

Seven—after all, why not? Almost competitively, as if they were making a claim for young Chris to which he had no special right, as if in this too he must be unique, Chris began remembering when he was seven. It was a long time ago. He had come a long way. He used to go to church then too, every Sunday morning with his mother. A bigger church, but the same smell: furniture polish and glue, the dry leathery smell of old hymn books. She would let him find the hymn and then they would hold the book together, both pretending he could read. Even later than that—till he was ten or eleven and they moved to Boyle Street. But never afterwards. Once, he remembered, she suggested it, and he had turned and stared at her a moment and said, "You mean they'd want *us* there?"

Seven was easy. He could have met his Maker pure then too, held his own with the best of them. Tired, this fellow was saying—every so often He wanted somebody young and innocent because He got so tired of so much sin. Jesus! Who didn't? If that was what you called it; the jobs you didn't have the guts for, the big-time act you tried to fool yourself with, the people you knew that you wanted to spit on—the only ones you *could* know—the unwantedness, the envy. Jesus! Did they think you planned your life that way? Did they think it was what you wanted?

At that, maybe they did. All along, right up to the last week or so, *he* had thought it was what he wanted. He had had to run away from Boyle Street to realize he had always been afraid of it. Just as he had to sit here listening to Elsie Grover play the organ to realize he was ashamed and sorry.

It wasn't like him. It wasn't the old Chris Rowe. Maybe it didn't pay, taking yourself serious and trying to get a new slant on things. One thing led to another and here's what had happened. Here now he'd knocked the props out and brought it all down around his ears. Everything he was, had taken pride in being.

But somehow it was a good ruin. Watching her across it he began to wonder what she would really say if they ever met again. There was strength there too. Enough, perhaps, not to mind. To take him as he was, to believe in him, to suffer and go on suffering. He hoped so. Leaning forward a little in the pew, his fingers locked, his lips wincing, he kept his eyes fixed on her as if waiting for a sign.

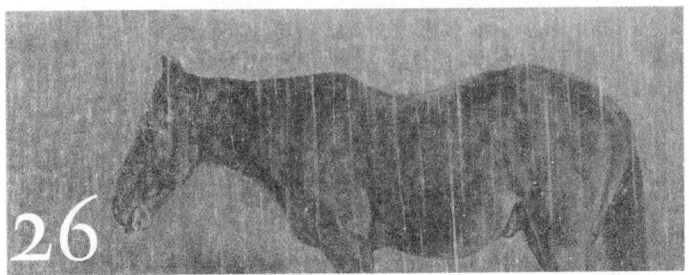

26

A COLD DRIZZLE HAD SET IN, and only six or seven cars followed the hearse to the cemetery. The service at the grave was brief. The minister stood shivering and inaudible, facing the mourners across the grave and speaking into the wind. When they began throwing in the earth Ole and Mrs. Paynter tried to lead Bell back to the car, but thrusting them away she waited dry-eyed and sullen till the grave was filled.

Then, fussily, her grief taking refuge in irritation, she began complaining about the way they had arranged the flowers. They had placed a wreath of white roses at the foot of the grave and she wanted it at the head. Mud was smeared on another wreath. She pointed it out to Ole, and obediently he got down on his knees and cleaned it off with his handkerchief.

The rain was heavier now, but everybody waited patiently. It wasn't until she was satisfied and turned to the car that they noticed Larson had wandered off to the far side of the cemetery. He was on his knees too now, busily clearing away grass and weeds from one of the graves. There were quick, uneasy glances. Leaving Bell to Mrs. Paynter, Ole came back and whispered with Sylvia. She stood irresolute a moment, biting her lips and twisting her handkerchief. Then she said, her voice worried but distinct, "I was afraid something like this would happen. I've seen it coming for the last month. No—you'd better let me try."

She walked awkwardly on her high heels. She had neither coat nor umbrella to protect the new fall suit she was wearing, but instead of hunching her shoulders against the rain, or putting her hand to the bit of white ruffle at her throat, she made her way across the cemetery deliberately, with what seemed caution and anxiety. This was serious, she seemed to be saying. There was no time to worry about such little things as clothes or rain.

She did it perfectly, and thinking how sharp and clear her mind must have been to seize on Larson's behavior as something to be made the most of, turned to advantage, Chris felt the admiration that was Boyle Street's tribute to such control and wiliness. But there was uneasiness too, a kind of premonition. The determined, tottering way she walked along the gravel path—it had something unerring and grim about it, like the gait of a winged bird stalking its prey clumsily on foot. Her mind was made up now. Things were coming to a head.

Three or four feet away from Larson she halted, leaned forward slightly, apparently trying to persuade him to come back to the car, then edged closer and touched him on the shoulder. They saw him straighten stiffly, shake a fistful of weeds at her. She glanced round with a little movement of helplessness as he resumed his tending of the grave, then reached out and touched his shoulder again.

This time, using the weeds as a switch, he began striking at her legs. It was plain he didn't want her to set foot on the grave. Again she looked round, and suddenly Chris set off along the path at a run. The old fool—in front of everybody! If he only knew how he was playing right into her hands.

He motioned her to step back, then seized Larson under the arms and helped him to his feet. Larson looked confused and frightened, but made no resistance. He still held the bunch of dead flowers and weeds in one hand; the other he extended, palm upwards, to feel the rain. For a moment his eyes had a lost, groping look, as if he were regaining consciousness after a blow or fainting spell. Then he turned them on Chris and smiled slyly.

"Come on, you're getting soaked," Chris said, but ignoring him a moment, Larson bent over and slapped at the muddy patches on his knees and drew his trousers out where they were sticking to the skin. Then, with a little shake to each leg as if he had wet his pants, he let Chris take his arm and lead him to the car.

Ole and the others moved aside for him. No one spoke. Larson, like a prisoner taken into custody, kept his eyes lowered until the three of them were in the car and Chris was starting the motor. Then, as they were driving through the gate, he turned with the same sly smile as at the grave and shook the weeds almost in Chris's face. "Fooled you, didn't I?" he said. "You thought I'd forgotten—you thought you were going to get round me. But I know who you are. I'm as smart as you are and maybe then some."

He only meant he knew he was a stranger, Chris told himself as they drove home, someone he had met for the first time a few weeks ago. He had tricked himself into half-believing he was his own son come back; but the funeral and the sight of the coffin had finally brought home to him that his own son was dead and buried. He had half-accepted Chris; now he was swinging round to accuse him of manoeuvring for acceptance, was laughing because he had outwitted him.

That was all. It made sense that way. He couldn't *know* anything; you would never tell a story straight in your sleep, even though you might drop little things. But supposing he had run across an old paper, had heard something in town. He glanced sidewise, feeling the need for verification, and Larson, as if aware of what was on his mind, was waiting with the smile turned on full.

It was only about four o'clock, but the rain and clouds were bringing the night early. There was the time Larson ran at him with the pitchfork, and there was the paint he kept hidden in the loft under the sheaves. Staring at the road again through the wiper, he told himself that Sylvia was right—anybody that far gone didn't have much to lose. Old and mean and crazy, everything he had was just being wasted. She was right, too, when she said it wouldn't take much to make him turn. The pitchfork had been one warning. The way he had smiled just now was another.

But when they reached home he wondered if he had been imagining it all, if his eyes had deceived him. The lost look was back on Larson's face as he stepped out of the car. He didn't seem to recognize his own buildings. He stared a moment at the weeds he was still holding, then slid them guiltily down the back of his leg. He looked like a man who hadn't so much as smiled a sad or timid smile, much less a sly one, for the last twenty years.

And before he quite realized what he was doing, Chris was at his side and helping him up the back steps. Perhaps it was because at the sight of his helplessness he felt a kind of remorse for the thoughts that had been running through his mind, for his own hostility that had gathered in retaliation; perhaps because, at a level beneath that of actual circumstance, his peace of mind and sense of well-being depended on the old man's good will. It was a kind of paradox: his need for strength—strength to lean on, to sustain that part of him which was orphaned and immature—revealed itself in a display of strength. Ignoring Sylvia he helped him upstairs and out of his wet clothes. He seemed all at once to realize that in order to believe in and count on him he must first restore him, fit him to play the role he wanted him to play.

Larson, for his part, was passive. He stood in apathetic silence while Chris undressed and rubbed him down, except occasionally to turn his head and watch Chris, furtively anxious, as if puzzled and embarrassed at not being able to place him. Chris in turn kept trying to catch his eyes off guard for signs of the hatred and distrust that had unnerved him in the cemetery. And finding none, he felt reassured, elated, just as he had while walking back to the church after parking the car. "Don't worry about the barn. I'll see to everything," he said to Larson when he had him in bed. "It's settling down for a wet night. You'd better stay out of it or you'll be stiffened up worse than ever."

Then he slipped Larson's suit on a hanger so that it would dry in shape, smoothed out some of the wrinkles in his trousers and laid them across the back of a chair. He liked it this way. It was the first time he had ever tried looking after someone, and it gave him a feeling of contentment and importance. Then, with the instinct of a tenement dweller, he turned to the window and drew the blind—there was not another window that could have looked in on them within at least a mile—and stood listening to the soft steady murmur of the rain. With the dark and wet shut out, the room looked sane and peaceful. Alone with the old man, doing little things for him, he felt safe, free to relax. As he put his shoes away it came to him that now Sylvia was the one in the way. Mentally eliminating her, he thought what a good winter he and Larson could have alone.

At that moment Sylvia arrived, hurrying in with a stiff hot drink and the phial of sleeping-pills. There was an unnatural, effusive kindliness about her. "That's right, a good sleep is just what you need," she said, setting the glass on the little table beside the bed and raising Larson's head to slap up the pillows. "It's been a hard day for you—now you've got to forget everything. Drink this down fast while it's hot. You won't know a thing till morning."

There was a kind of captive obedience about the way he took the pills without looking at her, then sucked at his cheeks to work up enough saliva to swallow them. Chris held up the glass of whisky for him, but it was too hot. Larson put his lips to the rim, then, with a slight nod towards the table, handed it back.

"All right, we'll leave you now," Sylvia said briskly, "but mind you don't forget it. I want you to get it down while it's hot so you'll have a good sweat. Chris is going to look in again in a few minutes to make sure."

Turning away, Chris caught his eyes for a moment, and they seemed beady and contracted with hate again. The smile, the voice, the way she had felt his forehead—he couldn't have missed it. Outside on the landing Sylvia motioned him to follow her downstairs, but instead he went to his own room to change back into his work clothes. A few minutes later when he looked in again on Larson he found him asleep and the glass beside him untouched. He shook him awake, helped him to sit up and held the glass to his lips. Larson drank meekly, only half-opening his eyes, and then, mumbling a little about the horses, sank back on the pillow.

Chris put out the light and went downstairs. Sylvia was waiting for him nervously. "Is he asleep yet?" she asked, wheeling away from the stove where she had been standing with her hands out to the heat. "I'm soaked—I've got to get into something dry—but I don't want to talk to him. I can't stand his eyes."

Her hat was on the table. She picked it up, examined it to see how much damage it had suffered in the rain, then dropped it and turned back to Chris. "We've got to hurry. It's our chance—we'll never be so lucky again."

"What do you mean, lucky?" He wanted to delay the actual moment of decision, whether to take a stand with or against her. "I had to wake him for his drink. He'll be asleep again by the time you're up there."

"In front of everybody today—that's what I mean we're lucky." She turned to the stove, in the same instant swung back and seized his arm. "Now they'll all know he's crazy, for sure. It's going to spread fast. The way he hung on to that bunch of thistles—nothing's going to surprise them. It'll be a big disappointment if he doesn't do something."

Her eyes were fixed on him, sunken and powerful. He wavered a moment, then laughed and shrugged. "You mean you're still fooling round with that idea of putting him down the well? Why don't you get smart? Like I keep telling you—take a trip yourself, play it safe and have your fun both."

"It'll be so simple. They find the truck at the station—there's only one thing it can mean. Everybody's going to go round looking wise and saying, 'What did I tell you?' But it's got to be now, Chris. Now—while they're all talking, ready to believe anything."

"You don't know what it would be like, right up against it. The trouble with you, you keep doing it in your mind."

"I've had five years of him—I know what *that's* been like."

"You're thinking about afterwards—I'm thinking about the job. What's riskier still, you're counting on me, and I'm not so sure I've got the nerve for it."

"It's not going to take much. Two minutes and it'll be over. All over. He'll never know a thing."

"Once you start something like that you can't leave it half done. You can't give it to him once and say 'This isn't going to be so much fun after all. I'll leave it a couple of weeks and try again.'"

"Once'll be enough."

"That's what they all say. They're going to be smart about it—keep cool and do it neat and fast. But a lot of times you read where they make a mess of it."

"It's coming, anyway—one of these days he's going to say something. I'll never get through another winter with him. You can stand just so much and then you don't care. So I figure it's better to do it sensible, so things'll work out the way we want them."

"And your little scheme—you call that sensible? Jesus! Even supposing I get the truck to town without anybody seeing me—you think they're not going to wonder how he's disappeared so fast? They'll get a search going. It'll be in the papers—they'll send out his description ..."

"I can stall a week before the hunt's really on. So when they don't find him a lot can have happened. I'll say he was talking a while ago about a trip to California, on account of his rheumatism and the winter coming on. I didn't pay much attention because he's always on about trips and trains, but the notion might just have hit him. Off having a little fling—I figure that's more likely. But don't worry, he'll be back all right. Just like you say, he couldn't stay away from his horses. And the time's going on; a month, and it's an old story."

"Better try California yourself." He stood rigid, setting himself against her, body and mind both. "Tell him the winters are too cold—you think you're coming down with something..."

"It's you, Chris—ever since you've been here. I can't go on. I can't keep it from him any longer."

"That's all right. I could stand a winter in California too."

"Not that way—even if you meant it." She pressed against him, seized one of his hands again. "Just think—we'll have everything, a good living for the rest of our lives. Or later on we can sell—fifty thousand easy, maybe seventy-five. Besides what he's got in the bank, or stacked away in bonds. A couple of minutes, Chris, and it's all over."

"Maybe you're right—maybe tomorrow." His voice sounded thin and papery. His knees began to tremble.

"He's up there now. He'll never even know."

"I've got to think first. Maybe tomorrow."

He stood motionless a moment, staring back into her eyes, then turned abruptly and went out. It was worth thinking about. It was a better prospect than catching another freight and starting out again to look for Rickie. She was thirty. He could have it all pretty well on his own terms. His farm, his money—all for two minutes' work.

But such dirty work. He was starting to let his mind jump too. And just as he had told her, his nerve wasn't up to it. He'd been through it once. He knew what happened to a man's face, what happened to your own insides. He didn't have the guts—not the right guts, not killer guts. He was soft. All along he'd just been putting up a front. Playing with the colt like a little kid—that was his real size.

He would have been ashamed to admit it on Boyle Street, but from here he could look back and see Boyle Street guts for what they were. It wasn't being soft that was his trouble now; it was having to start in again to play tough and hard. It was having to catch another freight, put on another act for Rickie, just when he was ready to be himself and settle down.

But she gave him no choice. Something about her voice, the glassy cold look in her eyes—all along he had sensed her determination; now he was convinced of it. Not only to do away with Larson, but to draw in and possess himself as well. The one was as implacable as the other. Just as she had said, he was her last chance.

So in the morning, as soon as Larson was up and around, he would ask him for his wages. It struck him that he owed it to Larson to stay—a vague feeling of responsibility, that he ought to protect, at least warn, him. But he shut his mind to it. It was their affair; he couldn't afford to get involved. She was smart and smooth. If he told Larson she would turn it back on him. Larson mightn't believe her, but again he might. In any case, she would say who's he to talk? What's he doing here? Who's Baxter?

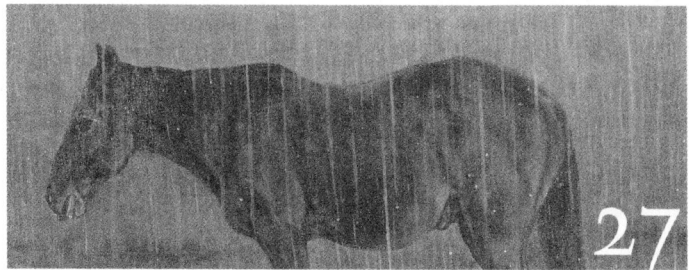

27

THE NEXT DAY LARSON SLEPT till nearly noon. It was two o'clock before Chris had a chance to be alone with him and tell him he had made up his mind to leave. Just for an instant a look of protest, almost dismay, spread over his face; then, squaring himself independently, he brought a grubby little notebook out of his pocket and said, "I thought you'd be going. I've been checking up on your days to see what's coming to you."

"But I didn't know myself. I only made up my mind last night." Chris hadn't expected him to be so unconcerned, and the perplexity in his voice had an edge of disappointment. "Maybe it was the funeral started me thinking about home."

Larson spat, then smiled again, the same smile, sly, with just a trace of malevolence, as yesterday in the cemetery. "I figured you'd about had enough. I'm going to town now and I'll see if I can find somebody."

"I know it's not much notice, after giving you to understand I'd stay the winter ..."

Larson turned and peered at him a moment, and then, as if still willing to be reconciled, dropped his eyes and stood toeing the dust. But Sylvia was watching. At that moment Chris glanced up and saw her at the kitchen window, and hardening in his determination to leave, his anxiety upon him again, he said curtly, "I can't wait till you find somebody. If you're going to town I want to go too."

Without answering, Larson turned and limped off towards the garage. Chris followed at a few paces, troubled again by the old stooped shoulders, searching for something to say that might make amends. But inside, fumbling for his keys, Larson looked round and smiled. "Nice car—suits you," he said. "You look right at home behind the wheel. Too bad I'm not going to hand it over to you."

Chris was silent a second, hurt and stung. Then, pushing up to Larson, he said threateningly, "Who's asking you? Just hand over my pay. I won't be around long to bother you."

"When I'm ready." Larson's mouth set. "You're not getting away that easy."

"I'm going today—and I want what's coming to me."

"What's your hurry all at once? What are you scared of?"

"I'm not scared. I just want my pay." An alarm went off. His voice was quick and rough. As Larson unlocked the car he seized the door, ready to push in and take his place beside him. "There'll be no trouble—unless you ask for it."

But now Sylvia joined them. "Wait! If you're going to town there are some things I want." She was breathless from running; the words came wheezily. Suspecting a quarrel, apparently, or that Chris was planning to leave, she had hurried out to interrupt. "Soap and apples—and we're getting low in coffee."

Chris swung round and faced her guiltily. In the same instant Larson slipped inside the car and pulled the door shut. When he heard the click, heedless for the moment of Sylvia, Chris tried the handle and then began rapping on the window. But he was locked out. Without deigning a glance at either of them, his face stony, Larson backed out of the garage and drove away.

"What was that all about?" The wind was cold; as she spoke, hunching her shoulders and crossing her arms, she started back towards the house. "If you want to go to town for something why don't you take the truck yourself?"

"I don't know what went wrong. He says he's been checking up to see how much I've got coming to me." When they reached the house he remained at the foot of the steps. He felt at a disadvantage looking up at her, but lacked the courage to go farther. "It was that look on his face—like I'd been trying to pull a fast one and he'd got wise to me. I got sore and said I was ready to go right now. But you saw for yourself. Even if he's got to go to town for my pay he could have taken me along with him, now that he's in such a hurry to get rid of me."

"He's always got a roll on him—plenty for you." She watched him shrewdly, but there was no hint of accusation in her voice. "It must be something else. What got him started?"

"He said he'd figured I'd had about enough anyway. No reason at all—just like yesterday. And then he started on about the car—didn't I wish he'd hand it over to me?"

Still there was nothing in her expression to suggest she realized he had been planning to run out on her. With a shrug he went on, his voice a little more confident, "Ever since the funeral, all at once he seems to think I'm trying to get away with something, pass myself off as the boy."

She nodded thoughtfully, looking past him. "We shouldn't have let him get away. When he gets to town if he's really through with you he'll maybe start talking. There'll be nothing to hold him. As soon as he comes back I'll try and get round him—find out if I can what he does this afternoon."

The last words were hurried, a dismissal, as if she had just thought of something she had to do and wanted to get rid of him. Before he could speak again she went inside and quietly closed the door. For a moment he had an impulse to follow and make her tell him what she knew; the shrewd, fast-thinking look in her eyes and the careful quietness with which she had closed the door made him certain that she did know something, either that or had a plan. Then, with a feeling of exposure again, and that she might be watching from the window, he set off at a quick walk for the barn.

There wasn't a great deal to do. He paced up and down between the stalls and worried. Minnie pawed and whinnied each time he passed, but it was too cold to take her out. The colt depressed him. It was no longer his, he could no longer take pride or satisfaction in it. Every few minutes he went to the door and looked nervously up the road. He didn't know what he was afraid of, but he felt trapped, plotted against, nowhere to turn. He kept going over what Larson had said, trying to account for the change in his attitude, the sudden, sly bitterness; wondering if it was because Sylvia, in an effort to bring things to a head, had dropped a hint of what was going on between them. The pup came in and for a while he squatted beside it, his face buried in its coat.

When at last the night began to close in he set to work at his chores. It was almost dark by the time he finished, but still he hadn't put on the lights. Then he crouched in an empty stall with the pup at his feet and waited. He was incapable now of thought or decision. He had yielded to his fear, let it possess him. The truck was there. If he was really afraid, there was nothing to stop him going to town and catching the next train. But he kept thinking of his wages—a hundred and fifty dollars or better, he wasn't sure. The winter was ahead; already he was shivering in his shirt and overalls.

It was about six o'clock when at last he heard the car. He went out and stood beside the barn and watched Larson drive into the garage, then cross the strip of light from the kitchen window and disappear into the house. No one was with him. At the sight of his hunched, familiar figure he somehow felt more sure of himself. It was the Larson he knew; he would be able to handle him. Sheltering at the corner of the barn out of the wind he lit a cigarette, then tossed it away and approached the house whistling. It would be better to put on a front. Stand up to Larson—he would be more likely to pay him his wages and let him go. Stand up to her too—once and for all let her see he had decided.

When he entered the kitchen Larson was washing his hands at the sink. The table was set, and Sylvia was moving back and forth from the stove to the pantry. Neither of them looked at him. When he had dried his hands, Larson sat down at the table with a livestock paper that had come in the mail.

A pan of meat was frying on the stove, the kettle was singing, yet there seemed to be no progress in the preparation of the meal. Chris, too, washed and dried his hands; Sylvia was still moving in and out of the pantry. His nerves were already frayed and twitching. Now the silence began to wear on them. It was like a conspiracy. It gave him a feeling of helplessness and exclusion. Suddenly he wheeled on Larson; his voice shot up harsh and loud. "What about my pay? You've been to town and you say you've got it all figured out. What are you stalling for?"

Larson creased back his paper, and for a moment pretended to go on reading. Then, without looking up, he said quietly, "You don't need to worry—you'll get your check for every cent that's coming to you, just as soon as I find somebody else."

"Look at me when you're talking to me." Conscious of Sylvia watching him—more, perhaps, to give the lie to the accusation of timidity and weakness that her attitude lately had implied than to impose himself on Larson—he reached out and snatched away the paper. "And a check's no good. There's a train sometime tonight—I want cash, so I can catch it."

"I told you—you'll get your pay when I get another man." Larson seized the paper and tugged at it ineffectually a moment, then struck the table with his fist. "You can't walk off a job any time you feel like it. I looked round town today, but there's nobody. Harvest's over, they're all leaving. And my rheumatism's bad, and there's a lot of work to be done before freeze-up ..."

His voice trailed off plaintively. It struck Chris that he didn't want him to go. Whatever the suspicions that had seized him yesterday in the cemetery and again this afternoon, they were subsiding, leaving him ashamed. Now he was simply trying to save face.

"So you not going till I say. The law's on my side. Start something and I'll start something too." Then with a slight movement of his hand, he indicated Chris's place at the table. "All this crazy talk—sit down and eat your supper."

But now Sylvia intervened. "What's he done?" she began angrily, stalking across the kitchen and taking her place beside Chris. Their arms touched. It seemed that with the pressure of her elbow she was trying to make some sign to him. "What are you chasing him away for? Every day you get crazier. Yesterday in the cemetery even—in front of everybody ..."

"Nobody's chasing him." Larson crouched back in his chair. His face went stubborn and hostile again. "He's been after easy pickings—you yourself said so. But he knows now he's not getting any, so he's through. I'm not chasing him; he came himself asking for his wages."

"Sure you are—you think I don't see through?" Her voice was choked and rasping. Chris felt the pressure of her elbow again. "And if he goes I go too. I'm not staying alone with you. Not another winter. Not for ten thousand a year."

The stubbornness in Larson's face gave way to bewilderment. "But what's it to you if he stays or not? You've been saying all along you didn't trust him—you've been after me to get rid of him."

"Never mind what I've been saying all along. Now I say he's got to stay. You've been having things your own way long enough. Now it's my turn."

"Sure he can stay. It's what I've been trying to talk him into, ever since he came." His eyes blinked off the implication of what she had just said as if it were a fly trying to settle. "But you were the one—just yesterday, when we were getting ready to go to the funeral. You said you didn't like the way he kept looking at you."

"Just looking for trouble, making up things!" Her words now were simply for the sake of sound, to drown him out. "Ever since the day you went at him with the pitchfork—I've been watching. Now it's the car, saying he's trying to get it away from you—like nobody but you ever had a car."

Her face was convulsed. Chris touched her arm restrainingly, but she shook him off. "Telling me he's hiding out here—on the run. How do you know? What's it to you anyway? Just lies and lies, because you're scared!"

"No, Sylvia." He half-rose from his chair, then slumped back heavily. "It was you kept saying he must have done something and was lying low. I said if he had then this was just the place for him."

"Scared on account of me—that's why you're trying to get rid of him. Scared I'll look at him and see the difference ..."

"Shut up, Sylvia! You don't know what you're saying!"

Chris tried to push her away, but she pressed against him and shouted over his shoulder. Her eyes had a hot, bulging glare. Frothy spittle was gathering at the corners of her mouth. She had probably begun deliberately, to hurry things, but now her rage was running wild and reckless on its own momentum. "I *have* looked. That's why he's got to stay. Because I want him—you hear me? Because I want him. It's been going on now for weeks now—for weeks!"

Chris stood numb and helpless. Somehow it was inevitable, what he had been waiting for. He felt a sick, strangling fear, and he also felt a kind of relief—an exhaustion, a willingness.

"You look at him too, so maybe you'll see *why* I want him." She thrust Chris aside, bending forward again to spit the words into Larson's face. "Why I'll never let you start in again—never let you put your dirty old hands on me."

"No, Chris, not you ..."

Their eyes met, and for a moment Chris thought he was going to cry. His face collapsed, as if he were sucking in his cheeks. He put up his hand beseechingly, then let it fall back heavy on his thigh.

"Sometimes I wondered if you were, but I always made myself stop. I'd say to myself quick, 'It's just because you're getting old—everybody you see you're jealous.' One night I had a feeling in the morning that I'd been asking her for something and she wasn't there. But I didn't know for sure. I figured it had just been a dream. And yesterday at church when we were coming out—I saw her give you a look. And then at the grave with Cora and the boy I was ashamed of myself for trying to make you do. You weren't right, and I knew you never would be. But still I kept fighting it. Right up till now I've been fighting it. Because I want somebody real—because pretending's no good ... I get so tired ..."

There was a second or two of silence, the kettle singing and the meat frying. Then swiftly the stricken look gave way to an old man's fury. "Whore!" he shouted. "Filthy whore! And you—taking you in like I did—trusting you!" There were no words for Chris, he could only shake his fists. "Trusting you—even giving you my clothes!"

"What are you going to do about it?" She was quiet and hard again. Her rage had subsided to a sneer. "Why don't you phone Ole? He'll believe you. Nothing would suit him better than to see us both go. Tell him what we were talking about the other night, that maybe Chris shot this man Baxter and the police are after him."

"I will—I'll tell him everything. You think I'm too ashamed, but just watch me."

Heaving himself to his feet, he lurched past them to the telephone. Then, unhooking the receiver and clutching it as if it were something intended to fight with, he glared back hunched and wild-eyed. "They can laugh—I'll tell everybody. It's nothing to be ashamed of—not when your wife's what you are."

"Quick, Chris—now!" As she spoke she nudged him, slipped something into his hand. "Quick—he's starting to ring—before they take down the receiver and hear anything ..."

He drew back from her, looking down dazedly. A gun—that was right. He remembered now, she had told him there was one, had said it would be the easiest. She had brought it with her from the pantry or the stove. All the time she must have been holding it at her side, hidden against her skirt. It felt suddenly familiar in his grasp. His fingers closed on it as on something of his own that had been lost. A glow of power spread through him like the glow from a drink.

"He's ringing. Quick, Chris, *now*, you fool—before they answer!"

"I'll show you who's running things." Larson had finished ringing. With the receiver to his ear he turned and faced them again. "Taking you in and making things easy for you, like you belonged here—letting you ride Minnie. Just wait till Ole gets here—he'll handle you. He's never had any use for you, right from the first ..."

And then he saw the gun. His eyes had been blazing; all at once they went glazed and cold. His jaw dropped and he crouched back against the wall. Without turning round he felt carefully for the hook and hung up the receiver.

So now Chris had to. Larson had seen him, so he had to. It was suddenly as necessary to extinguish the look of stunned fear in his eyes before it spread to judgement and accusation, a sense of final betrayal, as it would be to tear down and stamp on a burning curtain before it set the house on fire. His fingers tightened on the gun. There was a lap of heat across his eyes ...

"Give it to him—now! Don't just stand there!"

But her voice, even as a twitch of obedience ran along his nerves, jarred him back to reality. Its spit and scream cleared his eyes as a solvent clears a glass. He saw Larson again, old and hunched, blanched with terror, and in the same instant, with a spasm of revulsion, he dropped the gun and kicked it under the table.

She stood rigid a moment, seeming to swell and rock a little, then with a curse dove past him. She was crouched on one knee, clutching the barrel, when he reached her. Something like relief swept over him—it was the way a little girl would take hold of a gun, she didn't know what it was for. And then as he bent towards her she swung viciously and caught him with the butt on the shin.

He gulped with pain, hobbled backwards a few steps. For a blurred second or two he felt sick and drained. The room reeled, went out like the reflections in a shivered glass. Then there was a little croak of protest from Larson. "Don't, Sylvia, don't—I'll go away, anything you want ..." Suddenly alert again to what was happening, he saw her raise the gun and aim.

She fired as he sprang. He caught her wrist and the second bullet struck high above the telephone.

Larson went down slowly, his hands to his belly, his mouth working sidewise as if his teeth were entangled in a piece of candy. Chris stood numb a moment, cold and hollow. It was as if *he* had done it—done it again; as if some secret part of him had actually yielded, dazing him a moment with the lightning of its spring so that he could not yet see he had turned and foiled it. And then, as the realization burst upon him that he was not the one, he stared at Larson a moment without even seeing him, dazed a second time by the lightning of release. He was free—there was room for nothing else. He had been living under a spell—of what he was, always had been, always must be, a doom of Boyle Street cheapness and frustration—and now the spell was broken. He had not obeyed. Even with the gun in his hand, he had not done it. On the floor a pool of blood was gathering again, but this time there was no need to run—no need to find someone and explain that he hadn't meant to do it, that it had been an accident.

But only a moment and then it was Larson's blood, and Larson, still with his hands to his belly, was crumpled moaning in it—slowly, with a grimace, was turning over on his back. He knelt beside him, shook his shoulder, and then, at the sight of the sucked-in lips, looked up at Sylvia. "You'd better phone—I think he's hit bad." Involuntarily he trusted to her competence again, forgetting for the moment that she was the one who had done it. "Maybe there's still time if we get a doctor."

There was such hatred in her face that he thought she might shoot him too. But even as he leaned back, steeling himself, she shrugged and put the gun on the table. "I got him all right—it'll take more than a doctor. Watch out, or you're going to get it on your overalls."

"Phone, Sylvia! It'll be all right! You were just fooling—you didn't know the gun was loaded."

"Hold it a minute. I've got something for you." She stepped over Larson's legs into the pantry and came out with a glass half-filled with Scotch. "I knew you'd crack so I had it ready. Go on—maybe it'll take that sick look off your face."

Still on his knees beside Larson, he drank obediently. "Don't worry—everything's going to be all right." She bent slightly and gripped his shoulder. "It's going to be just like we planned it. We'll carry on from here. All you got to do is keep your head and do what I tell you."

She took the glass and began to crowd him. "But you've got to pull yourself together—look at the way your hand's shaking. We've got to get rid of him, and you've still got to drive to town."

"No—you're the one that did it." He drew back and half-shut his eyes, as if expecting her to strike him. For a moment there was an impulse to run. "I'm not helping you to get rid of him. I'm not driving the truck to town."

She stepped back a little the better to meet his eyes. "Who says I'm the one? Who's going to know? Your word against mine—no witnesses."

"*He* knows." He looked down at Larson and touched his arm. "I threw the gun away—I tried to stop you. And he saw me."

"Look at him—a couple of minutes and it's not going to make any difference what he saw."

"But I didn't." His voice was taking on a panic-edge. His hands were clenched at breast level. "You tried to trick me into it, but I didn't."

"There's no time, Chris. If we don't get rid of him fast it's going to mean the police. Your word against mine—which one are they going to believe?"

"No, I won't go through with it. Nothing'll make me." For a moment he had been free; all at once life had opened before him, clear to the skyline; and he clung hard to the memory. "I tell you I won't—it's nothing to do with me."

"Stop the funny talk—you've got no choice. I'm telling you, it's going to be just like we planned. First we get rid of him, then you drive to town."

He faltered, dropped his eyes. His knee was in blood now, and roughly, in desperation, he began shaking Larson's shoulder again. Larson hitched his body a little. His lips worked a time or two, as if there was still something sticky in his teeth. Then he whispered, his voice so faint Chris had to bend to hear him, "I heard her and she's right. It's her word against yours. They'll never believe you."

"But you can tell somebody—tell Ole. I'll phone him to come over right now ..."

It was as if instinct rather than senses warned him: even as he spoke he leaped to his feet, reached the gun only a second or two ahead of her. "That's right—I'm going to phone Ole." With defiance his sense of freedom returned. He squared himself. The words came with a little smack. "I can use a gun too if I have to. So don't try anything before he gets here."

They faced each other a moment, the meat still frying, the kettle singing. Then, at a whisper from Larson to come closer, still keeping her covered, Chris took a few steps backwards towards him and squatted again at his shoulder.

"It's no good phoning. I can't hang on that long." He was breathing now in wheezy gasps. With one hand he groped along the floor as if feeling for something on which to brace himself. "There's a pencil in my pocket. And you'll find paper on the shelf by the window under the catalogue." His voice faded, but pinching his lips he raised himself again. "Maybe if I write something it'll help—so you can show them. Watch her. Try and not let on what you're doing."

With the whole side of his face he winked, a slow, contorted movement as if something were in his eye, then put his hands on his belly and lay back flat again. Chris glanced at the shelf as he straightened, trying to estimate the distance without appearing to plan a move. But Sylvia wasn't watching. Intent upon the telephone, afraid he might still try to use it, she made a little detour towards the sink, then slipped past him into the pantry. By the time she reappeared, a knife in her hand, he had reached the shelf and found the paper. She brought her head up with a start at seeing he had moved from Larson, but gave no sign of even noticing the writing pad. Instead, taking her stand defensively beside the telephone, she held the knife to the cord. "Just try phoning Ole and see how far you'll get," she warned him, voice and jowl thick as she drew her chin down tight against her breast. "We're going to do it my way. You might as well make up your mind."

It was a small, thin-bladed kitchen knife. He didn't for a moment doubt she would use it, either on himself or Larson, with as little hesitation as she had fired the gun. Larson would have to be propped up and supported before he could write; to kneel beside him would be to expose his back to her. Besides, there was the gun. It took one hand, and he couldn't risk laying it down.

Deliberately, though, in the hope of throwing her off her guard, he set it back on the table and then, with a shrug of helplessness and defeat, stood looking down at Larson. The telephone was seven or eight feet away. He stepped over Larson, back again. The manoeuvre cut the distance by nearly two feet and brought him to a position where he faced her. The writing pad, as if accidentally, slipped from his hand. He bent to pick it up, steadied himself and the next moment, counting on the surprise, sprang and caught her wrist a second time.

The knife clattered to the floor. She struggled a moment, kicking his shins, clawing with her free hand at his face, till with a wrench he brought her to her knees. "Out you go now." Easing his grip just enough to let her regain her feet, he propelled her, still doubled over, to the door. "You can come in again when we're finished. But maybe it would be smarter if you kept going."

He thrust her out, slammed the door shut and locked it. For a minute he stood braced against it, not trusting the lock against her pounding. Then, with a faint feeling of satisfaction at having disposed of her with such speed and ease, he propped a chair under the knob and returned to Larson.

There wasn't much time. His face was ashy, his mouth a lipless slit. When Chris tried to lift him to a sitting position, supporting him against his knee, he only groaned and pressed his hand against his belly. The sound froze Chris. His concern vanished before an awareness of his own predicament, of where he stood if Larson didn't clear him. "Try—you've got to do it." His voice quaked, went sharp and desperate as the pounding on the door began again. "Just a little—here's the pencil. I'll steady you ..."

There was another groan, another slow contortion of the stiffening lips. Staring at them, Chris read rather than heard the word "Water."

But instead, he brought Scotch. "You've got to try—this'll bring you round." In the pantry, at the sight of the bottle, his hope had flared wildly. Now, as he held the glass against Larson's clenched teeth, there was a tortured moment of suspense, almost anger. "Swallow—it'll be good for you. Don't fight it—swallow!"

A few drops spilled over Larson's mouth and down his chin. He licked his lips, seemed to hesitate, not quite sure of the taste, then with a whistling sound, like a child trying something hot, began sucking at the glass.

In his eagerness, Chris tipped it too far. Larson gagged at the harshness of the liquor, slobbered and turned his head. But a little flush spread over his face. His breathing grew steadier. And then, almost greedily, he turned his head back to the glass and took two or three swallows.

"I'll try now." His eyes were clear, his voice firm. "Keep holding me just like that and I'll try and bring up my knee. Take one hand if you can and steady the paper."

For Chris it was still torture. Larson put the words down letter by letter, as if he were a child just learning to write. The pencil slipped, jerked back, made a long meaningless scrawl, started carefully again. Chris had to bite his lips to keep from shouting at him to hurry. His own hand was so shaky he could scarcely hold the pad. The sweat was trickling from his armpits.

"*Chris didn't do it, it was Sylvia,*" Larson wrote. "*He kicked the gun away and tried to stop her but she was too quick for him.*"

"That's enough—sign it." The pounding on the door had stopped. Now he was afraid she might be making her way in through the basement or a window. "Don't try any more—just sign it."

Larson slumped back and let the pencil fall. "But it's no good like that—you've got to sign it too." Chris thrust the pencil back in his hand, tried to tighten his fingers round it. "Try—you've *got* to—or they'll believe *her*."

"It's all right, I'm just resting." Chris held up the glass and he took another mouthful. Then, gripping the pencil, he felt blindly for the pad. "No sense signing till I finish. You just show me where to start again."

Chris took his hand and set it back on the paper. "Anywhere—but don't take long. Better if you signed it just as it is."

With the same slow, letter-by-letter care, Larson continued, "*Everything is to go to Chris except what Ole's farming already. He's to keep that. But Chris is to paint the old house. Like Cora wanted, white with green trim.*"

"Sure, I'll paint it—sure I will—but now you've got to sign." His voice was desperate again. As Larson slipped back he shook him roughly. "Quick, try hard!—right where the pencil is ..."

"I'm just resting, so I can sign it right. It'll be no good if they think maybe you did it yourself."

Chris held up the Scotch again but he shook his head. His mouth puckered and set; he closed one eye and squinted at the paper as if he were sighting along a rifle. Then, firmly, all in a breath it seemed, he signed and made a satisfied little clucking sound with his tongue. "There—they'll know now. That'll stand up anywhere—just as good as I do on checks."

As he leaned back there was another thud on the door. "Fooled her!" There was triumph in his voice; his eyes shone bright with malice. "Let her in so I can tell her, so I can watch. But see she doesn't get round you again. She's smart, Chris—all kinds of tricks. No matter what she says, go straight to Ole."

The words ended in a wet, gurgling sound. The pencil slipped from his fingers again and rolled across the floor. There was a little spasm, a sudden rigidity.

Careful not to look at his face, Chris eased him back flat on the floor, then tore off the sheet of paper and folded it away in the watch pocket of his overalls. As yet there was no sense of loss, no anger. The margin had been too narrow; his response to the feel of the gun in his hand had been too prompt, too willing. Nothing was alive within him but relief. Nothing mattered but survival and escape. The hammering began again, and seizing the gun he spun round as if guilty, afraid of being caught. His throat tightened at the thought of facing her. Already she seemed to loom over him, to press in and dominate the room. His knees were shaking as he opened the door. The gun in his hand felt dead and heavy.

But she walked in sniffing, and without so much as a glance at Larson, walked straight to the stove. "Couldn't you smell it?" Seizing a towel she jerked the pan of charred meat off the fire. Her face showed nothing but a housewife's irritation. "Lucky there was plenty of water in the kettle."

It wasn't what he expected. Her calm reminded him of Larson's warning, suggested reserves of guile. She glanced at the gun and he felt foolish covering her. He slipped it into his pocket quickly, and then, folding his arms, tried to put on a front of unconcern.

"I was watching you for a minute through the window." She kept busy at the stove, her back to him again, and spoke quietly. "Whatever it was he wrote for you, do you really think it'll do you any good?"

"It can't do me any harm. He signed it."

"And the shape he was in—you think they're going to *believe* he signed it?"

"There's a chance they will. Even if it is shaky—they've got special men that can tell."

"Naturally he cleared *you*—put it all on me?"

"Just what he saw."

She glanced at him obliquely, then laughed. "The way you say that and the look on your face he must have left you everything too."

Involuntarily he nodded. She put her hands on her hips and laughed again. "A nice night's work, Chris. Sitting pretty, aren't you? Right from the start I knew you were soft, but I didn't think you were a fool too."

"Sure I'm sitting pretty." Her contempt stung; he met it with a smile, retaliatory and thin. "It's a good farm—just watch me. Just see if I don't make a good farmer too."

"Maybe you will at that. He said you had a way with horses."

It was almost like defeat—the sagging shoulders as she stared down at the body, the hand to her eyes as if to brush the sight of it away—and for a moment he felt safer. Safe enough to let the meaning of what Larson had written sink in, to wonder a little at his trust and acceptance, to hold up the thought of possession, inheritance.

"But it'll never do you any good, Chris." She scarcely moved—a slight tilt to her head, a narrowing of her eyes—but her voice sent a shiver across his skin. "My way's better. Even supposing they do believe that piece of paper, still they'll want to know who you are. Just like I said, they'll start checking. You'll have to come clean."

Because he had relaxed a moment, dropped his guard, he was vulnerable. There was no time to look away or draw a screen. She caught his eyes, held them relentlessly. "You're on the run—you've done a job somewhere. Do you want to go back and face it? Life, maybe—or the rope?"

"*You* say I'm on the run." He tried to throw it out lightly, with a laugh, but his lips were numb. "Go ahead—if it makes you feel better ..."

"That's what you said to me a while ago, remember? What good's the farm going to do you if they give you life?"

For a moment he maintained his front of defiance, erect, lips drawn and smiling, then backed away and gripped the edge of the table. She was right. She held all the cards. Either get rid of Larson her way, or start answering questions—try explaining to *them* that right up to the last minute he hadn't intended to put bullets in the gun.

"It'll work out all right, you'll see—for both of us." Pressing her advantage quietly, she gripped his arm. "But we're wasting too much time with all this talk. You'd better get the horse now—a quiet one, that'll stand."

He stared at her a moment, an appalled, sick look in his eyes, then nodded. "But there's the truck—wouldn't it be easier?" Now it was the thought of hanging the body across the horse, head and arms dangling, that made him shrink. "And faster?"

"Even if we didn't put the lights on somebody might hear us. Somebody riding or walking that we didn't know was there. They'd say what's the truck doing parked in front of the old place at this time of night. And the same night him to disappear."

Still he hesitated. She waved him angrily to the door. "Don't waste time arguing. I've got it all planned—we can't start changing now. A quiet one—that'll stand."

Her eyes held him a moment, then he obeyed at a run. Just to do what she said, close his mind to everything but the mechanics of obedience—for the time being at least it shut out the meaning of what had happened, absolved him of responsibility.

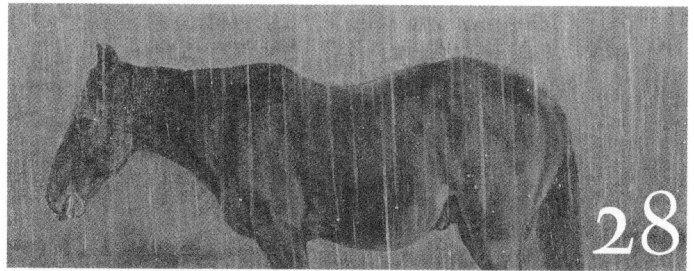

28

WHEN HE RETURNED with the horse he tied it to the railing of the back steps and went into the kitchen again. She had put on one of Larson's caps and was buttoning herself into an old sweater. "I'll lead," she said, "and you steady him. See you get a good grip—if he falls off we'll have a time getting him on again."

She turned as if to bend and take hold of Larson by the shoulders, instead swung back suddenly on Chris. "First, though, let's see that paper he's written for you." She counted, evidently, on catching him off guard. Her voice was sharp and quick, yet at the same time offhand, as if it were a matter of small importance, not worth arguing about. "It's no good—it'll only give you more crazy ideas."

She did it so well that he actually put his hand to his pocket. But Boyle Street was to be reckoned with. A low-down to everything—it was one of the rudiments. And even in his defeat, even admitting that what Larson had written was worthless, he sharpened and said, "Why?" Turning his head, he watched her slantwise. His face took on a crafty look. "If it's no good what do you want it for?"

"Like I say—just so it won't keep giving you ideas. There's no time. You've got to keep your mind on what's in front of us. So long as you've got it there you'll think maybe you can work something."

"No—it's mine—even if it's no good. He wrote it for me, and sometimes maybe I'll want to look at it again."

This was himself now, not Boyle Street. All at once the bit of paper was important simply because it was written by Larson, represented their relationship, because with a kind of foresight he knew there would be times when he would need it to help justify and accept himself. "I'm ready now." He put his hand to his pocket again, this time to assure himself that the paper was thrust in deep and safe. "Let's get it over with."

"It was just so later on you *wouldn't* have it to look at—so you wouldn't keep remembering." There was no time to argue; if she angered him he might resist again, turn stubborn. "Anyway, before we start we'd better get the key. The well's padlocked, and we'll never be able to pick it out in the dark."

She knelt by Larson and felt for his key ring, then went through his pockets methodically. There were nails and matches and coins, a package of tobacco, a red handkerchief, a roll of bills. She began to flick through the bills, then—as an inducement, perhaps, to keep his head, a foretaste of the prosperity that would be his if they came through the next few hours successfully—tossed them impatiently to him. "Here," she said, "you've got better pockets. And now the key."

She stood up and selected a key, then, keeping it separate from the others, handed him the ring. "I think this is the one. No—I'll take it off the ring, so when we get there we won't have to pick it out. But keep the others too, in case it isn't right. In a different pocket. Now—open the door and take him under the arms. I'll take the feet. The door—Christ Almighty!—the door *first*, Chris. *That* way you'll have to put him down again."

"Are we going to leave the lights on? What if somebody comes and we're not here? Or if they're waiting when we get back?"

Squatted between Larson's legs, she stiffened a moment and stared at him. "Supposing they are—we'll be careful when we get near. We had a row. I was scared and ran out.

Something like that—I'll think up something while we're walking."

Then her voice took on a sudden gnash of anger. "Just do what I tell you and stop looking for trouble. The face on you!—all your guts in your eyes. Get rattled and you'll spoil everything."

The horse sniffed nervously as they came down the steps. There was a little difficulty getting it to stand while they heaved up Larson and balanced him across its back. Chris thought they ought to tie him on, but he was too cowed now to suggest it. "Take a good hold," she said, "and see he stays there."

It was a dark, cloudy night. Chris could barely make out the shape of Sylvia three or four paces in front of him. The horse was still nervous, and kept pressing forward at a half-trot. He stumbled along awkwardly, clutching one of Larson's ankles. There was stubble, then soft heavy summer fallow, then stubble again. Twice Larson fell off. The second time, at the feel of the limp, cold body, Chris turned sick at his stomach, and Sylvia, as soon as she realized what was wrong, drew close to make sure of her aim, then struck him across the face.

The horse took fright and kept wheeling away. She cursed savagely because he hadn't brought a quieter one. Finally, leaving him to struggle with the body alone, she went round to the other side of the horse and prodded it back when it tried to swing away. "Put the arms over first—so I can pull while you lift." That way they succeeded. Then she hissed at him to be careful and keep a good grip of the leg. He promised. They went on again.

There was no track of any kind across the field. In the darkness it was impossible to keep their course straight. When finally they reached the fence they had to follow it nearly half a mile, post by post, until they came to the piece of white rag which several days before, in anticipation of a dark night, she had tied on as a marker.

"We're all right now, it's straight across." She clutched the wire a moment and drew a deep breath. "You get through and pull him under while I hold up the wire. Tie the horse first."

As if afraid of what he might do, to encourage him, she groped for his arm and squeezed it. "It's a dirt road, and likely soft after the rain, so we'd better carry him. If we dragged him it would show. And we'll carry him again from the fence to the well on account of the weeds. They'd show too, all flattened down."

His hands shook as he tied the horse. Crawling through the fence he thought he was going to be sick again. But she went on firmly, insistently, "Everything's working out just fine. Not a hitch. Another couple of hours and you'll be back from town. It's all as good as yours right now."

Afraid of his voice, he didn't answer. He was so weak that as he dragged the body under the wire he had to rest and pretend his foot had slipped. But she knew, and whispered desperately, "It's so close, Chris—just hold on. Just keep saying to yourself we've done it, it's all over. If you don't it'll be the rope. You know that, don't you? The rope—you're the one they'll hang for it."

He crumpled beside Larson and began to sob. She struggled through the fence, cursing as her skirt caught on the barbed wire, then struck him in the face again. He turned away, his hands up, and she aimed a kick that caught him in the ribs. The pain sobered him. He got to his feet and took Larson under the arms again.

On the other side of the road was a second fence, the new one, without a gate, that Larson had put up just that spring; and the strands of wire were strung so taut and close that they were several minutes getting through. Then, just as they were picking him up again, the horse whinnied. Away off, like an echo, another answered. Chris started, went rigid, and sensing his fear she said, "It's a horse, Chris. Listen to me—just a horse. We're almost there and it's over. As soon as we get back we'll have another good stiff drink."

"I'm ready—you go first. You know the way."

The clouds now had lightened a little near the horizon, and he could just make out the blur of the old house against the sky. The knee-high weeds around them shook and rattled in the wind. The horse whinnied again. In the distance there was the faint rumble of a wagon.

He gave another start that ran through the body. "For Christ's sake, you're not going to start worrying about that now! It's a mile off—on the highway—somebody coming home from town. Here, Chris—here we are. Put him down and give me the key. Careful—in this sand we'd never find it. Hang on tight till I say. All right, I've got it now. Let go."

There was windy, wagon-rumbling silence a minute, then the click of the lock, then the creak of the cover as she lifted it and turned it back.

"No!" All at once he saw it. "No, you can't. There's six feet of water."

"Easy, Chris." She turned to him quickly and seized his hand. "You just stand there a minute and don't worry. You're cold. You should have put a coat on. No time at all now and we'll be home having a drink."

"We can't—we haven't got a rope ..."

"It's all right, we don't need a rope. Here, you hold the key. Tight now, for all you're worth. And keep listening to the wagon. Tell me if you think it's coming closer."

He closed his fist on the key as if it were something alive that might escape. And understanding that she had given it to him to hold for something to do, to keep him quiet and controlled while she finished, he was vaguely grateful. He listened carefully, just as she had told him, and decided that the wagon was on the other road.

Then there was a swishing sound and a faint splash. He caught a whiff of the old rotten cribbing, and heard Sylvia slapping her hands together again. A moment later there was the bump and scratch of the cover being fitted back on, the snap of the lock. "We can go now," she said quietly. "Here's my hand. Put the key back in your pocket."

When they were through the second fence she walked ahead and let him follow with the horse. He was cold. His mind began to clear. Afraid where it might lead him, what it might make him face, he tried to concentrate on the drink she had promised him, of warming his hands at the stove. But even the thought that it was his own land he was walking on, that when he drove to town tonight it would be in his own truck—even that was not enough. He owned nothing, least of all himself. Between the dead horror behind him and the living horror striding on in front he was a prisoner.

When they reached the house she made him coffee. "You've got to drive, and keep your wits about you. There'll be plenty of time for a drink afterwards."

He had been counting on the drink. As he watched her pour the coffee his face hardened. Instead of sitting down when she nodded him to the table, he backed away and clenched his hands.

"Go on, drink it while it's hot." Scarcely glancing at him, she brought a mop and began cleaning up the blood. Larson's blood—and to see her it might have been spilled tea. There was nausea a moment, then pounding anger. "No!" That he raised his voice revealed the power she still exerted. "No—you can't make me."

"Suit yourself. Nobody's trying to make you." She shrugged as she put the mop away, pretending to miss his meaning, perhaps in order to gain time, decide on her next move. "But if you're cold it'll warm you."

"I tell you I won't—I'm through!" This was a shout again, but on the next words his voice levelled off, met her cold and steady. "I've been crazy to go along this far, but it's still not too late. I'm going to call Ole."

"Don't be a fool! Take hold of yourself." There was no pretense now of not understanding. Her face went white, took on a twist of fear. She put her nails to her mouth a moment, then sprang to him, her hand out to seize his arm, but he struck it away as if it were something that might sting. "Listen, Chris—there's no time. You're just going to spoil everything. It's done. A couple of hours and you'll be back from town ..."

He set himself, his face stony. His lips worked silently a moment, as if there were no words for his loathing. And all at once she seemed to see him, to understand. Her fear itself might have been dissembled, so swiftly, with such violence, she threw it off. For a second or two she crouched before him, fingers crisped like talons, then charged with her head down straight for his belly. Winded, he staggered back against the wall. She followed, went in with the same bull-like bunt. They clinched a moment; then, in the same instant as her knee caught him in the groin, she reached for his face and eyes. Her nails clawed down, drawing blood. He put his hands up and she made a grab for the watch pocket of his overalls. It was a deep, narrow pocket with an opening near the top at the side. Struggling with him, she was able to insert only two fingers, but her yank ripped it nearly to the bottom. This far he had only been trying to control her, hold her off. Now, his blood up, he caught and held her by the throat a moment, then flung her backwards to the floor.

She turned slowly on to her hip and elbow, and huddling low, as if expecting him to strike or kick her, glared up with tight, bitter eyes. His own were wary, hard, but with a look less of loathing now than release. He had thrown her off so easily; she was not really strong at all. And somehow, in asserting his own strength, he had defeated her completely. As he stood over her, revolted, yet faintly pitying, what had been formidable and monstrous was suddenly just cruel and cheap. There had been a collapse, a deflation. She looked ugly and old.

"So that's it—you really *do* think you're going to get away with it!" She rose stiffly, a hand on her hip, her rage subsided to a snicker of contempt. "Holding him up like you had to— that far gone, and still you think you're going to get them to believe it!"

The rage had been easier. All at once he wondered if he really were a fool, throwing away the chance of a lifetime and running straight for the noose. "It's proof—it says you're the one." His voice rose, angry and uneasy. He slapped his hand two or three times against the watch pocket. "It says you did it, and I tried to stop you."

"Yes, Chris, but be reasonable." She took a deep breath, pushed the hair off her forehead wearily. "First of all, it's not witnessed, and that means it's not legal. Anything important—a will, say, or a mortgage—it's got to be witnessed or it won't hold in court. And the shape he was in you could have done it yourself. I was watching through the window—it was all he could do to hang on to the pencil."

"They'll know all right. They've got experts that do nothing else."

"But supposing they do—there's still Baxter. One's enough. They'll still hang you."

"I shot Baxter, but I didn't kill him." It was less an answer than an attempt to feel his way forward, to come to terms with his situation and his chances. Ever since it happened he had let his mind look only to the escape side of his future. The other side, for the simple reason that he had refused to look at it—the side of arrest, trial, conviction—had taken on the terrors of the unthinkable and unknown. It had filled half his sky, had piled up behind him like a thunder cloud. But now he turned and met it squarely. "They said on the radio he had a better than fifty-fifty chance. Just before I left—I heard it myself. He'd had a good night. So it won't be a murder rap. Not likely—not unless something went wrong ..."

"It'll be life, though. Shooting to kill—armed holdup—they'll throw everything at you. Life, and the lash maybe too."

"Not that long. Ten years—fifteen at the most. And time off if I watch myself and take it easy. Maybe I won't be much over thirty."

"But there's the well—they'll know you did it. They'll know I could never have got him down myself."

"I'll explain what happened. Maybe they won't believe me, maybe they will. I'm going to risk it."

"Even supposing you're lucky, they'll be the best years of your life. Say it is only ten—you don't know what it's going to do to you. The way they kick you around and make you crawl—you won't come out thirty like you think, Chris. You'll come out mean and ugly, all beat up inside."

She drew closer, touched his arm almost timidly. "I've had five with him, Chris—look what they've done to me."

This time he paid no attention to her hand. His eyes were fixed past her. "No," he said, "free. I'll come out thirty and I'll come out free."

"You're the one that's jumping now. Like a while ago you said about me—instead of looking at the couple of minutes it was going to take to do it, you said I kept jumping over them. But you can't jump, Chris—it'll be by the day. It'll be beans and porridge and maggots in the pork—sweating it out in the kitchen or the laundry ..."

"There'll be lots of to think about. All I've got to learn: crops and machinery, all about alfalfa—"

"But I tell you it's no good what he's written!" There was a spurt of rage. Her voice shot up again, cracking at the scream. "Leaving you the farm—*that's* spoiled it for you. They'll know you tricked him. Because you're nobody—just a no-good bum, a killer and a bum. There's no reason why he'd want to. Never mind me—first he'd leave it to Ole or Aunt Bessie."

"He did leave part of it to Ole—the part he's on already. If I'd been tricking him I've have tricked him out of everything. And that puts Ole on my side now. He'll want them to believe it. The way you've been talking for years about trains, scared he'll catch one—it'll fit in with my story."

She stood motionless a moment, white and blank-eyed, then took a deep suck of air as if coming up from under water. "No—you're not going to get away with it. I'll swear you made him. I'll swear you threatened to set the barn on fire—with all the horses in it." She stamped. Her nails came out again. "I'll tell it so they'll believe me. All kinds of things. Try a trick like that and I'll show you. Anybody that's done one job will do another—that's the way they always figure ..."

It was only bluff and bitterness, he knew, but at the shrill panic in her voice he winced and shrank away. "I'll risk it," he repeated slowly, forcing the words out, not quite believing them. "Even if they do figure that way—I'll risk it anyway."

"And that sly little Grover bitch—" She stamped again. For a moment the words choked her. "You've got it all worked out. You think she'll be waiting for you too!"

The Well

"I don't know—she might be, though, at that."

He stared a moment at the froth on her lips, then looked past her again. All at once it was possible. The way she carried the blanket up the hill, the look in her eyes as she warned him of the Campkin crap games—all at once, just thinking of her, he felt steady and serene. He knew it was crazy, tried to bite it down. She was eighteen and he would be in for at least ten years; they would plead and reason with her, and finally she would see it for herself. But for the moment he believed. Just to know she was there, to remember—for the moment that was enough. Somehow it was an affirmation. Somehow it touched the squalor of his life, just as her cool slow hands had touched his throat and hair, and brought a sense of peace and vindication.

"She might be at that—I hadn't thought about her but she's just the kind."

He knew, too, confusedly, that she was less and more than this, that he was shaping her to serve his need and fear, an idealization without fault or weakness of her own, but that now was of no importance either. Just so she helped him through—helped him to go on believing, to shut his eyes and leap clear, heedless of the landing. "If I can take it there's a good chance she can too."

"You think it's a good gamble." Sylvia quietened, veered to a tone of reasonableness. "Ten years and then the farm, seventy-five or a hundred thousand dollars. But supposing they had it wrong on the radio, supposing Baxter did die after all. Or like I keep telling you, supposing instead of ten years they give you life?"

"What about here?" He came back sharply, his face thrust out unsparing and intent. "Wouldn't it be life here too?"

"No—you'll do what you want to. You're still young—I won't try to hold you down."

"Hiding out for life—that's what I mean. On the run, scared." He squeezed his knuckles into his eyes a moment, then looked down at the floor where she had just mopped up the blood. "Seeing him there—thinking about the well ..."

"But me, Chris—what about me? It'll be the rope for me too!"

All at once she seemed to see it. Her eyes bulged again, went blank. The veins in her forehead stood out dark and twisted. She leaned towards him, peering into his face, then drew back and braced herself against the table. "What you really mean," she said slowly, "you'd take the rope rather than me. It's not being scared, or thinking about the well—it's me ..."

She put her hand to her mouth, then with a clutch of breath ran to the door and disappeared into the darkness. He started after her, caught himself up short at the steps and came back to the telephone. Half an hour later he greeted Ole calmly. There was a raw spot where he had been biting his lip; his face had already taken on a haggard, strained look; but as he talked to Ole his voice was clear and resolute. The worst was over. He had leaped and made his landing.